Villa Sara

by Mancebo

Armadillo Niche
505 Pleasant St., Suite 202-E
St. Joseph, Michigan 49085

Villa Sara/Project Seek
© 1990 Armadillo Niche

Original Cover Art: Brenda Fulton Design
Cover Design: BJ Graphics
Typesetting: Sans Serif, Inc.
Printing: BookCrafters, Inc.

ISBN 0-9626993-1-4

Library of Congress #90-062235

In Memory of

Sara

(1892-1979)

Table of Contents

Villa Sara

Chapter 1

It was a hot July day when word came that Santiago had fallen. The sands of Santiago were shifted into shape once more by the sea breeze. From Boston to San Francisco whistles blew and flags waved.

To some it seemed an ideal war; its casualty lists were short, the national debt was not greatly inflated, and it raised American prestige abroad. The nation emerged with its pockets full of booty. Newspapers rushed their correspondents to Cuba to see the fun, and these writers trumpeted the renown of new national heroes. One of these heroes was Theodore Roosevelt, leader of the Rough Riders. Others were heroes only to those they went home to. They were never seen by the correspondents. The Spanish-American War had ended.

Yet when scrutinized closely, records show a victory of another kind. Friendships were bonded through vision and creative thrust. One of those heroes, overlooked by the media, was George L. Grantley, Confederate Cavalry Leader and Volunteer. He had been thrown from his horse in the march up San Juan Hill. The sounds he heard on that hot July day were not those of victory.

More horrifying than ten weeks of artillery firing and face to face combat were the cries of anguish—the screams, moans, groans, and gasps from other wounded comrades.

George pushed aside the torn, useless mosquito netting. The large rips and unrepaired holes no longer kept the insects away. The flies, too numerous to count, had long since invaded the cot. He struggled to keep them from his face and was wary of opening his mouth, he did not want

1

to swallow any. He cursed his stupidity for having lost control of his mount. He lay there for a while assessing his surroundings. His sleepless eyes saw row after row of cots, all filled with wounded and flies. Everywhere were the hordes of flies circling the three walls, entering and leaving a large open space about three feet by five feet that served as both window and light source. The fourth wall had the center section missing, and through this open walkway, he saw more cots filled with more sick and wounded, and more flies.

He saw a young soldier sit up suddenly and look at the end of his cot. His legs had been blown away. He sat there rigidly for a second, gurgled incoherently, then slumped backwards.

Grantley could see the empty place where legs should be and the soiled wrapping covering the spots where legs once were. Maggots crawled over the soiled area and the sight sickened him. The stench of burned and rotten flesh everywhere filled his nostrils. He closed his eyes and made every effort to cease to smell.

Abruptly he was filled with panic at the thought he also may be limbless and full of those crawling bastards. He sat up slowly and lowered the Army drab covering and sighed with relief. Both of his legs were there. He could move his left leg, but the right was wrapped from the crotch to the ankle. He tried to move his toes then fell back in excruciating pain, his thoughts a mass of confusion. How bad was his leg? How long had he been there? Had the shipment of sulphur arrived in time to keep his wound free from gangrene? Just thinking the word he could smell the pungent sweet, vinegar gone sour like, smell of rotten flesh.

"Oh God," he prayed. "Don't let me die in this Hell Hole."

"Mr. Grantley?" The low-pitched, cool, calm voice and rustling sound startled him. His deep grey eyes opened wide and looked into the watery ones of a matronly nun. She was followed by a platoon of green and white uniforms with children's faces attached, all cautiously making their way between each cot.

"These are children of San Andres Mission, Mr. Grantley. One third of them anyway," the nun said and smiled.

"The rest of the drill team are with their teachers in other wards. It is *Dia de los Flores* here in Santiago. It's a day when students bring flowers to patients and to put on the graves of brave fighting men."

She moved aside so the procession could move quietly, in single file, up to the cot.

"Thank you," Grantley managed to murmur, still puzzled and somewhat embarrassed by the giggles and whispers as each pair of hands laid a single flower on the cot.

The smallest child at the end of the line had now reached her turn to greet the wounded *Americano*. She almost missed the cot as she stumbled forward, but caught herself in time. Tears filled the darkest eyes Grantley had seen since his wife had pleaded with him not to join the Rough Riders. The little girl straightened herself and silently placed a crushed yellow sunflower in his open palm and started to move away.

"What, no greeting?" He watched her small, graceful hands plucking at the starched uniform.

"But, I don't know you, Sir."

She spoke in perfect English with just a trace of Spanish accent and that startled him. He had not expected the perfect English or the beautiful voice.

"Tell me your name then," he said.

"My name is Sara. Sarita Hernandez Garcia Bocan de Ke. . . ."

She stopped abruptly when she felt the heavy arm of Sister Domingo wrap around her frail shoulders.

"*Basta*, Sarita," said the nun. "Enough, my child. We mustn't tire Mr. Grantley and there are others we must see. Your name would take up all our time."

She patted the dark head with affection. "I'm sorry, Mr. Grantley. Sarita makes a game of adding to her name those she finds impressive."

"It's okay, Sister. I have a son about her age who lives in a fantasy world most of the time.

"I hope you'll come again, Sarita Hernandez Garcia Bocan de Ke. . . ."

Now he could see only two almond colored legs in uniform socks and shoes. The rest of Sarita was concealed within the folds of the nun's massive wings and robe. He looked around and could see the pain lessen in the faces of his comrades as the multi-colored floral gifts temporarily chased the flies and the smell of death away.

For some time after, hands clasped behind his head, he would look at the crushed yellow sunflower and the images of his shattered life collided with one another in his brain.

He was a babe himself when General William T. Sherman laid waste to farms and towns in a broad swath of destruction all the way from the mountains to the sea. That swath cut through the heart of Georgia and left cities gutted by fire or battered by bombardment. It left bridges down, roads neglected, and railroad track torn up.

The eyes of the veterans in gray reflected shattered dreams and the pain of the fathers and brothers who did not make it home. He never knew his own father. He did know that he and his father had never had much and he now wanted better things for his own son.

He wanted his son to not be overly concerned with the actual accumulation of wealth yet geared to get the most from life. Neither he nor his father had much schooling so he wanted his son to go to college and to develop a fondness for learning.

Perhaps most of all, he wanted his son to enjoy the sweet flirtations of Southern belles and yet dare to look elsewhere for a girl who could match his dreams.

His imagination thus fired with dreams, he lay on his cot, forgot the flies, and thought of how he had crossed the rough Atlantic and landed on the Georgia shores. Shores scented by magnolias and inhabited by people living in a lace and leisure era. The Southern belles were beautiful but he married a young woman of the Creek tribe.

By August, his hours of exercise paid off and he only had a slight limp left. Today he felt almost whole again. To work off the frustrations of inactivity, he often walked across the plaza to join other Rough Riders at the hotel where Roosevelt had set up command headquarters.

It had rained during the night and the streets were open sewers. Since the town was nearly all downhill, the water washed the rubbish into the bay. The heat of the sun was soon high enough to hit the cobblestones and reflect against the third floor balcony where a robust figure was leaning over the railing.

"Bully for you, Grantley," Roosevelt yelled down at his clean, crisp, khaki-clad figure.

He had been standing still and deeply inhaling the freshness of the Cuban air after the cleansing rain of last night.

"Come join me. The view is spectacular."

Grantley limped up the stairs and joined Roosevelt. He leaned his walking cane against the railing and accepted the lighted cigar. He observed closely the man soldiers would go through hell for, and a second time at that, if needed. Roosevelt's breeches were tucked into leather boots, and a heavy cartridge belt girded his waist with a holstered pistol in plain view. His genial face was crinkled in a smile.

"You're looking damn fit, Grantley."

"Thank you, Sir. I'm ready to ride again. Just name the time and place."

"Let's hope there won't be a next time, son."

He exhaled a trail of smoke as he carefully examined the countryside.

"Savor that sight my boy. Man can make it a battle zone and Mother Nature bounces it right back, alive and green. Working on a ranch conditions you to appreciate such beauty.

"Being a country squire you know that."

"Look over there, Colonel," Grantley said and pointed out a wagon road winding along a railway about a mile from the bay.

A tall dark figure pedalled a bicycle built for two. Behind the rider sat a smaller one, hidden under a huge straw hat, with legs too short to reach the pedals.

"Whoever they are they're in a mighty big hurry."

"That would be my friend, Juan Bocan and his daughter. I met him in the East back in 1884 when I had proclaimed myself as only a private citizen and literary feller. I had retired from public life for awhile.

"He spends about half his time climbing these hills and trampling the streets spreading his special brand of religion. His triumph over misfortunes far exceeds my own.

"In fact, at his hands you're soon to feel your first tug toward cultivation since we arrived."

"How's that, Sir?"

"You'll see."

The abundant foliage of the Cuban terrain blocked their view of the two riders, but Grantley thought he saw a flash of metal now and then.

"The hills steepen soon as the railroad makes that turn yonder," Roosevelt said.

"We'll lose sight of them then. They'll reappear on that path south of the wagon road headed this way."

"That's a long climb for such a little girl."

"Bully for her, I say," Roosevelt said while puffing deeply on the cigar. He directed Grantley to the doorway.

"We'll wait downstairs."

From the first floor balcony they watched the two riders dismount and prop their bicycle against the cement alley wall.

The tall man, dressed in black, leaned on a cane to climb the steep steps to the entrance. The little girl flapped a big yellow sombrero against her flowing blue skirt to fan some of the dust away. She pushed a damp strand of long black hair back from her face and leaped the steps two at a time. She was stopping after each step only long enough to make sure she let her father remain leader. She was a beautiful child radiating energy and life.

"It's her, Sir," Grantley blurted out. "The little senorita from San Andres Mission. She was with the children who brought us flowers in the ward.

"Allow me, Sir, to introduce her to you."

The colonel gave him an inquiring squint while reappraising the man with the clerical collar who still appeared white and clean after a long climb. He extended his hand in greeting. The firm handshake in return reassured Roosevelt his friend had not changed very much.

"How long has it been, Juan? Ten years?"

"More like thirteen, T.R.."

"You don't look much different than when I last saw you, a little heavier, a little older. Then we are all a little older," and the Frenchman laughed. Roosevelt responded in kind. He started to say more but was interrupted by Grantley.

"This, Sir, is Sarita Hernandez Garcia Bocan de Ke. . . ."

The three men laughed, but Sarita ignored them except for a dainty curtsey. She scooted a long wooden bench into the far corner near the window, hoisted herself toward one end, and pushed a hand-woven silk pillow to one side. Her ankle-length, button-down, gray shoes reached halfway to the tiled floor. She smoothed out her dark blue skirt after removing a small drawing pad from a big pocket. She began to leaf through the penciled drawings.

"It's indeed a pleasure, Sarita."

Roosevelt sent a salute in her direction. He gave the sergeant on duty instructions to see that she got whatever she needed and to bring her a cold drink. He led his visitors down a small passageway to his quarters.

They sat facing each other. Bocan and Grantley in cane highbacks at each end with Roosevelt across from them and seated at the large mahogany desk. The room was festooned with maps and diagrams pinned to the walls. The colonel leaned back and placed a hand on one knee. With the other he adjusted his rimless glasses and then offered the men cigars and matches.

"I'd hoped our next meeting would be under more pleasant circumstances, Juan. Maybe a Sunday breakfast and a ride into the hills? A day of recalling past times?

"Unfortunately military duties beckon, as you can see."

He sifted through a stack of official papers, their seals freshly broken.

Bocan smiled and a twinkle spread to the ends of his deep blue eyes.

"Ah yes, life was good at Sagamore Hill those years but, as I remember, you were never one to nurse depression or yearn too strongly for times past. You always accepted what you got.

"By the way, do you still feel that tug toward politics?"

"You in politics, Colonel?" Grantley looked admiringly at his commanding officer.

"Does it surprise you, my boy?"

"Just that I picture you as galloping the range or commanding troops, but you'd make a damn good president, Sir."

Roosevelt beamed through the cigar smoke, leaned back in his chair, and propped himself against the wall.

"I don't think Juan's comment included the White House Grantley, but I support your choice."

They laughed and paused in their conversation when a Cuban lad of twelve or so brought in a pitcher of cold papaya juice.

The conversation drifted from one person to the other. It ranged over experiences in New York to North Carolina, Pennsylvania to the western plains, Georgia to Florida and back to Cuba. All places where at least one of the three men had been.

"It says here, Juan," Roosevelt said as he picked up a British communique, "that you have won quite a place for yourself on this island. It seems the Spanish, French, British, Jamaicans, and Americans, all hold you in high esteem. So you're the ideal choice to give the benediction at our victory assembly. I would feel honored to be standing beside you when we raise the flag to lasting peace."

"Thank you, T.R." Bocan nodded. "I support your choice."

They sat in silence for a moment and looking out toward San Juan Hill.

"I wonder how your daughter will take this honor," Grantley said.

"Let's go find out," answered Roosevelt.

The sergeant was posed rigidly behind his desk and grinning.

"You can move now," she said.

Her quick fingers smeared some shadows in the sketch she'd just finished and then she turned the tablet toward him.

He snapped to attention as soon as he saw the group approach.

"That's me, Colonel," he said.

"At ease, soldier. I can understand your enthusiasm. She's very good. Your daughter has a talent worth developing, Juan," he said turning back to his companions.

"Maybe she'd consent to record some fine memories of the victory celebrations," he continued while admiring the other drawings in the sketchbook.

Sarita gathered up her sketches and turned to her father, tugging on his long coattail.

"Papa," she whispered, "ask him for dinner."

"Colonel, it seems my daughter's inviting you to share our evening meal."

"Under other circumstances I'd jump at the chance, my dear." He winked at her.

"But military matters are urgent, and I apologize for having to leave so soon to compare reports with Shafter's unit at El Caney.

"Grantley here can fill me in later," he said.

He clapped Juan on the shoulder, returned Grantley's salute, and strode off down the hall.

Grantley's mouth opened wide and his eyes flashed questions as the robust figure disappeared down the corridor. Sarita reached up and took his hand.

Chapter 2

By the time the siesta hours had passed, the sun had bleached the color from everything. The extra thick masonry walls looked like they were wilted and sagging into the street. The walls were all covered with tiles and could only be distinguished from each other by the various tints of cream, green, pink, or yellow. They lined the narrow Reloj Baja Street. Grantley was walking down this narrow street next to Juan and both behind little Sarita.

When they were close enough to home, one without a veranda, Sarita ran back and grabbed him by the hand. She broke into a run which made George merely lengthen and quicken his stride.

At the door Sarita released his hand and, by standing on her tiptoes, grabbed the heavy, ornate knocker and gave it a series of sharp, quick raps. There was some kind of squawk from inside and Sarita giggled.

"*Adelante. Adelante.* Come in. Come in."

"A ritual we go through," Juan said as he caught up.

"It's Pepe, our pet parrot. She delights in hearing Pepe welcome anyone in Spanish and English. It's never the other way around.

Sarita rapped again on the door. Pepe again called out his greeting.

Juan tapped her gently on the shoulder with his cane.

"Enough Sarita. Ampara's short legs are not as swift as yours."

"She's almost as tall, though," added Sarita, looking at Grantley for approval.

"Sarita," Juan said rather sternly.

"I'm sorry, Papa. It slipped out." She was going to add, "and she's just as wide" when the sounds on the other side of the door ceased.

9

The door opened into the parlor area and revealed Ampara's welcoming smile. It didn't seem possible the slow moving, little round shaped figure could have made so much noise, then he looked at her feet. The wooden clogs she wore had made a rhythm their own. She gave a curtsy in recognition. Then just as slowly as she had come, she returned to the task of preparing dinner.

The mosaic tiles on the thick walls cooled the inside and deadened the outside street noises. If the window had been closed in the parlor, they would not have heard the rattle of a vendor's cart as he yelled about his produce, or the sound of the trolley roaring arrogantly down a nearby street.

"You know what you must do, young lady," Juan said as he gave his daughter a nudge.

"But, Papa, we have a guest. Do I have to practice my violin? A whole hour?"

"Half an hour then this time."

He removed his hat and put the cane into its brass stand at the entrance to his study.

"I'll show Mr. Grantley where he can wash some of the Cuban dust back into the bay."

"I'll show him my turtles."

She threw the words over one shoulder as she leaned over to open the violin case.

"After you practice," Grantley said and smiled.

"I'll be listening."

She set an hourglass on the piano bench nearby so she could watch the sand flow freely from the upper to the lower half. She carefully positioned the violin, supporting it against her shoulder while she pulled the bow a few times over a resin wax bar. Tucked under her chin with such assurance, she and the instrument became one with the music, sending throughout the house scales that would baffle the trained adult ear.

From the study Grantley heard brief pauses now and then and could imagine Sarita giving the hourglass a few shakes to speed its calculation of time. When he came into the parlor, he found she had left the violin on the piano bench and moved over to a corner table.

"Sarita. Sarita," came her father's warning. She offered no objections, and, although she skipped over some measures, the lower bulb of the hourglass was more than half full when Bocan joined them with glasses of fresh papaya juice. He offered Grantley a cigar and light."

"Your daughter was distracted by your building plan," Grantley said, pointing to the scale model. "I can see why. This is a beautiful Spanish villa. It's magnificent."

"My dream once," Bocan said. "The plot is paid for in Vista Alegre overlooking the bay. It was my wife Anna's dream too."

"It's mine now." Sarita snapped the violin case shut.

"See." She jabbed a trembling finger at the cardboard sign arched over the entrance: "Villa Sara." My Papa can build anything." She leaned over and planted a kiss on the strong hand resting on the table.

"Sarita won't let the dream die. She spends every kilo of her allowance on books. I've promised to build a shelf for her birthday."

He fingered a book called *Suburban and Country Homes*. It was a book of nineteenth century building studies by William T. Comstock of New York. He handed it to Grantley.

He looked at the much used book and turned to an ear-marked chapter of "Suggestions on House Building", by architect A. W. Cobb.

Sarita was busy rearranging the mini-patio of her villa.

"I'm getting her to think of buildings not as separate architectural entities, but as parts of an organic whole which include the land, the community, and the society," Juan commented as he watched his daughter.

"Sarita is very perceptive. I know she will direct her genius in the right direction." Grantley said and smiled.

"Someone has said 'Genius does what it must, talent does what it can.' I haven't decided which slot Sarita fits in yet."

"She strikes me as the kind of girl to create her own space, Sir."

Grantley crushed his lighted cigar into a copper ashtray and turned to Sarita. "How about those turtles? When do I get to see them?"

Sarita plunked the three empty glasses on a dining table and planted herself between the two men as they moved toward the patio. It was a long rectangular courtyard with doors and windows opening onto it.

She pointed out the four bedrooms, servant quarters, the kitchen area with food bubbling over an open fire, a large utility room with shower stall and two smaller rooms marked "*Damas*" and "*Caballeros*." Far back, a flock of chickens shared a fenced-in area with a vegetable garden. She halted the tour when they reached the sweet lemon tree protected on one side by the neighbor's cement wall.

It was a magnificent tree standing fifteen feet high. It had a profusion of the beautiful fragrant flowers accenting the glossy green leaves.

"Papa planted his own tree so he could get all the lemons he wants. And he won't get spanked anymore." She giggled at Grantley's puzzled expression.

"I'll explain later, Grantley," Juan said.

"Sir, I'd like very much if you'd manage to call me George," said Grantley.

"After all, we're about the same age."

"And about the same length, too," said Sarita.

"Height, Sarita, not length."

"Yes Papa."

They all sat down next to the lemon tree and enjoyed its shade. Also underneath it was a large cement tank the size of the two bathtubs filled with gallons of water and oozing sea smells. A miniature castle extended out from the tank, its drawbridge lowered into the water. A little way away from the shadows was a floating platform supporting a turtle sunning itself.

"That's Pedro. He's the leader." Sarita introduced him as she reached over to tip the raft. "It's not good for him to get too wrinkled from the sun. There are three more," she looked up at Grantley, "but they're hiding." She reached for a long bamboo pole with a net, hoping to dredge for the sunken reptiles.

"Shall I, Papa?"

"Let'em be," her father answered. "George has seen one turtle and they all look the same. It's almost time for dinner."

Attached to the main house on the north by one of its octagonal sides, an all-white gazebo faced the sun. He unlatched a small gate and motioned for them to sit awhile. "What's on your mind, George? You have a faraway look."

"This reminds me of the pavilion back home. Ours is built on a site affording an enjoyable view of the river in Georgia."

"Hear that, Sarita?" He put an arm around Sarita and pulled her closer. "We're honored to have a Southern gentleman enjoy our view and one who's going to start calling me Juan—now that we've established our ages and height. Right, George?"

"Yes, I will," he said laughing.

"You know, ideas come easily out here, Juan. You've made a place for dreaming I. . . ."

He stopped abruptly when he noticed the random arrangement of sunflowers towering above a mosaic of salmon, apricot, pink, rose, blue, purple on red, yellow-centered, and silvery-white tropicals pushing up out of an assortment of containers. There were clay pots, antique and glass vases, tobacco cans and old storage jars, all filled and touching each other with feathery, plumed, wiry, and glossy, or fanlike foliage.

"Is this where you got the flowers you brought me in the hospital?" he asked Sarita, who seemed fascinated by a hummingbird hovering over the peonies.

She nodded, got up quickly, and raced out into the sunlight.

"And your dream, George? Surely you have one or two?" He kept a close watch on Sarita as he spoke.

"Not at the moment, Juan. I just want to savor this moment."

He then watched the little girl stop in her play, squat down, and pull a bug from a stem and squash it between two fingers.

"Sarita, go wash up for supper," Juan called.

"Sometimes I lack the strength, George, and the fortitude to transcend the loss of her mother. She was all that is pure and good in this world. But malaria picks its victims as those sunflowers their spot to grow, at random. Sarita is so like her mother. She has her mother's talents and her beauty."

"Something good always follow after the bad, my mother used to tell me. We just have to let ourselves believe it," Grantley said.

"Bully for your mother." They both laughed and went into the main house.

Ampara was used to putting out the finery with or without guests. The white Irish linen cloth and napkins in brass rings nicely set off an array of cut flowers, in many colors, brought in fresh from the patio. She had even managed to insert a silk butterfly.

The miniature garden of exotic flora with the light opera music filling the room from the victrola with its life-size ceramic black and white dog, lured Grantley deep into thought. This was giving him his first taste of civilization since he came to this war.

"Do you like the opera?" Juan asked, directing Grantley to the master's chair.

"Of the fundamentals I know a little," he said, "but music, whatever kind, has a message. Someone's sweat and blood is being played for our benefit."

"Poetically stated, my friend."

They started the meal with *Sopa de Huevos* — a rich broth, full of egg bits. Ampara removed the dishes and replaced them with large platters of French bread, steamed rice, corn fritos, and *escabeche* — a perfectly prepared dish of pickled fish in onion — potatoes, green beans drenched in olive oil and garnished with pimentos. They washed it down with a bottle of red wine. For dessert they had the traditional Spanish flan, a vanilla wafer topped with custard with a cinnamon stick. Somewhere between the "Tales of Hoffman", first produced in 1880, and the Gilbert and Sullivan composition following, Juan leaned over and whispered in his daughter's ear. She nodded, smiled at Grantley, folded her napkin, inserted it in the brass ring and excused herself politely. She moved toward the upright piano, turning off the victrola as she passed.

"Sarita and I have a little surprise for you. A little something to cap your first social evening in Santiago." He smiled.

They finished their demitasses, lit fresh cigars and moved quickly to seats in the parlor. Sarita had selected the music, adjusted her position on the piano bench, and had given her long delicate fingers a proper warm-up when the advance applause began. She shifted on the bench, pushed her hair behind her ear, smiled and struck up a medley of tunes. First a jiggy ditty of the 1850's, "The Irish Jaunting Car." Then a flood of patriotic reminiscences of "Battle Hymn of the Republic", "Tramp Tramp Tramp, the Boys are Marching," and closing with, "Rally Round the Flag, Boys."

When the applause subsided, she bowed and shifted again, announcing: "Just one more Papa." She chose a ballad, "Mother Kissed Me in My Dream," expressing feelings of loss and evoking the memories of home, all feelings she did not seem to know at her young age. When she finished, she rushed over to her father and pulled him to the piano.

"I get the feeling I'm witnessing a preview of concert stardom," said Grantley as he applauded approval.

He watched Sarita grip the violin with a sureness that delighted him while her father slid onto the piano bench. With the piano as backup, or due to her father's deep interest, the little girl glowed with an indomitable joy. Their gift to Grantley: two extraordinary musical favorites of the South—"Dixie," and "The Old Rugged Cross."

"I wish we could freeze this moment with you," Grantley managed to tell them through tears of gratitude as he said his good-byes later that evening.

"What, and miss Sarita's notable future?" Juan laughed and put an arm around his new friend. "I'll get my hat and cane and walk you to your quarters. It's still not safe on the streets at this hour."

Sarita pleaded to join them, but her cries were unheeded. Grantley crouched down to wipe her tears away.

"Thank you for a most enjoyable evening, my dear. I'll see you again."

"Soon?"

"Soon."

"Promise?"

"Promise."

They were to spend many more afternoons and evenings in the pleasant courtyard with the beautiful lemon tree casting its welcome shade and perfuming the air with its fragrant blossoms. Finally, early one morning, Grantley's ship sailed westward. He would have plenty of time at sea to think out plans to alter his own son's life of isolation. Plans about selecting the right school, even if it meant sending him to New York, and other plans for bringing more culture into their home.

One thought, above all others, from Bocan would remain forever with him—the dream the father fails to accomplish one of his children will bring to full bloom.

Chapter 3

*T*he artillery began again. A shell whistled overhead, reaching across the country to a wooden structure high in a walnut tree on a plantation in middle Georgia. A motley crew of uniformed men cocked their carbines, ready to fire on command. There was another volley of gunfire in the distance and a loose branch shaken by a frisky squirrel landed a barrage of walnuts against the tin roof of the treehouse.

A frightened, lean boy of eight shot upright flinging his arms over his head in protection. He had soaked his oversized flannel shirt and homespun breeches in sweat and his face was white against the worn boards of the tree house. He was sputtering.

"Pa. Damn him to hell," he said as he came completely awake.

He thought he could still smell the gunpowder as it mingled with the scent of bacon and eggs and fresh baked sourdough biscuits coming from the farmhouse nearby.

It had been a dream. He was home. He had spent the night in the tree house, at home.

He got up, went to the door, and pushed aside the climbing vine that blocked most of the daybreak. He stood and listened for his mother's call to breakfast. At the sound of his name, Earl W. Grantley straddled the vine like a giant walking stick and he bounced to the ground.

He raced into his father's chair at the end of the wooden kitchen table, plunked bony elbows down on each side of his place and propped his chin in his hands.

He lingered over the food, pushing kernels of hominy into two drill teams as he studied the tall, heavy woman rattling pots and pans, unnecessarily he thought. Sometimes she did that to break the silence around the place. A woman like his mom was used to having lots of people and children to care for. Now, it was just him and . . . best not to think of anything right now.

"Will we ever have to eat mulesteaks, Mom?" he said.

"What did you say, Baby?" She stood twisting one end of her apron with her strong firm fingers and stared at her youngest son.

"Eat your breakfast, Baby, don't just play. You don't have enough flesh on your bones to keep you from shivering in the early morning hours."

"Mulesteaks good for you?"

"Where do you get all these questions? I declare, Earl." She went around the table and took the chair next to him.

"Pa's always talked about the infantrymen parching corn and braising mulesteaks. Ain't no harm askin'."

His eyes narrowed as he examined the larger ones under the concerned brow before him. He saw the smooth tilt of the nose, the thick pale lips, and her dark-brown hair with faint specks of white that was twisted into a bun at the back of a large head. The part in her hair looked like one of the ridges in the creek bed after a rain shower.

"No harm askin'," she teased as she pushed aside a piece of spider's web caught in his corn silk white hair.

"That was another war, another time. Your pa knows how to take care of himself. Now you eat up. We want more meat on those bones so's to surprise your pa when he gets home."

She tried to sound confident and brave to protect him, but in her heart she knew this son was wiser than his years. His pa was in a war and there was always the chance he would not come back. He would change the subject just to try to please her. She would try to answer all his questions, but there were chores to do, never mind, though, they managed.

He began to fidget like a piglet pushed from its nursing place. He knew he had to change the subject, but would the next one bring more grief to the surface? He had to try anyway. He was not a quitter.

"I could see it, Mom."

"See what, Son?"

"The creek. It's gettin' over the rain. I saw it clear as glass from my crow's nest." He examined her dark eyes fixed on his hazel ones. He paused a moment, then dared go on.

"Looked safe enough for fishin' I'm thinking."

"No fishin', Baby." She wiped away a tear on the edge of her apron. "We promised your pa. We can't chance losing another son to that creek."

"Didn't Pa love me?"

"Of course he did, and still does. That's why he doesn't want the creek to get you, too." She took him in her arms.

"It's just that your brother Calvin was about your age when he drowned. That nearly killed your pa. Only thing kept him from an earlier grave was the call for volunteers, men willing to ride with Theodore Roosevelt. Men who knew horses and guns.

"Your pa was one of the best. He saw to it that we were taken care of before he joined up at Tampa.

"He'll come back and take you fishing. Just keep that thought in that lively brain of yours." Her arms tightened around him, pulling him ever closer.

He had all sorts of suspicions about his father, but none of them marred the overriding feeling he got that his mother loved him and cared about him. He snuggled deeply into her warm comfortable arms.

He only wished she hadn't made that promise to his father. How could she watch him day after day as the hurt deepened when he saw the field hands go by with their cane poles and tin cans? Some boys, no older or bigger than him, were returning weighted down with their catch. It hurt him most when one would stop at the house and give his mom a few choice ones just for the privilege of letting them fish in their creek. His creek someday, and he couldn't even fish in it, because of some hasty promise.

Well, it wasn't his promise, but it would take some shrewd thinking to convince his mom he was big enough to take care of himself. She might need visible proof that her son could provide their own fish. Some very shrewd thinking indeed.

His thoughts were interrupted by a rapping along the side of the kitchen wall.

More loose shingles blown from the smokehouse?

The rapping continued, and then they could hear a man's deep breathing.

Earl looked at the musket over the kitchen door. He knew that his father would not have hesitated to use it.

"It's only Bill George, Son," his mom said and then he recognized the sounds too.

"Why don't you go let him in while I dish up another plate? Then you wash your face if you still want to go with him to the store."

He raced out to meet Bill George. Bill George stood in the doorway shifting his feet. He had an open, friendly face, not old, black, and lined by the weather like the corrugated road he traveled each morning from his cabin to the Grantley's back porch. He had a twinkle in his sightless eyes, and as he spoke, he tipped a worn felt hat.

"Mornin', Ma'am. Mornin' E. Somethin' cookin' smell mighty good," he said, grinning. His accent was thick with dialect.

Earl beamed. Bill George was the only one who ever called him 'E'. The boy's quick eyes surveyed the bulky frame standing there in the kitchen. Bill had on large worn brown brogans. He had slightly bowed legs encased in leather to the knees, and the faded blue trousers were supported by sweat-stained suspenders. His tattered work shirt's sleeves were held in at the elbow with huge rubber bands, its color long since lost in washing.

"Don't just stand there, son," his mom said. "Let him in. Sakes alive, chile'." She placed a platter heaped high at one end of the kitchen table for Bill George.

Earl watched the big man devour a second serving of bacon and eggs, fresh baked sour-dough biscuits, hominy and lots of gravy. He watched him sop up the gravy with whole biscuits, shove them in a giant cave size mouth, and lick each finger, even the ones that never touched the plate.

"You starvin', Bill George?"

"Not anymore, young feller," and he snapped his suspenders and laughed hilariously.

"Then let's go." Earl handed the huge man his crude thick walking stick and pulled at his sleeve.

"I've been ready for hours."

"Is he tellin' the truth, Ma'am?"

"Afraid so. He's thought of nothing else all week, unless you count the war dreams he keep having.

"Seeing Mis' Mattie and her sister again might get his mind off fishing and especially that creek."

"Don't you fret none, ma'am." He tipped his crumpled hat. "I'll take care of him and see he acts proper and stays away from that creek."

"I know you will," she said. "We've trusted you ever since you came here, and there's no reason to stop because his father's not around."

"Look like a good day, don't it, Mom?" Earl smiled hoping to erase some of the worry lines from her still young-looking face.

"Doesn't it," she corrected, cupping his eager face in her hands and slipping a few coins into one tight fist.

"You mind Mis' Mattie and her sister now, you hear? And keep your hands off 'them valuables'."

A three-member chorus of laughter followed those last six words. They were like a trademark branded in large bold letters on the swaying shingle above the tiny general store.

Left alone now she shivered in the bigness of the old colonial hall-way as she moved to the front porch to watch her baby match bold strides with the only companion he had.

He needed friends his own age. Even an older brother or sister would help, or a father who wasn't tormented by pain. She and Grantley had faced and survived the most bloodcurdling personal war of all—that between whites and the Creeks in the South. But their love had been strong and their isolation had sheltered them from later harassment and exclusion from the educated genteel society of the day.

What pained her more than the loss of one son, more than the absence of her husband, was the stigma, the half-breed label, slapped on her children by a civilized nation.

Earl needed to be in school and she prayed that his father, in the mid-Atlantic somewhere, would have found an answer to their problem. If it meant sending him away, she could learn to loosen the apron strings a little.

Even now she was testing that strength to let go, knowing full well that Earl would return with legs and arms swollen from the bites of pesky mosquitoes, sand gnats, and the deer flies that were everywhere on a July day like this.

She thought of Bill George, back when most of his people took to the roads—moving out from the run down farms to the mill villages, taking with them their labor habits and attitudes developed in farming, long hours and the whole family sharing the work. But young Bill had decided to stay.

A faint breeze rustled the oak leaves against the porch railing. She shaded her eyes and looked out towards the burning sun. A hint of a breeze brought a trace of relief to her tear-stained face, and an optimistic silence followed her back into the farmhouse.

She stopped and turned back when she heard the soft, long mongrel baying far off in the distance and realized old Patch, foraging for food, must have scared up a rabbit or partridge in protest of the meager breakfast of scraps she'd served him.

"He'd better pay attention to protecting my child 'stead of chasing off like that, if he knew what's good for him," she said to the breeze and empty space.

*   *   *

Emerging from the high pine forests where he'd gone to relieve himself, Bill George heard the old dog sniff his way back to Earl and smother him in wet, hot saliva. He was excited from his run after whatever animal he had been chasing.

"How did you know it was old Patch, Bill George?" The boy let a growl rumble from deep in his own throat, teasingly.

"The eyes ain't the only part of the body," he said. "Why everythin' from the balls of your foot to the top of your head has feelers. Of all people, the Indians know that."

"I'm only half Indian and you aren't Indian at all."

"That's true," he said. "But I can still see the world with more than just my eyes."

They didn't talk for a while, just walked in the sun and the dust of the road.

Earl's mouth felt dry and hot from the taste of the swirling dust settled over the wagon trail. All he wanted now was to soak his tongue in some of Mis Mattie's sweet water.

When they got to the clay-packed, more traveled road, a tenant farmer slowed his mule and offered them a lift. They sat in the back and dangled their legs off the rear of the battered old wagon. Its wobbly wheels, screeching rhythmically, carried them to the country store. As they approached the small, whitewashed one room structure, the old mule's ears perked up.

"You think ole Joe hears somethin' we don't, Bill George?" He reached for a sleeve, tugging playfully.

"He knows there's water and shade up ahead. Mis' Mattie most likely got company, so it's time for you to straighten up that collar and mind your manners.

"Damn, Bill George! That's goin' to take all the fun out of our venture."

"Watch that, E," Bill George said more firmly, then reached over and pulled the boy closer to him. "Your mom would want you to be a gentleman, and I know you can be. She also wouldn't approve of that kind of language and neither do I."

"Why can't I be both? A gentleman and myself," he sighed, then cocked his head to one side to listen to the medley of tunes coming from the tinny upright in the store.

"You have to ask your pa the answer to that one," Bill George said.

"I hate my pa!" Earl snarled.

"You don't really mean that. Your father's only doing what he thinks is best for all of you. If you grow up to be half the man he is, you'll make us all proud. Now say you're sorry for making that remark and let's go get that sweet water while it's still cold."

Earl's nose twitched at the sound of 'sweet water', and reluctantly mumbled a 'I'm sorry', then followed at Bill George's heels as they climbed the wooden stairs.

Chapter 4

Inside the old general store was a tall, thin woman with white hair pulled back on a slender bobbing head. She wore a simple blue print dress. Her nervous fingers were clasped in the lap of a flour-sack apron, and her eyes were fixed on the piano, as though mesmerized by the Beethoven-Brahm medley. She ignored the two new customers.

Seated next to her, in a twin hardwood cane rocking chair, was a well-dressed younger woman. Her light brown hair was frizzled and short. Her dress was crisp looking, and light green. She toyed with a lace hankie and was tapping her tiny feet in rhythm. She was all smiles and cast many approving glances in the direction of the piano.

At the piano was an elegantly dressed young man with a moustache. He had a straight, strong back and played with a great deal of expression. He seemed to be totally unaware of anyone.

"You be quiet now," Bill George cautioned his uneasy companion.

"Shhh, and watch your feet." He led the way to two empty wooden crates near the potbelly stove.

For two years now, since he was six, Earl had been allowed to buy candy at the store with Bill George. They had been coming once a month and he never had to sit very long. He looked at the old pendulum clock near the piano, wishing he could move the long hand forward. He fidgeted and leaned back on the crate. He would have certainly stopped the concert if Bill George, sensing the danger, had not reached out for his hand and held it firmly. Getting a stronger grip on his walking stick, Bill George held it close against Earl's legs so he could quickly detect any movement. The boy groaned quietly and rolled his eyes around at the surroundings.

The display case, most of its glass missing, stood to one side. It was nearly empty except for a few cans of peas and tomatoes, old cracker tobacco, and tea tins, and a flour sifter. On top stood some old jars, old kerosene lamps, and old scales, old everything. One of the displays near the center of the store had a few items in all sizes of cardboard boxes. Some held cakes of soap, others hairpins, combs, shoelaces, and plugs of tobacco. The hard candies half filled four apothecary jars near the brass cash register.

Earl felt the coins in his pocket. He was anxious to place them on the counter and select his favorite candy from each jar. He turned completely around with his back to the piano. He found his image staring threateningly back at him from a large ornate mirror over a marble counter top. He spent a few minutes practicing some of his better glares, then lost interest.

He then looked at the newspaper clippings, cracked and yellow with age, that plastered the walls and spilled over onto the counter. The American and Confederate flags were the only things that added color to the magazine portraits of presidents Grover Cleveland, Benjamin Harrison and William McKinley.

Earl's eyes finally riveted on a twenty-four inch bronze statue of a man on horseback leaning against the largest, most colorful shield he had ever seen. He had not even heard the music when it stopped, nor felt Bill George when he first nudged him. The shield and the man on horseback had not been there on any of his previous visits or he would have seen it. Somehow he felt he was involved or would someday like to be a part of that world of chivalry. He did not have enough time to really get into any good fantasy about slaying villains, because he was interrupted by the piano player.

"My name's Curtiss Timms," the pianist said and extended his hand.

A little embarrassed by his inattention, Earl sheepishly accepted the stranger's introduction with a silly grin.

"I'm not the artist," the soft-spoken but animated Curtiss Timms insisted. "I'm an antique dealer and genealogist by profession. I did bring the statue with me. I got it in Atlanta. It's Don Quixote. Does he inspire you with his lofty but impractical ideals?"

"I don't know, Sir. I don't know who he is," Earl said. "I just know that I like it."

When Bill George and Earl left the store, their pockets were loaded with candy, tobacco, shoe laces, a curled up catalog or two and memories of two hours of learning. They had to lengthen their stride under a crushingly hot sun to get back to the Grantley place for dinner. Earl's mouth was tasting the dry dust again.

"That Cola Mr. Timms brought from Atlanta was better'n any ole sweet water, I'm thinkin'," he said.

"Can't argue with you none there," Bill George said. "How did that huge Coca-Cola sign read?"

"It reads 'Relieves Fatigue Five Cents.'"

"Thank you, Count Earl of Grantley."

"Only fittin', Sir William of George."

They both slapped their knees hilariously, and paused a moment to wipe off the streaming sweat from their faces.

"You believe all them things Mr. Timms said about Mis' Mattie's ancestors being killed by Indians, and some Mr. Hampston being at a tea party in Boston?"

"I'd say some is true and some ain't," said Bill George. "I had no learnin' myself, but I bet you'll come back in a few years from one of them fine schools knowing more than that Mr. Timms. You can tell me then what's true and what's not."

"I don't wanta go away to school ever," he said and stamped one foot in the dust.

"I'm going to help Mom here. She can teach me all the stuff I need to know. I can read and do numbers now."

He studied the face of his friend carefully. He was expecting a lecture of some kind. When none came, he laughed playfully.

"That Mr. Timm's sure a rib-tickler, wouldn't you say? And Mis' Mattie's sister, Lizzie Anne, sure's pretty as a hummingbird sitting there tapping her pretty feet to the music. Bet if she was standing up, her whole body would flutter.

"Bill George, you listenin' to me?"

"Hush up now," barked Bill George. "Hear that? I think old Patch has scared up more'n a rabbit this time."

The mongrel's baying had turned to a howl—a penetrating howl of a dog in pain. Before Bill George could get out a word of warning, Earl sprinted into a wild run through the snarled underbrush. His arms and legs were thrashing around as if somehow they would help him go faster. He stumbled over an old rotten oak log and felt something sharp stab his right jaw. He raised himself to a crouching position and looked at his dog.

Patch was in a boxing match with a three foot copperhead. He was circling the snake and attacking when he thought he could. They were trading blow for blow and stirring up a storm of dust and debris. Patch was slowly losing strength but did not seem to know how to quit.

Earl quickly grabbed handfuls of sand, small stones, anything within reach, and tossed them at the snake. He was hitting the dog about as often as the snake. He was looking around for a bigger rock, when Bill George finally reached them. He gave Earl his hickory cane with instructions to break the snake's back, not hit just the head.

"It's the back that controls the brain, don't you see," he said. "Your father taught me that once when I got bit by a rattler. Reason I wear leather boots now. Why your. . . ."

He stopped when he realized Earl was not listening.

Uttering snarls of curses, Earl hacked viciously at the venomous reptile. Soon nothing but pieces of copper, red, and brown flesh were left quivering in the dirt. Patch, sensing his safety now, sniffed at the raw meat and pawed it deeper into the earth. Satisfied at last, he ran off whimpering with his tail between his legs.

"Let'em be, E," Bill George said. "Patch will go wallow in the swamp mud. Best medicine there is according to the Creek Indians, and they lived here long before us. Did you get hurt?"

"Only my jaw when I fell. It's swelling up on me." His words were slurred and he was trying to be brave.

"But that wasn't from the copperhead. I got stung by something."

"I saw some hornets back there. Probably had a nest in that rotten log. Show me where they got you."

He took a large chunk of the moist Brown Mule chewing tobacco from his mouth and plastered it on Earl's jaw. Then ripping the faded sweat band from his felt hat, he asked the boy to press it firmly against his swollen face. When they got on the main road again, Earl collapsed in a heap. Bill George struggled to get the boy in his arms, dropping his stick while doing so. He then carried the unconscious boy home.

*　　　　　　　*　　　　　　　*

"Your quick thinking probably saved his life," Mrs. Grantley told Bill George later.

"Doc Stringer said he was okay. I've given him a tonic and he's resting quietly now. Thank you for carrying my baby all that distance."

She sat down at the table across from him and covered her face with her apron.

"Don't cry, Ma'am. If you could have seen that little feller pounding at that snake to protect his dog, you'd be awful proud. He didn't even ask to go near that creek, if that's what crossed your mind. That snake was near the road."

"I am proud, Bill George," and she nodded from habit. "I'm proud of both of you. You're a good man and a very faithful friend. I just worry so."

"Don't fret, Ma'am, everything's going to be just fine, you'll see."

"Yes, I know you're right. Why, you haven't touched that food and you need some more coffee."

She got up, bustled around getting them both fresh coffee and composing herself, then sat back down to talk about their day.

"Now tell me what all that jabbering about knights and counts, color shields and armor, means. Who is Mr. Timms and what is Coca-Cola and. . . . Well, I'll hush and let you talk."

Time passed quickly in the quiet kitchen and soon she refilled their coffee cups.

"He really talked about music for hours? You know how I struggle to get him to sit at the piano for just half an hour to practice his scales, and he's hardly touched that harmonica since his pa left. Well, will you look at us still sitting here talking, and you must be exhausted. There's nuthin' more you can do here, so you might as well go on home when you've a mind to."

"We lucky he didn't get snake bit, Ma'am. Maybe he could find some of them leather leggings like I got in one of them catalogues he brought home." Bill George took another sip of hot coffee.

Suddenly he slumped forward, dropping the cup into his empty plate. Gasping for breath, he clutched at his chest.

Mrs. Grantley ran to the sink, came back with a damp dish cloth to press against his forehead and took his wrist in her hands.

"I'll get you a tonic and you sit as long as you like. Earl would never grow up to be the fine young man we hope for if you go leaving us. You oughta be seeing a doctor, too," she scolded him gently when he seemed to be okay.

"I'm all right, Ma'am. Don't fret none.

"It's just my ole ticker. I 'spect I live to see your boy all grown up and fretting over his own children someday."

"And sprouting his own gray hairs." She laughed and Bill George joined in.

"I can almost see him now. He be graduated from a fine school and finding a good woman. Yes, he sure appears to be happy," he added.

"Enough of that kind of talk," she interrupted. "Let's let him enjoy a boy's life a little longer."

She laughed, but deep in her heart she knew those days, and years, would pass all too swiftly with lots of pain mixed in.

NEW YORK 1912

Everyone stopped what they were doing and gave her their full attention as she stepped from the Manhattan hotel elevator. If she was not an important person she should be. She was slim and erect in a sunflower yellow lace dress. Her ankle-length, full skirt was snugly fitted in all the right places to accentuate all her best qualities. She tried not to appear to notice the attention. She glided through the lobby swinging a violin case in one hand, a small, beaded, silver purse in the other, and entered the open door of a swank black limousine. She left a light trail of French perfume behind her.

"Who is that?" a young waiter whispered. He nodded his head in the direction of the departed beauty. He still held the tray of long stemmed crystal goblets in one hand, a fact he seemed to have forgotten.

"Never mind," the manager snapped. "She's way out of your class. What you need to do is get those glasses to the dining room." He then turned to include the rest of the immobile help.

"Get back to work, everyone. Show's over."

"Hey, sprinter," someone called out to the waiter. "Here's your chance to use that burst of speed you've been bragging about in them distance relays at that southern high school."

"Yeah," another joined in. "If you hurry, you just might catch that limousine at eight hundred and eighty yards." He slapped his hip and laughed at his joke.

"He said he was in second place. He ain't a champion," a bellhop corrected.

The young waiter continued to set up the glasses around the table, trying to ignore the carping remarks, only half hearing them at best. He could still see the raven-dark hair piled in an upsweep, the exquisite face, the appealing long lashes, and he was almost positive they fluttered at him only through the shaded window as she rode from the hotel. He surprised himself when the words spilled out of his mouth. He was even more surprised at what he said.

"She doesn't know it yet but, by my next weekend off, I'm taking her to Atlantic City." The reaction from his fellow workers startled him even more.

"Thought you were saving your money."

"Giving up school, are you?"

"Can't prove to your father you be 'prudent' that way."

"Dreamer."

He tried desperately to shut out their words by imagining what her voice might be like. Did it have an innate softness and delicacy in keeping with her appearance and personality? In spite of the coolness from the overhead fans, he felt a dampness spread over his body. He walked to a window and stood staring into the darkness. He trembled with surprise when the manager's heavy hand rested on one shoulder in a firm grip and he turned to see the look of urgency on his round scowling face.

"Get to work," was all the manager needed to say.

*   *   *

The applause was full and long. Men in fashionable suits, women with fox scarves and flyaway hats, had hung on to her every note. The young violinist closed her eyes and felt tears forcing their way out and could not say whether she was blissfully happy or devastatingly sad. If only her father could have been here to hear her.

The bright lights and the glare distressed her somewhat, but not the performance. She was not a bit nervous. She was a professional concert pianist and violinist. Playing before an audience at New York's Hippodrome, the biggest and most expensive theatre, was much like the mission schools, musicals, or governor's balls in Santiago. Her father had taught her well.

"Never let the public intimidate you. Always remember it's the music that endures. Seek out those the music can speak to," he'd say.

She stepped delicately and proudly across the mammoth stage to stand next to the accompanist. He was a big success with his first show, "The Firefly", and she had been a part of it. He kissed her hands and thanked her profusely, wishing her luck in furthering her career in America.

"My father would have enjoyed meeting you, Sir," she said. "He taught me of your work at Prague and is totally convinced that Rudolf Frime hears a different drummer."

"God be with you both, my little firefly." Frime let go of her hand, they both bowed again to the audience, and went backstage.

Like the nocturnal firefly, she had let her light shine. During the pause she heard a distinct voice call: "Savor this moment, Sarita."

*   *   *

After hitting a backhand passing shot down the line, the young tennis player flung his racquet down in triumph. He was feeling good about himself physically and mentally. At last he'd won at something, even though just a game to satisfy a hotel guest. He inhaled the early morning air deeply. He looked much different with a tennis racquet instead of a tray of glasses.

"They all beat me back home," he said. "It can be frustrating. But that sliced return, Brett, was superb."

"Perfect some of those wild shots and you could make tournament history, my friend. Thanks for the workout. I needed the competition if I'm to meet the champions next season."

"How do they play under a scorching sun and with temperatures sometimes at one hundred degrees for over three hours?"

"You learn to control the pressure from your opponent and to ignore the weather." Brett started for the stairway then turned back.

"Two sets enough for tomorrow?"

"Tomorrow. Same time." He watched the tall, blond Australian disappear from view, then hurried to the registration desk to get his work assignment. With an exaggerated action he spun the racquet, letting it hang almost vertically from his hand.

"Dressed for your Long Island tennis party?" the assistant manager snidely asked while sliding a worksheet in his direction.

"You're late again."

"I was entertaining a guest of this hotel," he retorted and looked up at the clock above the assistant manager's thinly parted hair to confirm the time. As he did so his eyes were drawn to the far end of the long walnut counter to a Dresden doll like figure dressed in blue and white.

"Has Dr. Jacobs called from the embassy?" she asked the desk clerk.

"No messages at all, Miss Bocan." He shuffled through some envelopes,

"If you're going to be on the veranda, I'll let you know as soon as he comes in."

"Her voice is soft, delicate, and just as I'd imagined it would be," the young man said softly to himself.

He searched for other words to express his feelings. When none came, he smiled. The effect must have been appealing and magnetic somehow, for she looked up and acknowledged his presence in a sincere and compassionate manner.

As a sprinter, he knew a burst of speed could come at any point during a long race, and he was nearing the finish line. It was mid-week and he had only got as far as her last name—Bocan. He slid in closer.

"Hey, Romeo," barked the manager, "get to work or you're fired."

She brushed pass him, eyes beaming radiantly, into the arms of a tall elegantly attired gentleman in white. He was more tan than an Aztec Indian.

On her way through the lobby, later that evening, she searched for the lively young man with the tennis racquet. Her own keen perception of people had alerted her. There was also a lively brain and keen mind behind that awkward behavior. She felt a little nostalgic and sensed a tingle of romance. She pictured him as a knight of the old school off on some crusade.

When she did not see him, the monotonous, painfully boring events at the garden party swept her pleasant thoughts of the young man away. Her assisting Dr. Jacobs in the task of soliciting funds to fight yellow fever in Cuba had accomplished little. She had worked long hours to perfect the music, yet no one could have heard it over the clinking of glasses and idle chitchat.

She was now exhausted in body and spirit, but there were letters she still had to write. "Manana," she whispered to herself. "I'll casually ask about him at the desk tomorrow."

Chapter 5

His nose twitched at the smell of steam and hot oil as he gripped the platform's brass railings. A clap of thunder erased the quiet charm of the landscape as the passenger train roared into the yellow-gray light, and Earl Grantley looked down at the glassy rails. The straight lines of track were like the brief hotel message on its yellow page:

URGENT . . . FATHER HURT . . . COME HOME.

It hadn't taken him long to pack his few belongings: a change of clothing, harmonica, tennis racquet, two favorite books: *American Poems* and *Age of Greek Fables* and one his father had brought from Cuba that he had yet to read: *Don Quixote* by Miguel de Cervantes.

In his haste to leave a note for Miss Bocan, he had forgotten all his toilet articles. But it did not matter, he was going home. Already Manhattan was a fading dot on his social map. His only regret was that he had not reached the finish line with the beautiful, elusive violinist. He didn't know her full name, where she was from or who the handsome man was she met that day.

Now, when he should be worried about his father, he could not help but wonder if it was fate, or his father's plan, to deny him happiness. He remembered his father had found a safe exit by physically removing himself to Cuba when disaster first struck at home. For Earl the only escape was mental.

He stood and watched the Georgia countryside pass and visualized the rail ties being stacked like cordwood into bonfires. He imagined how a group of Sherman's men all might have carried heated rails to the nearest trees and bent them around the trunks.

Then his mind wandered off to his own small piece of Georgia and he traveled through denser forest, winding over dusty wagon trails, and into the woods by his creek. The creek he never got to fish in.

He and his father had bailed hay together, ridden horses, mended fences, herded cattle, fed livestock, and sometimes read together far into the night. His Father had never let him fish in that creek. After that first year of constant pleadings, he just gave up in; hopeless frustration.

Now, when he got into these moods of hopeless frustration, he conjured up an image of Miss Bocan. A picture of her in the yellow dress, a picture he had framed and hung in his mind. In his haste, he wondered now if he had signed his name to the bold love note he left at the desk.

The locomotive gave a lurch and began to rock, sending a rippling effect through the friction plates connecting the line of cars. The pine stubbled hill country swayed in unison. Earl could hardly hear the conductor's voice above the piercing whistle and clicking wheels. He took out his gold chain watch and checked the time.

"The farmers around here will be setting their clocks about now too, Sir," said the stocky, uniformed young man.

"It looks like we should be expecting a sudden summer storms." Earl said and smiled. It was more a statement than a question and the conductor seemed impressed.

"That sky is a sign recognizable to any Georgian, Sir," he said. "We're asking all passengers to stay inside until the weather clears. You might prefer the diner, though."

At his first dinner out of New York, Earl shared a table with Jeff Browning, a blond, tanned Australian tennis player on a world tour. He was much like Brett. It came to him suddenly that he had not left a message for Brett. What would he think of him when he didn't show for practice? He wanted to tell this young man about Brett and some of his own plans, but he didn't. The stranger seemed so full of pent up reflections, that Earl held back and let him talk for an hour and a half without interruption. He knew more about the United States after a two-week tour than most natives with two years of college.

Suddenly there was a thunderclap so loud it shook the diner. A dark, pretty woman across from them jumped stiffly to her feet and gave a half scream. Her two small children shrieked half in fun, and half in fear, while hugging each other.

Earl thought it humorous how she so quickly changed her behavior from fear to attempting to calm them in a language foreign to him. The Australian promptly told him what it was.

"The accent is Afrikaans. That's a language of South Africa developed from the speech of 17th-century settlers from Holland and still very like Dutch, South African Dutch. However, she is French, but married to an American."

"How did you know all that?" Earl asked, eyeing the young man.

"A hobby of mine, you might say. Truthfully, I overheard her conversation with the gentleman you see seated alone at the table near the exit. Now he's what railroader's call a 'spotter'. He's employed to keep the conductors honest. Some are known to skim the top off the fares they collect on the train."

"Boy would Bill George snap his suspenders at that."

The words rolled off his tongue so smoothly they startled him. A lot of changes had gone on in the ten years since he had last shared a moment of real 'reckoning' with the negro companion of his childhood. He wondered if he would be up to the challenge of social changes. Did true friendship need re-cultivation. He thought of. . . .

"Are you thinking of home?" asked his companion interrupting his thinking.

"Someone I haven't thought of in a long time. Someone who was closer to me as a child than my own father. We did everything a father and son should do, but go fishing. He is blind."

"You look like you have a problem. Do you?"

"I'm wondering how much of that camaraderie has been damaged by absence, or, perhaps I should say, growth and maturity."

"Your eyes show me how much you thought of this man. Sometimes it's very hard to go back to something you had as a child. Sometimes it's not possible at all.

"So perhaps the simple truth is that if two men have something they're enormously proud of they should meet on that common ground, the pure joy of inspection."

"Inspection?"

"Inspection.

"Take the brakeman on this train, for example, when he inspects a wheel. If a hotbox, an overheated—axle bearing—develops, the crew will detach the damaged car and leave it on a spur track for repair."

"Are you suggesting that if I find our friendship broken, I should just detach myself?"

"Don't let the damaged car slow the whole train down. Don't let the loss of a childhood companion get you down.

"You have a destiny, Grantley. Follow the tracks that lead you there."

"Is tennis just your disguise? You sound like a Bostonian philosopher or an Indian guru."

They raised their wine glasses in mutual admiration.

The rain continued to drip down the window glass but the air seemed less heavy, as did the conversations around them. Earl checked his watch, alert to the jolt that was sure to come as the train's slow movement shortened the distance to the next terminal.

CHICAGO 1912

A few weeks later, when Roosevelt announced, "My hat is in the ring," Sara Bocan joined the twenty thousand of his followers in Chicago to form the Progressive party and name him its candidate. She remembered his use of the "big stick," his love of nature, his robust stature, and his smoking cigar. She really liked his favorite phrases: "savor the moment" and 'bully for you.' She thought back to that day in Santiago when she had gained, and lost, a friend in a few hours. She wondered if Mr. Roosevelt would have any news of George Grantley. She longed. . . .

"You look as if you are thinking of home. Are you?" asked the nervous, elderly man who called himself Otis Miller.

He had played a bit part in *The Great Train Robbery* made in 1903 and now at seventy-three, with an invalid daughter, he worked in the coffee house. He did not wait for an answer, but hastily introduced her to a tall well-dressed stout woman as though rehearsing a role.

"Many women are active in the leadership of the progressive reform movement, but you'll never find a more capable example than Jane Addams.

"Miss Addams, this is clergyman Juan Bocan's daughter from Santiago, Cuba."

Welcome to Hull House, my child." She extended a white-gloved hand. "If she is half as talented as she is pretty, Theodore is sure to win many more votes."

"I've read your book, *Twenty Years at Hull House*, Miss Addams, and can appreciate the problems of life you deal with in the slums. We face the same ones in Cuba."

"Otis, my good man, the child has class. If I had a daughter, I'd want her to be exactly as you are," she said and patted Sara's hand.

"And after reading about your life, your suffering, your father's influence, I sometimes think, had she lived, my mother would've been much like you," she said and took a deep breath.

"We have a lot in common and I'm here to help in any way I can in the campaign for our Mr. Roosevelt."

"Bully for you."

"Bully for us all."

Otis joined in the brief gaiety with a little soft shoe of his own rendition.

"Enough," Jane Addams said and clapped her hands lightly.

"I'd like for you to see more of Hull House. Since it began as an educational and recreational center for working mothers and their children, we've grown to include this coffeehouse, a gymnasium, a children's building, and even an art gallery."

"An art gallery? I'll savor this moment," Sara said.

"You're a connoisseur of the arts, my dear?"

"With my father's help, I've designed a villa that combines the architecture of my home and America. Among other things, it's a symbol of my dream to help bridge the gap between all countries."

"A tremendous undertaking. When and where do you propose to build your villa?"

"*Quien sabe?* If dashed hopes were cement blocks, I'd have a superstructure by now. Twice now a war has interrupted my plans. One thing I do know for sure. When I do build, it must be near water.

"I can't give a reason. Isn't that strange?"

"Not at all strange. You hold tight to your dream, young lady. Dreams have a way of sliding off written pages into reality. You're looking at someone who knows first hand," Jane Addams said.

They both got up and started off on the tour of Hull House. They moved into a lecture room/laboratory facility where three young women were working on some drawings. An older woman bowed as they entered the room and slipped a folded message to Miss Addams. She stopped, read the note, re-folded it, and then looked at Sara.

"I'm sorry to have to leave you so quickly, Sara, but Melanie will introduce you around. These sisters are from Atlanta. Someday their efforts will stir that sluggish legislature in Georgia into action. You'll find our group has the vision and creative thrust to accomplish that and more." She unfolded the message a second time.

"Now let's see what our Mr. Curtiss Timms, a private contributor, has up his sleeves to further our cause." After giving Sara a warm embrace, Miss Addams strolled confidently from the room.

"Don't worry," one of the ladies addressed the shy young lady left standing. "She'll not desert you."

"I was thinking more of what she has to endure," said Sara. "My own experience with private charity has been so discouraging. I think the more vital work is done by the working people themselves."

"Bravo," another cheered. "She's one of us."

They all applauded and offered her the empty seat near them.

Chapter 6

GEORGIA 1912

*T*he old mildewed fishing boat struggled to support its nearly two hundred pounds of cargo. Earl sat hunched over, protecting as much as possible his tennis racquet and valise from the seeping creek water, while alternating the stroke of two long poles. Why he chose this means of sneaking in the back way he could not really justify.

It had something to do with Jeff Browning's pep talk about following his own tracks. He had to have time to prepare himself for confrontation with his father and perhaps by defying the creek on his first return home, he could ease some of the unsettling thoughts in his mind. He also wanted to see Bill George first. With his help he'd know more about what to expect.

The smell of fatback, eggs, and sweet potatoes baked in the ashes, permeated the air through the north portion of the never-ending green meadow. Now Earl could see the smoke hovering over the crumbling chimney of Bill George's one room ramshackle cabin among the pines. Inside he would be scurrying about to get his supper fixed. Nothing in the appearance of the cabin or yard had changed over the years.

As he neared the backyard he shifted the traveling bag and reached up to pluck a ripe, deep purple fig from the bushes by the fence. He had become accustomed to more exotic and faraway fruits at the hotel, things like pineapples, guavas, mangos, and avocados. A fleshy fig on a morning like this had its own special charm and taste.

Earl moved to the boulder that served as a front step, to sit for a moment. His chest pounded so he buried his face in his strong hands before knocking. He wanted to catch his breath and compose himself.

The door was open and Bill George appeared, shifting his bulky frame slightly. He looked out past the young man's shoulders. Between his long, bowed legs, Earl could see fiery tunnels in the coals and ashes of the fireplace.

"Hey, Sir William of George, mind if I turn a few potatoes for you?"

"E, that you? I declare," he said and snapped his sweat-stained suspenders.

Earl threw an arm around the old man's stooped shoulders and suddenly they both were wiping the tears from their eyes.

"You're a sight for sore eyes, you are. Your pa told me you'd grown even taller'n him."

He stood there a long time waiting for Earl to speak, feeling the arm slacken on his shoulders.

"I haven't seen any of them yet, Bill George. I wanted to see you first."

"I'll get us some coffee," he said and soon dropped down beside the young man on the boulder.

"I've been thinking about you. Your ma reads all your letters to me. She's doin' real good but your pa, he's real bad off."

"What happened, Bill George? The message I got didn't give any clues."

"They had a big fire over in Haddock. The whole town burned to the ground, the way some tell it. Why you could stand on the tracks in Gray, six miles away, and read a newspaper; that's how big that fire was. According to Mis' Mattie and them, some night watchman was responsible. Apparently he left a half-finished cigar in a windowsill." He stopped talking and took a long sip from a tin cup.

"But my pa? How'd he get hurt?"

"Well, as soon as those big dinner bells from all over started clanging, which always means trouble, your pa rode out on Trader to help. He was as proud and eager as a Rough Rider charging San Juan Hill. Just outside of town he was thrown from his horse. But ole Doc says that's only part of it."

"What do you mean, Bill George?"

"You'll have to see for yourself."

"Will you go with me, just up to the house?"

"What kind of question is that? You don't still know how much your father cares for you, do you? You don't need Bill George to intercede for you any more.

"Your ma suffering the pain inside her now that she's got a hurt man at home and you the one's been away. What'd you learn at that school anyway?"

"I'm glad you haven't changed, Bill George. Don't know what I'd done if someone else had answered my knock this morning. You always were good at telling me what I needed to hear."

"Hush up now. Someone else knows you're here."

A nondescript, earth brown dog with one eye streaked in from the woods, tail wagging frantically, and tongue dripping saliva all over Earl's hand. He thought immediately of ole Patch.

"Who's this?" he asked.

"That's Ojito. Your pa named him . . . says it's Spanish for 'Little Eye' because of the one eye. Looks to me like he's come to make your going up to the house easier." This struck them as funny and they both slapped their legs, hilariously.

Chapter 7

The excited first yelp alerted Mrs. Grantley that the lanky figure coming over the rise onto the massive lawn was not that of Bill George.

"Who've you brought home this time, Ojito?" she asked, rubbing her gnarled fingers behind its ears. As her weakened eyes focused, she gasped. Racing forward with open arms, she showered her son with rivulets of tears.

Ojito barked again sharply, then relieved himself nervously against a rotting board near the walnut tree. He turned around in frantic circles until he finally settled down and sat nearby. The two humans laughed at his showmanship.

"How you been, Ma? and Pa?"

"He'll be mighty glad to see you, Son," she said. She held him at arm's length and admired his handsome, more mature face and healthy body.

"Gracious me, how you've shot up there. Don't waste another minute. Your father's in his room. Doc Stringer was just here and changed his medicine."

"Ma, there's something I gotta tell you first."

The look in his eye, the sound of his voice and the way his grip tightened on her arm, let her know how serious this was. Jeff Browning would have said, "Lay your cards on the line, pal, stay on track." His pause lengthened.

"What's on your mind, Baby?"

"I won't have to endure his brutal comparisons, will I. His throwing at me all the accomplishments of that Cuban filly he met in the war, and why can't I do all those things?"

"Young lady, not filly, Son. He hasn't mentioned her for years." She smiled with as much assurance as she could.

"He frightens me and makes me angry when he talks about her, and I know I should love him because he's my father. But Mom, there's someone else now. I met her in New York. She's so beautiful, Ma!"

Earl spoke with such tenderness and conviction, his mother felt a surge of pride. Her son was a man now and in time he would be aware of his father's finer qualities, when he got to know him better. She gave Earl an admiring glance.

"You must be patient with him. I think the obsession is only concealed not forgotten. But I'm happy for you, Son."

"What exactly is wrong with Pa?"

"Just indulge an older man's wishes, for my sake, please. Doc says the gunfire of the war has damaged your father's nerves and taken away his ability to hear high frequency sounds."

"But the fire? You mean it's a war wound?"

"His right arm is healing nicely. He got some smoke inhalation, but Doc says his lungs are clear.

"The war damage is in his ears. A ringing started about ten years ago. He never said anything to me. For the past several months the ringing has gotten much louder and is causing him great discomfort."

"Ma, that's awful."

"It's like having a train whistle going off in your head constantly.

"I try to get him to read. I offer to read to him, but he says he can't concentrate any more. He sleeps twelve hours a day because that's the only way he can get away from the constant noise. Our friends don't like to come anymore. They don't understand when they can't see anything wrong." She tried desperately to hold back the tears.

"It's all right, Ma . . I'll see what I can do." He planted a kiss on her moist cheek. "I'll put my full force behind it!" He wished Jeff could have heard him say that.

Taking the steps two at a time, he raced up the winding staircase, paused briefly at the top to muster his courage, then rapped softly on the open door to his father's room. When he did not get a response he entered the dark interior and gasped at the gaunt, weak, skeletal figure smothered by layers of covers on the huge canopied bed. Only the white head propped against a soft goose down pillow was visible. His face was turned toward the heavily draped oversized windows. The room had the heavy smell of the sick. It reeked of turpentine, vinegar, and camphor rub. The kerosene lamp was lit even in the daylight. Nothing, except for open windows, a stiff breeze smell and the fragrance of fresh cut flowers could have concealed the smell of illness.

His father was breathing peacefully, however, but when Earl touched the marble cold hands, he made no movement, his eyes glued together.

"Pa, it's me, Earl." He brushed the fine white hair back from the face and felt the aged hands begin to relax in his, but his father did not answer. He gave a cough from nervousness, and in hopes the sharp sound would get a response. None came so he then moved cautiously to the windows and drew back the heavy brocade drapes to let in the mid-morning sun.

"Jessica? That you, my love?" His father's words were muffled and weak. His eyes, though, were half open now.

"It's me, Pa. Earl. Here, let me straighten your pillow out."

"Son, is that you?" He reached for Earl's hand, his eyes now filled with tears.

"You came back!"

"Yes, Pa. I'm here, to stay."

"I can't take any more wars. Dash the lights, Son," he said as he squeezed Earl's hand as tightly as possible. His eyes were darting around in their sockets, looking for something no one could see.

"Don't try to talk now, Pa. I'm home to stay. We can . . . look what I brought you." From a worn brown paper wrapper, he removed a pair of dark sunglasses.

"They're to help you enjoy nature's warmth. I know how much you miss being out in the sun with Trader, but he's hurt, too, inside. You and I at least have that in common, we can talk and understand the animals. Trader would never disappoint you, Pa."

His father, even after several attempts, still failed to keep his eyes open and in focus. He tried to speak, but no words came.

"Here, Sir, try these." Earl had asked the salesman on the train for a child's size, but even so, the glasses jutted from his father's ears like quills on a porcupine. A faint smile slowly crossed his father's face and he knew his gift had been worth the money he paid.

"Army issue, Son?" His father groaned then and began to shiver violently. Earl pulled the thick handmade quilts tighter around his shoulders and held them there until the shaking stopped.

"No more talk. I'm . . . so . . . tired."

"I could read to you for awhile. Would you like that, Pa?

"One of your favorite passages, maybe?"

The old man nodded and the glasses slipped off on to the pillow. "You won't be needing these for now. I'll adjust them to fit later."

His eyes scanned the well built shelves jammed with his selection of literature. There were some volumes dating back to pre-Civil War days. Their leather backs were beginning to crack from the hot sun. The newer books had paper covers to protect them. Their covers were also in bright colors to attract the reader to them. The shelves took up one wall and overshadowed all the other furnishings in the room. There was a bed and stand, a dresser with an ornate mirror, and a couple of rocking chairs that were casting twin silhouettes across the oak wood floor. The other two walls facing the windows were bare except for one glass framed picture near the bedpost. Had Earl been less preoccupied with track and tennis at school, less into mathematics and literature, and more serious about the Arts, he would have been attracted to this painting by Charles Dana Gibson. It was *The Gibson Girl with Violin* and was away from the sun's direct rays. He hadn't noticed it. Had he seen it, it would have reminded him of his Miss Bocan. Instead he made his choice from the worn volumes and began to read to his father.

" 'Nevertheless,' answered Don Quixote, 'at the present moment I would rather have a quarter-loaf of bread, or a cottage loaf and a couple of heads of salted pilchards, than all the herbs that Dioscorides has described. But, good Sancho, get up on your ass and follow me, for God, who provides for all, will not desert us; especially, being engaged, as we are, in His service. He doth not abandon the gnats of the air, nor the worms of the earth, nor the tadpoles of the water, and He is so merciful that He maketh His sun shine on the good and the evil, and He causeth the rain to fall upon the just and unjust.'

" 'Your worship,' quoth Sancho, 'were fitter to be a preacher than a knight-errant.'

" ' 'Knights-errant' Sancho,' said Don Quixote, 'knew and ought to know somewhat of all things, for there have been knights-errant in past ages who were as ready to make a sermon or a speech on the king's highway as though they had taken their degrees at the University of Paris; whence it may be inferred that the lance never blunted the pen, nor the pen. . . .' "

His father was asleep. Earl finished the passage, put the book on the stand, still opened to the page, and began to straighten the covers on the bed before leaving. As he reached for the brass doorknob, he remembered something Jeff had said.

"The French have a proverb," he said. " 'A door must be either open or shut.' Life is a series of choices and the only way to live it is decisively."

He left the door open, anxious to share a few quiet moments with his mother in the kitchen.

"Just you and me again, Mom," he said, sipping coffee and eating a wedge of hot, freshly baked pecan pie.

"Looks that way, Son, but not for long." Her hands trembled as she lifted her cup.

"Mom, I'm staying. Pa thinks I've been to war; he's never going to get better," he stammered.

"Don't ever lose hope, you hear! One year, Son. No more, then you're going back to that school. Someone in this family is going to get a proper education," she said, reaching over to cup Earl's face in her hands, as she had when he was small, "and that someone's you. And it won't do you any good to change the subject."

"Then help me get started, Mom," he pleaded, "help me to make the right decisions."

As his mother began to tell about all the improvements made and jobs left to do, Earl felt the confusion and frustration mount inside him.

"I can never be the Rough Rider Pa was, Mom, but I'm going to try to make you proud of me. I just have to do it my way." He kissed her gently on the cheek and headed for the barn to saddle Trader. He had some deep thinking to do and he knew just the right place to do it.

He tied Trader to a low limb of the cottonwood tree and sprawled out beneath its branches, looking out over the recently swollen creek. Time to think and the right place to begin. He let his mind sort the events for him. He would be functioning on a local level as an inspiring business farmer. He would need to check on the workers at the top-ranking sawmill in these parts. He would need to build up the herd of Holsteins, and see that the payroll for the hired hands was accurate and on time.

On a broader level, he would need to learn new methods to help the few tenant farmers they had, to investigate the reason the South had to pay higher railroad rates, and study more carefully any new Federal land policies.

Most satisfying of all, he would get to inspect the country club and see that it was being run properly. His father had built the log structure off the dirt road and nestled in a grove of pines for 'poor people.' He had wanted a place for them to be able to get together after work, relax, have good food, and drinks. Of course, he had never been allowed to go there before, even with his father. But now he would be expected to.

They had a fine big house, still isolated by five miles of dirt road, with Bill George as the closest neighbor. It was the way his father had wanted it and that was the way it would stay.

He worked hard in his new life and the only complaint now became his romantic life and his strong need for the elusive beautiful violinist. He dreamed of her sharing this life with him—this life at the edge of civilization yet apart from it. A life less than one hundred miles from Atlanta, where he'd heard the women were the most beautiful. He would polish up on his courtly manners at some of those garden parties with his cousins, but his heart would be in Manhattan, or wherever she was.

By the end of the year, he had developed quite a reputation around the state as a ladies' man. He had also, with his mother's help and faith in him, managed to have the estate in such shape that it could practically run itself. Now it was time, again, to make a decision about school and he'd left on Trader early that July morning—to think.

His mother and a few close relatives had had their heads together for months, planning a lawn party of some kind: it was the peak of watermelon season, and Earl's birthday. Such occasions and fussings were more Atlanta's style, he thought, and he had no intention of making a big thing out of it. Since Claudia Brighton had been invited, whom he did not care for, he knew he'd stay away as long as he liked and sneak in the back way toward the end just to be polite, explaining the urgency of his business deals and the time slipping by.

By noon the tables were filled with food. They had been set up under the walnut trees and dotted the spacious, freshly mowed lawn. Floral arrays and green clippings made a path through the garden and into the ballroom itself which was ready to accommodate the hundred or more dancers.

Model Ts and touring cars lined the dirt road for a mile, coughing and shaking their lovely occupants in preparation for the jarring they would be getting shortly on the dance floor. The men, in full evening dress, after greeting their hostess, deposited their cousins or sisters in small groups of giggling maidens and went to seek out the ladies of their choice to share their food and whatever followed.

The Bumphrey sisters wove in and out among the crowd, introducing their special guest and returning compliments about each other's fashionable gown. They had a special surprise for the evening that many knew about.

Fanny Brighton's daughter, Claudia, fidgeted and squirmed, eager to break away to seek out Earl.

Time passed quickly for some, not so quickly for others, Mis' Mattie and her sister, Lizzie Anne, had planned that all would enjoy this evening. Being in charge of the entertainment, they had persuaded Mr. Curtiss Timms to give some readings and play for the dance. Even the grand piano, its curved, graceful legs polished to perfection, stood ready in its rosewood frame.

"He'll whet your appetite for more," Mis' Mattie had said to all who asked about Timms. Since Earl had met him so many years ago, he had become a regular visitor to Mis' Mattie's.

Claudia was still craning her neck above the heads of the others, hoping for a glimpse of Earl, long after the music had started.

Timms had selected a spirited march to move the group indoors where most, in the excitement of the evening, soon forgot what was to be the highlight of the gathering, the introduction of the Bumphrey sister's special guest. The Latin rhythm was a cue for the Bumphrey sisters to get everyone ready and a signal for someone else. The music climbed the spiral stairway to the top and from the open door of Grantley's room stepped the young lady in green taffeta and lilacs. Most of the guests had been introduced to her earlier.

Under the soft glow of lighting she could have been the *Gibson Girl* who had stepped from the painting while leaving her violin behind. The shouts and cheers from the polished dance floor led by the Bumphrey sisters alerted Earl's ears.

He had slipped in the back way through an outside passage to his room and was struggling to button his evening shirt. He ran sweaty hands over his thinning hair, grabbed his black tie and tails, and raced out the door. In an instant, he saw that his earlier, brief assessment of the young lady's beauty had not been exaggerated. He gasped with embarrassment.

"You?" he stammered.

"I hope so," she smiled, dark eyes flashing.

"What're you doing here?" He lowered his voice and smiled at the gawking faces below.

"It's your birthday." She lifted her skirt and started down the stairs as the guests began to sing the birthday song.

Earl beamed nervously, a little like a small boy caught with his hand in the cookie jar, but he held firmly to Sara Bocan's arm.

"I need some answers," he whispered, through the pasted on smile.

"What were you doing in my father's room to start with?" His grip tightened.

"I don't owe you answers but they will come." She pulled away, still smiling for the spectators, but pleased to see Earl display the same attitude, personality and demeanor he showed at the registration desk. The worst thing that could happen was that he could not dance.

"Well, are you going to ask me to dance, or just stand there until Claudia catches your eye?"

"Claudia? Who's Claudia?" he whispered in her ear as he guided her deftly around the floor, one palm cradling hers, the other arm encircling her tiny waist. Their bodies turning and gliding in perfect harmony. They swirled by his mother, who saw only a blur of black tie and taffeta.

"He didn't waste any time," chirped Fanny Brighton as Claudia stood by her side, fuming, and feeling faint.

When the music stopped, the Bumphrey sisters were the first to reach them.

"I see you like our birthday surprise. Happy birthday, Cousin." Melanie stood on her tiptoes and planted a kiss on Earl's flushed face. She stepped aside so her sisters, Malissa and Malinda, could offer their congratulations too.

When the stream of well-wishers had dwindled, and Sara had been spirited away during a slow waltz, Earl made his way to his mom's side and gave her a kiss.

"It's her," he said proudly. "The girl I'm going to marry."

"Then thank your father, Son, as I have."

"What's Pa got to do with it?"

"If you had seen his face light up when she entered his room you wouldn't need to ask that. I'm thanking the Lord for His blessings today."

"You can't mean she's that 'filly' with the unpronounceable name?"

"The same. Now go on and waltz with your darling and be a gentleman."

"I'll be a gentleman and myself," he assured her. "There's someone special I want her to meet before this party is over."

"Bill George is waiting in the garden," she said, smiling. "You know how he hates crowds, but loves any kind of music."

* * *

In the garden later that evening, Bill George did not have to give his oral approval, the joy for Earl was clearly seen in his sightless eyes. They all sat close together on the cast-iron bench laughing over old memories, sharing enthusiastically with Sara who joined in, as though she had experienced them too. When the rollicking hodgepodge of music grew increasingly louder, both Spanish and English tunes, Bill George slapped his knees and snapped his suspenders.

"Spanish and Irish eyes smiled this night."

Then Earl and Sara vanished into the shadows of the walnut trees. The dreams of what they both had always thought they wanted began to merge with the reality of getting it.

The music stopped. The lamplights flickered. The party ended.

Chapter 8

GEORGIA 1917–1919

In the following years, the United States trained and equipped an army to send to France in time to stem the tide of German advances, and Earl was still waiting for his dreams of wife and home to materialize. Finally on another hot, humid July night he reached for his diploma. He heard his mother's words ringing in his ears as he accepted it.

"As long as there's a university where any student can study any subject," she said, "you're going to finish school, Son."

"But, Mom. . . ."

"No argument. Your Sara has her heart set on earning a fine arts degree. She told me all about it, and it's not just to pacify her father." She brushed a strand of silky red hair away from his face.

"She'll wait for you, Son. She as much as told me that too."

Then I might as well volunteer for service. . . ."

He choked on the words when he saw the hurt they brought to his mother's eyes. Then he, too, felt the pain of the two decades before when his father had gone to war. He did not volunteer and as sole male heir he was not required to serve.

In rebellion, he raised a storm or two but somehow endured the boring, aimless academic life. On this graduation night his eyes were the only dry ones in the vast assembly.

That same week, while a small army with red, white, and blue flags tossing about, marched down the Champs Elysees, Earl was deep in conservation, as he and a few tenant farmers marched down rows of seedlings for a new pine forest. While the column of khaki-clad regulars found crowds of men, women, and children covering them with flowers, Earl found a ready and profitable market for his cotton, trees, and meat in England and France. Serving by at least providing food and supplies to the government made him less guilty asking Sara to share a lifetime with him. Her main preoccupation since her graduation had been helping the poor and unfortunate in the Caribbean. From the letters she wrote, he knew that her intentions were as serious as his. He had written Juan Bocan and had formally asked for his daughter's hand in marriage.

Father and daughter arrived by train on his twenty-fifth birthday. A few days later Juan was giving his daughter to the son of the Rough Rider he had met in Santiago two decades ago.

The bride wore white brocade, with ruffles at the wrist of old Irish lace. Around her neck hung a gold locket and inside, under the glass, was a miniature yellow sunflower that Grantley senior had just given to her. He had offered his blessings and, with Bocan's help and encouragement, had consented to being wheeled out into the August sun onto the lawn for the light meal after the ceremony.

Everyone had such a good time that many guests lingered long after the others had gone. These few busied themselves with a second examination of the wedding gifts as an excuse. When the dust of the last vehicle settled over the dirt road, the bride and bridegroom rushed to their room to change into something more appropriate. They embraced their parents and, while still holding hands, they raced to saddle Trader II and rode off for Earl's favorite thinking place. They both knew full well there would be, on this visit, less thinking and dreaming and more action.

The site by the creek, distinguishable even in the semi-darkness by its gracious surroundings, brought tears to Sara's eyes. Earl held her at arms' length and turned her face up to look her in the eyes.

"Why do you cry, pretty lady?" he asked, brushing a tear from the corner of her sparkling dark eyes.

"I'm just so happy and sad," she answered. He gave her a gentle kiss when he pulled her closer.

"Why sad?"

"It's too beautiful to last."

"What's too beautiful? You're too beautiful, and our love will last a lifetime." He kissed her tenderly.

"Not that, silly." She kicked the side of his boot gently. "I'll be silent and not share my thoughts with you."

"Brilliant idea. Come here," and he stretched out under the cotton-wood by the bluff with the wind in his hair. She walked to one side and sat on a boulder overlooking the creek.

"OK, tell me your thoughts then, pretty lady."

"You'd only laugh," she said, screwing up her face to give him a mean look. But he did not laugh. Instead, her account of her attempts to build "Villa Sara" filled his heart with blissful longings. When she showed to him the drawing, now faded and torn from so much folding and unfolding and dreaming and hoping, he would have promised her anything.

"You shall have your villa and this is a fine place for it."

"Honest?"

"Honest. Now come here."

Their wedding night started under the stars and was continued later as they entered the back passageway to their bedroom. The following morning they proudly hung their emblazoned bed sheet from the window as visible proof of the bride's virginity.

"According to some custom," Sara had informed Earl, "a new bride was considered to be a vessel for bearing sons and had to be untouched."

"It's a beautiful custom," Earl said. "Do you know any others?"

"Many of them," she teased as she twirled around in her petticoat. "Let's go for a walk and I'll tell you another."

"What'll we call our first son?" he asked, giving her a gentle pat on the rear. She did not answer just then, but two years later fate made alterations.

They spent their honeymoon in Cuba and Earl learned to respect and love his wife's father as much as he did his own. He also reached a new awareness of a foreign culture and saw what such knowledge could mean in terms of strengthening the relationships between the two countries. His sons would do more than fight in wars to bring about peace, of that he was certain.

Back in the United States, they resumed life at the Grantley estate. As a girl from a wide background of luxury and poverty, Sara found it never dull in her new environment, and Jessica Grantley soon became the mother she had never known.

When Earl was away on the more complicated tasks of running the estate, she and his mother would finish the house chores and talk for hours about things each had seen and done. Sometimes they would play the piano or sing together. And when she wanted to be alone or take a walk, she was free to do so. As the days went by, she learned to confide more and more in the older woman who seemed to glow in this new-found relationship. That relationship burst into full bloom when Sara told her mother-in-law a year later that she was pregnant. The birth of a male heir would make their lives complete.

By the latter part of October, Sara could barely fasten the upper two buttons on her light coat. Her joy was accentuated when all the signs indicated she was going to give birth to a boy.

On one of those early frosty mornings she decided to cut short her daily walk through the pines and around and instead she went directly to the barn to feed Trader II his daily apple. Ojito, the dog, had run ahead of them but, soon sensing her absence, he had come back to trail along beside her.

The events that followed occurred so rapidly that no one could completely piece together for sure what had actually happened. But everyone agreed that the culprit was a tom-cat.

The horse seemed restless when Sara and Ojito entered the building, but he calmed down when she extended the apple and gave him an affectionate face rub.

Ojito gave a low growl of warning, but the straggly orange and black cat had picked this particular spot to become enamored of a female in the loft.

When the two cats tangled and dropped from above, they took bridle, tack, lead ropes, and bits of hay with them. Ojito barked frantically and Trader lost control. He kicked the side wall and crashed through the gate to his stall. He pushed Sara over a fallen saddle as he galloped into the barnyard. He stopped at the barbed wire fence, whinnying helplessly as he pawed the ground.

Later, when Mrs. Grantley looked out the kitchen window, as she often did to watch Sara return from the barn, she saw only Trader and Ojito and went to investigate. "It's not time, God," she prayed. "The baby needs more time."

Earl heard the metallic boom of the iron dinner bell at a distance of two miles and pushed the Model T's gas pedal to the floorboard. When he chugged onto the lawn and saw his mother waiting on the porch, her whole being revealed the fear she felt. He leaped from the car, leaving it still running under the walnut trees, and raced up to her. The smell of formaldehyde confirmed his suspicions that something terrible had taken place.

"Mom, my baby?" he screamed, taking her firmly by the shoulders. "What's happened to my son?"

"Sara's been hurt," she sobbed. "Doc asked us to wait and pray and then closed the door to your room. It wasn't Trader's fault, Son, listen to me."

"I said where's my son?" He rushed past his mother and followed the smell.

What he saw just inside the kitchen door sickened him. He felt the ivory handle of the gun strapped to his hip and sailed out the back door straight for the barnyard, Ojito snapping at his heels.

"I knew I'd find you here, E."

He whirled around to find Bill George near the post where the barbed wire stopped at the crude wooden gate. He ran to the old man and buried his face into his sweaty flannel shirt, letting the tears fall without apology.

"This whole place has a curse on little boys," he said and shivered. "I don't know what to do, Bill George, I feel so useless."

"You hush that kind of talk right now, young man. If there's any curse put on anyone, it's going to be me wishing one on you if you don't hurry up to that room and look in on your Spanish lady. She's hurting inside more'n you and needs to see your strength." He gave Earl a friendly nudge.

"Now be a man, you hear?"

"I think that's easier than being a gentleman." He shook Bill George's cane for emphasis because he was drained of any playfulness.

"And in case you're wondering, I didn't shoot anything. I couldn't bring myself to hurt Trader, but I gave that old tomcat a good scare."

"You go back to the house, now, you ready?"

"There's one more thing I have to do first. You go on ahead."

Earl wandered through the sunflower garden purposefully searching for just the right arrangement of blossoms to convey his sentiments to Sara. When he started for the house he could hear the Model T coughing where he had left it running, for what now felt like an eternity ago. He turned the engine off and took laborious steps forward to fulfill a first task in his new role as father, even though for such a short time. The thought alone gave him inner strength. He approached their bedroom with confidence.

From the ornate, hand-carved brass doorknob down to the simple hooked rugs, from chintz draperies on the window to the carved cabriole legs of the side table, the room's mood was her own creation. His eyes roamed delightedly over the white walls freeing space for one family photograph of her father and mother. The bed and two chairs were made of mahogany as was the chest of drawers lined in oak.

"Mahogany is best," she had explained to him when her father had suggested furniture as his wedding gift. "Because of the grain and colors. It's light and takes a shape very well. Her talent for collecting and arranging objects about the room epitomized her belief in a simple but elegant way of living and it ignited his enthusiasm. The chipped blue vase and assortment of seashells and arrowheads held special meanings for them. Art and music and their love had its own method of healing.

He moved silently over to the side table where she kept her model of 'Villa Sara' and laid the smallest sunflower he had picked at the arched entrance. Then he went to her and gently put her cold hands to his lips and warmed them tenderly, kissing away the tears in her sad dark eyes. There was no need for a lot of words.

Just as there was life in the things of the room, there would be life for them. She dried her tears and asked him to read something to her, so he selected a message of hope from the Bible, (Job:14:7–9).

> "For there is hope of a tree, if it be cut down, that it will sprout again, And that the tender branch thereof will not cease."

She sighed deeply, thanked him and closed her eyes in sleep. He sat beside her for some time, thinking this was at least the start of a new beginning.

Mis' Mattie and her sister prepared the body. They laid the tiny baby in the cedar cradle Earl had carved out for him. With Doc Littlejohn and Mrs. Grantley senior they made the short trip alone to the family grave-yard to a fenced-in section near the sunflower garden. There they buried the tiny child.

CUBA 1919

They planned a vacation trip to Cuba to visit her father. They felt it would give them an added shove into a new beginning. Their doctor had been opposed to the trip. He wanted them to avoid the exposure of a long journey during the infantile paralysis epidemic of 1919. They ignored him and eagerly packed their things and were soon there and on the Cuban Special, an all Pullman train which made weekly tours between Havana and Santiago.

Only once did Sara break down on the long journey, and then she sobbed uncontrollably for hours. She was seated next to the window when, mid-way to the island, she saw a young couple with a baby waving cheerfully from a village platform.

Earl immediately exchanged seats with her and held her closely until the trembling stopped, grateful that the happy family was not aboard with them.

She recovered once they were involved in the hectic activities surrounding the anniversary celebration of her father's new school building in Suena. On other days they rode horseback high into the hills of the Sierra Maestra mountains. On other days they breathed deeply of the fresh sea breezes and filled their stomachs with exotic fruits. Their happiness was explosive until her father took them to Vista Alegre.

There they saw a dream crushed not by war, but by Nature's own hands. Hands of revenge or Divine purpose, depending on which side of the pulpit you stood. As they sat among the ruins of her father's country villa, Sara renewed her vow to build the dream of Villa Sara even if it meant performing the labor alone.

"A penny for your thoughts, pretty lady," Earl teased as he plucked a twig from her dark hair. She remained silent while they watched a green iguana blink down at them from the coconut palm then leap to a pineapple plant and turn brown.

"Papa worked so hard," she said. "It's just not fair. I'm afraid he's had one too many disappointments in his life." They looked at the tall, thin figure leaning on a cane and facing out into the bay.

"He's going to be fine," Earl assured her and reached for her nervous hand. "He still has that firm determined mouth that breaks into a laugh easily, just like you."

"You're teasing me again, just when I'm feeling nostalgic." She wiped a tear away with his hand.

"Go to him, pretty lady. Tell him he must come home with us."

"He'd never leave. Did you know he wants a grandson desperately?"

"Then, with your consent, we'll try to oblige him," he said squeezing her hand firmly.

She kicked him playfully on the leg and went over to her father.

"Papa," she said as she put her arms gently around him, "we're ready to go home now."

"It's a beautiful sight isn't it, Sarita?" he said, looking into the distance. He was trying not to hear her.

"*Si*, Papa, but you must see the one I've found in America."

"Is there really another so breathtaking as this?"

"Equally so, Papa, but you must see it to believe it. We want you to share our place and dream with us. Will you consider it, Papa?"

"In time, Sarita, in time. I have so much yet to do here."

"I understand, Papa. Let's go now. Earl is getting restless and we must see that our American visitor does not find us lacking in Southern hospitality."

The huge battered bus backfired all the way down the narrow mountain trail toward the Carretera Central, the highway that snaked its way across the entire length of the island. Earl wondered if they would make it. Once on the highway the *campesinos* aboard came alive—they had seemed to be sleeping—and noisy with chatter.

This made Earl most uncomfortable because he only knew a few words of Spanish. Only enough to get hot water for shaving, food to eat, or money exchanged. He saw little need to exert his energy learning the language when most of the islanders could speak English. He was also nauseous from the smell of so many bodies so close together. Body odors fused with cologne, hair oil, and live produce was overwhelming to his western senses.

"Try to think of something pleasant," she said, as she rested a hand on his shoulder, and smiled.

"Think of the tropical flowers and the towering monuments to the heroes of our island. Look at the dusky purples, blues, and mauve tones of the timeworn buildings and the. . . ."

"*Basta.* Enough, Sarita," her father said as he tapped her on the shoulder with his cane.

"I'm sorry, Papa, the words just slipped out."

A brief stop a short while later for drinks at Bar Ramona brought some relief. At last Earl could get out of the crowded bus and breathe deeply of the fresh air. He watched a mountain boy and his goat pass on the road and head into the hills with a vast round loaf of rough bread under his arm. He wondered what it was really like for his father to have climbed those hills on horseback with the Rough Riders so many years ago.

They rode for hours afterwards through village after village, and Sara pointed out the assortment of architecture with Moorish influence predominating. They crossed deep blue-green harbors whose bridges barely supported the bus and them, then they went down incredibly narrow and dirty streets and, at last into Santiago.

As they approached the dwelling without a veranda, Sara rushed ahead to be first to use the ornate heavy knocker. This time she did not have to stand on tiptoe as she had done when Earl's father had been their guest. Nor did she get the same response from inside, for Pepe the parrot had not returned after the last earthquake. She pounded a second time and Ampara's daughter, a replica of her mother's short, Buddha figure and of her walk, clogged rhythmically forward to unbolt the heavy latch from the inside. Sara hurried off with her to prepare a light meal.

They ate silently in the octangular building. The once all-white gazebo was sadly in need of paint now. They watched the sun cast its last shadows of the day against the sweet lemon tree.

"Aren't you feeling any better, my Son?" her father asked, seeing Earl push his food around and not eating.

"Just an upset stomach, nothing to worry about," he said, reaching over the bench to touch Sara's hand.

"We can take care of that, can't we, Sarita?" With his cane, he reached up and pulled down a branch of the lemon tree to select the richest, sweetest, and juiciest of the abundant fruits.

"Bite into one of these and see if it doesn't correct the problem in no time."

"Papa planted that tree so he could get all the lemons he wanted," Sara said, smiling. "He said he never wanted to get spanked again."

"I promised to tell your father that story once, but somehow we never got around to it. Now I'll share it with you and you can relate it to Grantley senior with my apology. You must also take back with you a cutting of my tree to plant in this place my daughter seems to think is a rival for Vista Alegre."

GEORGIA 1920s

Wrapped carefully in wet newspapers, the lemon tree cutting had formed some roots during their journey home. To assure a lasting transplant, Sara nurtured it for several days in a large mason jar of well water. She gradually added soil from the creek until the roots took hold, crowding and pushing to be a part of a larger plot of land. It was unusually quiet the day they planted the sweet lemon tree facing the sun and overlooking the creek. Wildflowers and ferns were gracefully stirred in an air current which seemed to flow from all sides. Then they heard a lone whippoorwill trill in the distance. They also heard a car in the distance which seemed to be arriving at their home. They dropped their tools against the cottonwood and rushed home to find Doc Littlejohn's Model A parked under the walnut trees. A chill swept over them.

"It's Pa, I know it is. I hope we're not too late," Earl whispered, breathing heavily.

"Your poor mom," she sighed and reached for his arm and held on tightly.

The silence that enveloped the whole house after the death of George L. Grantley became more penetrating with each slight movement. Earl began to feel the pressure of being the only male heir. He was frightened by such responsibility and could not understand his mother's complete control. After all she had suffered, she now held back her tears. Tears he expected her to shed, uncontrollably and for hours, did not come.

He suffered from his own muddled thoughts about his father as someone to be loved at a distance, or loved only because he was his pa. These thoughts became increasingly intense to the point where Earl soon began a routine of leaving the house earlier each morning and on some pretense or other stay away until later each evening. Both Sara and his mother thought Earl might be spending some of his time with Bill George, but that was not the case.

Bill George made a daily walk to the house but he always arrived after Earl had left. He never let the women lose hope but always encouraged them to be patient.

"E's got a big weight on his shoulders; but he'll figure a way to lessen it, don't you fret none."

"You're right, Bill George, something good always comes after the bad," Ma Grantley said. Then turning to Sara who was deep in dirty dishes and suds, she started a new conversation.

"Shall we let a certain someone in on our secret?"

"No, I'd like to find the right time to tell Earl first," she said, "when he's in a more receptive mood."

Doc Littlejohn continued to stop by to see them and began bringing some of Mis' Mattie's 'stimulating people' to keep alive their interest in the outside world.

One day, during one of his visits, he suggested that since they both had talents beyond that of a housewife, they should consider starting some classes in music and art. He said he knew a number of people who could not afford the private schools, but still wanted their children to learn some culture but at lesser fees. The idea was a brilliant one and came at the right time.

The two women had their heads together and were giggling like school chums when Earl came rushing in, a big grin on his face.

"What's the secret?" he asked, stuffing a hot sourdough biscuit in his mouth.

"I saw Bill George and he said you had something to tell me. Is your father coming to stay with us?"

"Not so fast," his mother said. "One question at a time."

"The lemon tree needs water," Sara added. "Will you go with me to see how it's doing?" "Now?"

"Now."

"Mom?"

"Go on, Son. She'll tell you. Then she and I have some planning to do to get ready for our new venture."

Earl was ecstatic. He waltzed Sara down a red clay path. Later he wandered through a blooming cottonfield, picked a few bolls and threw them into the air. He spent time in the kitchen baking corn bread and soda biscuits in the wood burning oven and, through the many months, he waited patiently for his son to be born.

In honor of his good fortune, he spent a considerable sum for a gold plate with an engraving to mount at the base of the lemon tree. He knew Sara would be pleased with the inscription when she was well enough to walk the distance again to see it.

Over the years their family grew to include five children, three sons and two daughters. The 1920s were a period of unmatched serenity in their lives. Her father came to visit. They decided to enlarge the house to accommodate their growing family. Juan was happy to supervise the construction, and suggested they try to enclose the back porch as a dining area and extend a side into more bedrooms. They had the foundation in and part of the section walls up when the tornado hit.

*   *   *

Ojito, the dog, sensed it first. He felt a difference in the air and whined through much of the evening meal while the family celebrated the progress made on the house by eating a second serving of homemade peach ice cream. Ma Grantley had an inner warning system too, and had tried to alert the family to some kind of impending danger, though she did not know exactly what it was. She was teased unmercifully to the delight of the children.

"Mom, you're not going to give us one of those Creek old wives tales are you? This is only the usual summer thunderstorm coming," Earl assured them.

"Don't dismiss those Indian weather proverbs, Son," Sara's father said. "They had logic on their side."

"What's the story, Nana?" the oldest boy asked.

Earl's eyes pleaded with her not to say any more.

"I'll tell you later, Baby," she said and smiled. Her smile took in all the children.

The rain and flashes of lightning continued long after the kerosene lamps had been extinguished and everyone had gone to bed. Ma Grantley still insisted on being prepared and promised to watch over the children. She tiptoed into their room later and found them with the covers pulled up over their heads. The baby was wide awake, cooing gleefully. She picked her up and moved cautiously to the Chippendale rocker as Ojito whimpered just below their window.

Sara's father now also had the feeling there was going to be more to this storm than just the summer thundershower they had expected. He knew from the feeling of the atmosphere, the sultry heat, the hideous darkness, and the smell from the lightning bolts that more seemed to be coming. He sat fully clothed at the study desk in his room with an open Bible before him.

The turning, shifting and whirling winds slammed across the country-side like a herd of wild horses magnified, carrying away fences, uprooting trees, and ripping the rooftops from their buildings to transplant in open fields. There was no time to scream, cry or even think, in some cases. Earl pulled Sara behind the heavy mahogany chest and restrained her from going after the children.

"Mom's with them; she knows what to do," he assured her, pressing her tightly against the wall and pulling the mattress over them. They heard something hit and what sounded like buckets banging against the walls. China and glass was sucked up and shattered. They could only imagine what the damage truly was and the imagination always produces the worst.

Sara's father got to them first when the danger was over. He pulled back some of the heavy boards and helped them to their feet. They were not hurt, but Sara's hair was caked with plaster and Earl's face was streaked with ashes. They stumbled over more boards and timbers to finally reach the children's room. They looked in the bedroom and immediately noticed the beds standing empty with the covers thrown off. They started ripping through bedding, mattresses and digging frantically.

"They're out here!" Sara's father shouted from the hallway. They found the four older children under the grand piano, each grasped tightly to his own curved leg.

"It's over," Sara whispered through tears of joy. "You can let loose now."

Dust filled the air and the children started coughing. Earl had to pry the two younger ones from their post and when he did get them to let loose, they held on then to their parents' clothing. All were too frightened to make a sound.

"My baby! Your mother!" Sara suddenly screamed when she realized they were missing. "We've got to find my baby and your mother!" She started wading through more bricks, broken glass, throwing boards aside, and sobbing uncontrollably.

"You two go ahead," Grandfather said. "I'll take the children out to the garden." The older two helped with the younger ones as they made their way through more debris into the early morning sun.

Earl and Sara retraced their steps to the children's bedroom. They saw a six-by-nine timber rammed through the seat of the rocking chair and into the floor below. They also now noticed one of the children's dressers was jammed against the closet door.

"Help me move this," Earl said. "God, let them be in here."

When he opened the door, his mother's body fell forward at his feet. The baby, safe in its cradle to one side of the closet, slept peacefully. Ma Grantley had quit breathing.

Doc Littlejohn later diagnosed the death as a coronary occlusion. But Earl would not accept that. To him it was the curse on the place. God was taking his loved ones away at random while he stood by helpless. It should have been someone else's turn to die, anyone else, but not his mother. When they took her body to Mis' Mattie's for embalming, he collapsed on her bed and sobbed unashamedly. Still later when they placed her next to his father and his first son in the family graveyard near the sunflowers, he dared not look at the earth, but kept his eyes toward the sky.

Sara's father stayed on to help pull the family back together. The children started to call him "*Abuelito*"—little grandfather—because he was so thin and seemed to be shrinking as they grew taller.

They did what they could to repair the damages done by the tornado. They straightened nails, piled up bricks, cleared away broken china, and gathered clothes and toys together to send to the neighbors. They did all of this while they bombarded Grandfather with all kinds of questions. One question brought back the terror with force.

"Why is Bill George alive," the oldest asked, and "Nana is dead?"

"It's God's will," came his hushed answer. "God's will be done."

His heart told him the little children needed more. So he would gather them around him and to tell those stories that added a lighter touch to the scary ones circulating around the countryside.

"As it crossed the creek the tornado carried the water up in a solid stream," he told them, "and dumped it on the earth in another spot leaving the creek an empty hole in the ground. It lifted up Bill George, bed and all, and put them in that creek bed. That's over a hundred feet from his house. He was untouched and with his mattress and covers still in place. Well, God must've wanted it that way."

"Will Abuelito be staying with us forever?" asked Calvin, the four-year-old. "I don't want him to."

They had named their fourth child Calvin as a compromise between christening him Juan, for Sara's father, or George for Earl's father. Any similarities with his dead brother, Calvin, that this child might have had long been buried in Earl's memory. Only his parents could have testified to a likeness in attitude, and Calvin was like none of the other children.

"Why don't you shut up?" snapped Santiago and he reached over and gave his brother a shove that sent him off the wooden bench. "I like him, no teeth and all." Santiago was four years older than Calvin so he could box him soundly when he had a mind to.

He got his name from the city that had brought the two families together and life for him was going to be very similar in many ways to the city he was named for. It would be without struggle, but all downhill. Any disagreements with other people would be washed away like the debris in Santiago after a rain—into the bay.

"Make them stop, Abuelito!" Earlito pleaded. "Go on with your stories and don't pay any attention to them."

The eldest son, at ten, was very much like his father in appearance, with his sandy hair and fairer complexion, but closer in his heart to this grandfather than anyone else.

"And what about you, little sister?" Abuelito smiled at the six year-old squeezed against him by the pushy Santiago. "Are you ready for more stories about 'tronadas'?"

"If you want to, Abuelito!" she said, snuggling even closer. As the middle child she felt even now pulled in two different directions. Baptised Juanete, she had more than her name in common with her grandfather.

The word "Juanete" meant 'Prominent cheek-bones' or in nautical terms, "A gallant sail." Water, even in a disaster situation, held a deep attraction for her. She turned a small freckled face toward his.

"I'll be glad when Espe's old enough to understand what we are talking about and stays awake more."

"Your baby sister needs her sleep," he said, "but she understands more than you think."

Esperar was her given name but she had quickly been nicknamed Esper. Esperar meant Hope, expectancy or, in nautical terms, "anchor of hope."

She was born during the 'Chinese Year of the Dragon' just as her father had been three decades before. Her calm in the wake of personal disaster would become her trademark. Of course, there was another meaning placed on the name as the depression years pressed harder. Her parents came to hope she would be the last child.

Grandfather continued with his stories about that night. He told about Ojito trying to warn everyone.

They found him later water-soaked and crouched against a brick column under the house, too frightened to come out, until much coercing and hunger finally brought him to his dinner dish.

The cast-iron dinner bell had been torn from its foundation and set down in the cornfield. The buckets from the hundred foot well had been lifted and hurled against a garden fence. The barn roof was swept away but all four walls and the latched door were intact. All the cows and Trader were found in a ditch near a pine grove, safe and dry.

"I don't see how they got out of the barn," interrupted Calvin, "if the door was latched."

"If the tornado can lift buckets out of a deep well into the air, it should be able to lift animals, too, I reckon," explained Santiago.

"But cows weigh more than buckets," Calvin insisted.

"Will you two stop it," said Earlito. "If the tornado lifted Bill George and his bed and the roofs of houses, why do you have to argue about it?"

"Just because they're boys I guess," Juanete answered.

"Enough for one day," Abuelito said. "It's about time for the baby to be getting up, and that blackberry pie should be ready for sampling by now."

The two older boys rushed ahead banging the door behind them. Calvin and Juanete helped their grandfather to his feet then each took a hand and led him into the now, after the tornado, one-story structure. Abuelito had installed a cove ceiling in the parlor that added about three feet to the height of the room. With the extension completed and whitewashed, happiness seemed to be returning at last. After a few more loose ends were taken care of, it would be time for a little celebration. It needed to be something the children would really enjoy. Their father came up with the perfect arrangement. He got tickets for all of them to go to the circus.

GEORGIA 1930s

The stock market crash and the following year of depression had drained everyone's pocket. There was very little money left for entertainment, until the circus came to town. The circus could take people back to their childhood again and for two and a half hours they would be boys and girls. It made them forget as nothing else could do.

The Ringling Bros. and Barnum & Bailey Circus had stopped for their last stand of the season at Waycross, Georgia, before closing up for the winter at their quarters in Sarasota, Florida. A circus meant lots of people and lots of animals that created a need for lots of sawdust and hay; good timothy hay.

Earl had lots of both, and he made a deal with the circus management to furnish all they needed. He hauled sawdust from the mill, now idle because of lack of lumber orders. The hay needed to be baled for stacking which required hiring more men and renting of more wagons.

The children flocked around the barn during the baling and celebrated when the last wagon pulled out of sight down the red packed clay road.

The Grantleys went early to take in everything from the jostling at the main entrance gate to the ticket wagons and brightly decorated booths. They liked the feel of their sawdust under their feet as they passed the side shows with the inviting posters of the fat lady, snake charmer, flame swallower, Siamese twins, and the midgets. They spent most of their time straining for a peek at the wild animals.

Sara wanted them to see some of the performers as they were getting ready for the big show, so she steered them to the area near the backside of the Big Top. They saw the clowns applying makeup, pretty ladies in sparkling costumes, and the marching band tuning up. But Calvin saw something else far from the dressing canvas tent.

The Siamese twins, born back-to-back, were sneaking onto the lot, apparently after having gone off exploring, and were now having difficulty scaling the wire fence.

"Look at that," he shrieked, and all eyes turned in the direction he was indicating.

"Help, Dada," Baby Espe said squirming around in her father's arms. Earl gave Sara the baby and started over to the fence. Before he got more than a couple of steps, one of the actors touched him on the shoulder.

"Let them be," he said. "They are performers, not invalids."

Within a few seconds, the two had lain down in a sleeping position on the soft grass. Then, as though seen in a mirror, one's right hand and then the other's left hand held the bottom wire high enough to hook it on the wire above. A left leg and a right leg propelled the bodies under the trapped wire until they cleared the fence. A wave of applause followed them into their tent.

A few minutes later the circus band, in full uniform, sounded the blare that announced the main feature would be getting underway in the Big Top and everybody rushed for his seat.

For weeks after the circus left, the Grantley Place became a mini-circus. The children were equestrians and Trader became a hundred white horses. They were acrobats and Santiago jumped from the smokehouse with an umbrella. When Juanete tried to duplicate the stunt she only managed to break a finger and became the first casualty of their performances.

They engaged the baby's help in getting powder and rouge from Sara's dressing table and transformed themselves into clowns, frightening a sneezing Ojito, who had become the dog of a thousand tongues. They tried pairing themselves off to be Siamese twins joined at the back. Calvin and Juanete never could get their legs to work in unison but Earlito and Santiago had perfected it to the point where they called their parents to see a performance at the back fence.

It turned out that Abuelito had to cut them loose from the barbed wire but, except for a few scratches, they were both well enough to pursue other acts. When Santiago came into the house later with a snake in a mason jar, Sara drew the line and canceled the wildlife show.

Watching their children at play, their curious minds absorbing so deeply the events around them made Sara realize their emphasis as parents had to shift to include the raising of educational standards. Many children their ages were now attending elementary schools.

She could not see any value in following traditional conservative methods of teaching a child at home to prepare him for his future life by learning to work with his hands. At least not after the child was ready for the sixth grade. Before then she did want them taught at home. The formal education approach had proven successful in all her father's mission schools, but to convince Earl was going to be a difficult matter. She and

Earl discussed the situation far into the night and, during the day, she also talked with her father. By the end of the week, they had made a decision.

At the end of his sabbatical year, Sara's father returned to Cuba and took their oldest son, Earlito, with him to train as an assistant. With this help other tasks could now be added to the many pastoral calls Juan had.

Earlito could attend school with the American, English, and Cuban residents of Santiago, and gain instruction in two languages. Earlito did not raise any objections to this, and the other children just accepted what had to be. The only condition to the agreement was that it was to be a one year trial only. They would both return to the United States and discuss any changes in plans during the summer break.

Although there was free public education in the elementary grades for the younger children, Sara preferred to teach them at home, at least for one more year. By then Santiago would be in the fifth grade according to the age standards used. She had already ordered, from a prestigious eastern school, the designated curriculum guides and materials for kindergarten through sixth grade. From another reputable company she expected a shipment of books on literature, art, and mechanics. Earl located an old jalopy at a car lot and hauled it home to put under the walnut trees so Santiago could learn first hand how to assemble and disassemble an automobile and, with luck, make it run. All of the children were already taking music lessons of some kind. They had a choice of piano, violin, or mandolin. Bill George, Mis' Mattie and her sister, and various other prominent people, including Doc Littlejohn, were deeply impressed with what was going on at the school under the walnut trees in this obscure little farm community.

The children spoke Spanish and English and when they came to words they did not know how to translate, they would make a game of it by adding "ito" to the English word. Broom became broomito, spoon, spoonito. They could do this until they had the baby hysterical with laughter. Sara would gently but firmly intervene and pointed out the seriousness of learning a language, or anything else, well. Often for their Spanish lessons, Sara would take them to the sweet lemon tree. There they would sit in the shade and she would teach them songs from her school days, and tell them all about their grandfather when he was small.

"Your Abuelito," she began, "might never have left his home town had it not been for his friendship with three young sons of the American consul. Across the street from our home was the small private school where the Adams children studied. They lived in what seemed to your grandfather to be a palace, like the palace in Cinderella. . . ."

The girls squealed and interrupted her.

"Girls." Calvin sighed. "Go on with the story, Mom."

"In their garden was a special temptation to a little Cuban boy," she said. "Your grandfather would climb the sweet lemon tree and snatch some of the fruit. He would get a spanking from Mrs. Adams, many such spankings because he was persistent.

"Anyway he vowed, then and there, at age eight, that he'd grow his own lemon tree. That way he'd never get another spanking."

"Now we have a cutting from his tree, don't we, Mamacita?" asked Santiago.

"Will we ever be able to climb it?" Calvin asked.

"When will it have some fruit?" Juanete wanted to know.

"Sweet lemon, taste good," baby Espe whispered and smacked her lips.

"I think we have another lesson all planned for us," Sara continued. "You'll each learn something about the lemon tree during the next week and we'll meet back here on Friday and share what we have learned. Fridays have a special meaning for Cuban children. I'll tell you all about it."

"I don't want to ever go to any other kind of school," Calvin said, taking in a deep breath of the soft mid-morning breeze. For once they all agreed with Calvin, but their fondest hopes were crushed within a few months.

*   *   *

By Christmas the children had advanced to the point where Sara talked to Doc Littlejohn about getting them the entrance examination for the closest public school. Doc Littlejohn supported Sara's methods of teaching her children, but as a school board member, he firmly suggested they enroll in a state certified school. When each child scored a grade higher than their classmates, the doctor did what he could to try to get the school officials to place them in the appropriate classes. He was not at all pleased with their response. They were assigned to the grades designated for their ages.

When school resumed that January, Santiago was in fifth grade, Juanete in third, Calvin in first, and, although Espe at four tested high enough for first grade, she was not allowed even into kindergarten because of her age.

"She's the only lucky one," sobbed Calvin.

"You said we wouldn't have to go to regular school for another year," said Santiago.

"And you, big sister," Earl looked up from all the forms the parents had to complete, "what do you have to say?"

"I'll go, but that doesn't mean I like it," answered Juanete.

The first few days they stayed close together after their classes, observing the other children at a safe distance, trying to decide just who might become a good friend. They compared notes and agreed the class work was both tiring and repetitious. Their minds were not challenged and their questions were never answered to their satisfaction. The two boys began to rebel against academia. Earl and Sara had to discipline them severely for the first time and they were not prepared for that. They debated about the proper kind of punishment and then finally left it up to the school officials who were trained for such things.

By Spring it was obvious things were not getting better. The dark cloud that hung over their once happy family now opened up in a shower of discontent. They had been harassed, which had then turned to name calling, and Calvin had hit another student in the mouth.

"It might help matters," admonished the principal, "if you'd give your children American names. You wouldn't call so much attention to their foreign ties."

"You must accept my children as they are," Sara said with firmness, "or not at all."

"Well, then," snapped the principal, "we have nothing further to discuss."

"We will take your problem to the school board meeting."

"My problem?" Sara's eyes flashed with intense anger. "I'd say you're the one who has the problem! My children are ready for more challenging subject matter, and you're robbing them of that."

"Then go back to Cuba, Mrs. Grantley."

"I'll pretend I didn't hear that!" Sara said and stormed out of the office.

During the evening meal she was still fussing and fuming, dropping dishes and scolding the children. She wasn't eating anything herself and serving the food mechanically. The children remained unusually quiet and Earl tried artfully to break the silence.

"So then," he said. "Tell me something good that happened at school today. Who'll be first?"

"I will" answered Juanete. "My teacher let me show the others how to cast out nines in arithmetic. That was fun."

"Wipe that grin off your face," teased Santiago. "Everything's fun in the third grade, especially for girls."

"I got to sit in the corner where the spider was," bragged Calvin.

"What were you doing in the corner?" Sara asked.

"Teacher sat him there," volunteered Juanete. "He didn't know his alphabet."

"I did, too." Calvin sniffed and tried to hold back the tears.

"Then why were you in the corner, Son?"

Earl reached over and touched him gently on the arm.

"I recited my ABCs backwards like Bill George taught me to. Listen, Z, Y, X, W, V, U, T, . . ."

"That's enough," Sara shouted. "We have a real problem, and I don't want to solve it by changing my children's names."

"It won't be so bad, mom," said Calvin. "I'll just keep mine if you don't mind."

"I'll take 'Jane' spelled with a 'y', as in J A Y N E," she said, grinning. "And Espe can be 'Elaine'; that's a pretty name."

"Nobody asked you to name the baby, potbelly" Santiago said and glared at his sister.

"There'll be no name calling in this house," Sara said firmly. "Now apologize to your sister."

"I'm sorry for calling you p. . . ."

"Son, that's enough," Earl yelled. Then, with more control, he said, "And what name would you choose?"

"I haven't given it any thought," he said. "I don't intend to go back to that old dumb school anyway. I'll join the circus before I waste another day there."

They did go back to school to finish the year out and were promoted to the next grades. Their certificates, however, were imprinted with their American names. Sara was so infuriated, she bought some black ink, erased the lettering very carefully and inserted the Spanish names. She was pleased with the results and glad she'd had Art classes in school.

*   *   *

As planned, Grandfather and Earlito returned that summer in time for the July fourth picnic at the fairgrounds. For the first time since the circus they were all together as one big happy family. What more could they ask for? Earl had driven up the day before their arrival in a pale green Studebaker roadster with darker green trim.

"We'll take her for a spin," he announced proudly. "We'll see how she handles the curves."

They all piled in with Santiago as close as a second person could get to the steering wheel.

Earl allowed him to rest one hand on the steering wheel as they drove along the packed red clay road. They had the top down and the breeze ruffled their hair.

Sara sat nervously next to Santiago, wringing her gloved hands and holding onto her favorite straw hat. The three younger ones were scrunched down in the backseat, bounced their feet rhythmically against the front seats.

"Keep those feet down," scolded Sara, eyes glued on the road ahead. "We don't know if this car is paid for yet."

"Of course, it's paid for," Earl beamed. "It's a partial payment on a loan deal I have with. . . ."

"Gosh!" interrupted Calvin, "Just look at that horse, will you?"

A paint thoroughbred, with its head erect and mane flowing with the wind, raced along the rail fence separating the animal from the road.

"Ain't it exciting?" giggled Juanete.

"Silly horse," giggled Espe and joined the others in the back to cheer the horse on in its imaginary race. Santiago urged his father to accelerate.

"Be careful!" Sara warned. "We're coming to a curve."

The children laughed as the car began rocking and lurching, swaying and swinging, bumping, and flinging them helter-skelter in their seats.

"Stop it. Stop it," Sara screamed.

They all saw the horse at the same time. Coming out from around some tall thickets, he made an abrupt turn at the curve, sailed up the hillside, then galloping at top speed, leaped the fence with a few feet to spare and touched ground in the path of the car.

"Hit the ditch, Dad!" shouted Santiago. The car made a few skids at the curve when Earl changed gears quickly and applied the brakes. The car came to a halt as the horse turned its head slightly, then disappeared into a farmer's cornfield.

"Wow, that's some horse!" exclaimed Calvin. "I wish Trader could jump like that."

"At least we know the brakes hold," Earl said, shaking his head.

"I can't say the same for my nerves," Sara stammered, reaching over to rescue her flattened hat.

"The roads are not safe anymore for man or beast," she fumed. "Everybody in back still breathing?"

"We're fine, Mom," they giggled. "Ain't it exciting?"

"Isn't it," she corrected.

"It sure is, Mom," said Santiago teasingly. "With a few adjustments I can eliminate some of the swaying and lurching. Wouldn't want to cut her speed none."

The next day the children were climbing over suitcases to get to their grandfather's lap and to stare at their sophisticated brother, who had grown taller. The experience with the horse, the engineering feat of the touring car, the parents' inquiries about the year's schooling in Cuba, and conditions there, all vied for equal attention. The younger ones smothered their grandfather with affection. Santiago could only gawk at his older brother, he now looked so grown-up and so quiet. Would he still be as much fun? Would he be willing to take the risk he had planned for him? Would he understand a need to get away from a kid brother who was always tagging along wherever he wanted to go?

Once they'd unloaded the car, Abuelito gathered them all around him in the parlor under the cove ceiling.

"I hope he don't pray too long," Calvin started to say when he felt a heavy hand on his shoulder, squeezing firmly.

Sara threw him a penetrating glare from her sparkling dark eyes that singed his delicate insides. The others obediently knelt in the circle. Grandfather smiled and read a short passage from the Bible, thanking God for all the blessings bestowed on the family, for the safe trip, and renewing vows to serve those less fortunate. He then invited them to join him as he unpacked the heavy baggage and pretended to search for hidden presents. He found Parisian perfume in fancy bottles, decorative fans and lace hand-kerchiefs for Sara and the girls, a box of Havana cigars and a carved pipe for Earl, coin banks of cast iron with clown images and leather pouches filled with various denominations of money for the boys.

The circus events of the previous year rushed over them as they talked far into the evening. They shared everything they could think of that had happened since they had last been together. Everyone wanted to talk at once. The baby was trying desperately to get a word in and to be first at something. She sat on grandfather's lap and reached up to tug on his clerical collar.

"*Basta, hijita!*" Sara choked a little on the words she had tried to say too quickly. "That's enough, dear! You'll get your turn."

"She wants to tell about the lemon tree," said Juanete. "She wants to know all about the spankings you used to get, Abuelito."

"You're the one that's going to get spanked if you don't stop butting in," said Santiago, gritting his teeth.

With the attention now focused on her, Espe babbled on about the progress of the "sweet lemon" tree, embellishing on what she'd absorbed from listening to the older family members. "It's not a dwarf anymore," she said, smiling. "Mom says it can branch out to ten or twenty feet high," and she flung both arms out to illustrate and everyone laughed.

"Will you and Earlito help us water it?" Juanete asked their Grandfather.

"It'll take more than water," Calvin said.

"We've gone through two seasons, Abuelito," said Santiago, "and still no fruit."

"Dad says it's a standard late lemon," Espe assured them.

"We'll see what we can do to help nature along," said Grandfather, "but now we'd all better get some sleep if we're going on that picnic tomorrow."

With the attention now focused on her, Espe babbled on about the progress of the "sweet lemon" tree, embellishing on what she'd absorbed from listening to the older family members. "It's not a dwarf anymore," she said, smiling. "Mom says it can branch out to ten or twenty feet high," and she flung both arms out to illustrate and everyone laughed.

"Will you and Earlito help us water it?" Juanete asked their Grandfather.

"It'll take more than water," Calvin said.

"We've gone through two seasons, Abuelito," said Santiago, "and still no fruit."

"Dad says it's a standard late lemon," Espe assured them.

"We'll see what we can do to help nature along," said Grandfather, "but now we'd all better get some sleep if we're going on that picnic tomorrow."

It rained at the picnic and most of the weekend. But early that Monday morning before the sun was up the two older boys had their heads together plotting their day's exploration. Shortly after breakfast they started out toward the creek with long cane poles and lunch pails in hand. They looked back occasionally at the only thing that could spoil their plan. Calvin had nagged his parents to the point where Grandfather had to intercede. Reluctantly, Earlito then pleaded with Santiago to let their little brother tag along. Calvin had to run at times to keep the two in sight. Ojito would yelp beside him for awhile, then leap ahead of the other boys, then back again with Calvin.

The girls had planned to take Abuelito to see the lemon tree even though it did not need water after the rain. By the time they were up for breakfast their father and grandfather had already ridden off in the touring car to check on some land deals with some contractors in another town. The girls, pouting with disappointment, moved slowly through the house chores and grumbled at their mother.

"I know how left out you feel, honey," said Sara. "But look at it this way. If you get your music practice in early, you'll be free for the afternoon to be with your grandfather."

"Earlito's too big to play with us," Espe said.

"He's too religious," added Juanete.

"He's your brother," said Sara firmly, "and you'll love him for what he is.

"Now get your violin and mandolin and you can practice outside."

They nodded and quietly slipped away to get their instruments. Bill George finally knocked on the side of the house. That was his signal to them that he had arrived. He was later today than usual. They would get him to eat faster, so he could join them on the front porch where practice came easier when he applauded and slapped his knees, which he did even when their sour notes sent Ojito whimpering for cover. It was just the two of them today with Bill George. The words 'just the two of them' would have a different meaning by nightfall.

Meanwhile the two brothers struggled to keep their weight balanced and hold their makeshift raft in place. The creek, normally no more than a few feet deep, had been swollen by days of rain. With their long cane poles, the boys fought the reddish water heroically.

"Move more to the center," Santiago ordered Calvin, "and do something about that dog."

"I'm holding on as hard as I can," cried Calvin. "I can't hold onto him and the raft, too."

"Stop your crying," said Earlito. "Just do your best." At the point where the creek joined the river, Ojito broke loose and jumped from the raft into a tide of swirling bubbles. Calvin reached for him and slid off screaming. A fisherman on the far bank upstream could only watch helplessly. The raft, spinning like a top, crashed against some fallen trees and the other two boys were thrown into the muddy water and disappeared.

An engineer with the water department, standing on a hillside, dropped his surveyor's level and ran for help. He assumed the fisherman would have attempted a rescue by the time he returned with a doctor. But later when they arrived the fisherman was nowhere in sight. Seeing a body still surfacing for air, both men, without a moments hesitation, dived into the furious torrent. Still later other men rowed out to help, but it was too late.

Back at the house, Earl and Grandfather had just finished their noon meal and were seated on the front porch, cigars in hand, when the battered Model T chugged onto the lawn and parked under the walnut trees. A rugged driver, breathing heavily, approached them.

When Earl spotted the familiar straw hat in the man's hand, his face turned white and his legs became paralyzed.

"I came as fast as I could, Grantley!" he said. "You better come with me."

"What is it, Man?" Abuelito asked as he stumbled forward to join them.

"They probably swam ashore or are rescued by now," he said. "I fished a hat out, but my boat wouldn't hold together in that whirl."

"You should have tried," yelled Earl. "They can't swim. None of them. Let's get going!"

"We're wasting time," said Grandfather.

"I'm sorry!" snapped the man. "But I don't know my way around your woods like I do the roads. To me this was the closest and fastest."

By the time they got to the river, rescuers had placed the two badly buffeted bodies under canvas and were diving beneath twenty feet of muddy water under the submerged raft for the other body.

"My God, what have I to live for?" asked Earl as he identified his two older sons. Grandfather stood rigid, praying, and stabbing his cane into the soft mud. They watched helplessly throughout the afternoon and into the night. The body of Doctor Littlejohn was uncovered from some debris that same day only farther downstream. The authorities refrained from telling the Grantley family for awhile. The engineer's body was never found. By the early part of the next afternoon, Calvin's battered form washed up on shore seven miles away.

Sara and the girls sat up for hours waiting with forlorn hope for some word. When the boys did not return for the evening meal and Earl and Abuelito had left without telling them anything, they felt more alone than they had ever been. Even after Mis' Mattie and her sister rode up with a stranger from town, they still felt all alone. Their mother was taken aside, told something, then, with much whisperings and sobbings, was led away, her bedroom. Mis' Mattie was asked to "look after my babies."

They remembered their mother had kissed them before she stumbled out of the parlor. Now their faces pressed hard against the window watching the car lights in the distance and they started to cry. Mis' Mattie reached out her arms to embrace them, but they broke away and ran under the grand piano, each grasped a curved leg. No amount of coercing would draw them out, so Mis' Mattie, feeling defeated, finally brought blankets and pillows and left them there until morning.

For weeks after the funeral the two girls never left Sara's side. In silence they held on to her legs or wrapped themselves in her apron when the many visitors came in to offer their condolences. Earl, who leaned on Sara for courage after his mother died, now invented errands to keep busy in the daytime. When the night came, he fought off sleep, but would nap, still sitting up with his newspaper on his lap and cigar still lit in his mouth. Each morning he would again think of more duties to crowd out any thinking.

His mother had always told him to keep busy and he would not have time to think about himself and how many troubles he had. It was real hard to keep that busy.

Grandfather stayed on as long as he could trying to hide his own deep hurt and wanting desperately to ease the strain on his daughter. He counted it a great victory when the girls loosened their hold on Sara and finally walked with him to see the sweet lemon tree. They could smell the sweet scent before they were even half way up the bluff. They raced ahead to be first to look up into leafy branches filled with small clusters of white flowers.

"Ain't they beautiful, Abuelito?" asked Juanete.

"Come see!" called Espe, jumping up and down with excitement.

"Can we pick some for Mama?"

"Not if you want the fruit," explained Grandfather.

"The blossoms come first and from the blossoms come the fruit. We've waited a long time for them. With luck, by late ripening season we'll have our wish for fruit."

"How tall do you think it is?" Juanete asked.

"I'd say about ten feet," he answered. "It will grow more. You've all done a good job taking care of it."

"Let's run tell Mama," Espe called from a ten yard head start.

"It would cheer her up," said Abuelito.

"And she could use some cheering up, right?" Juanete nudged her grandfather and helped him down the bluff.

The blossoming of the sweet lemon tree did bring some life back into the family. Earl was unhappy with the part he had played after the tragedy when he had just tried to escape. To try to assuage some of the grief the girls had suffered, and some of the guilt he felt because he had not done enough to heal anyone's hurt, he brought home a circus horse.

The horse had been injured and could no longer perform the circus acts, but it was a fine-looking horse, seventeen hands high, a trained thoroughbred, a palomino.

The girls named him "El Capitan."

For Sara, to try to ease some of her suffering, Earl engaged her father in a contract deal to build Villa Sara. They were in the process of ordering the needed supplies when an urgent message came from Cuba saying the church had problems that only the clergyman Bocan could correct.

Sara knew how deeply her father felt the loss of his grandsons and she did not want him traveling alone. She persuaded Earl to accompany him. She knew it would help him in his grief too. She assured them both that she and the girls would be able to manage for a few weeks. It would be Earl's first trip since the children were born.

While Sara packed his belongings and up until the day they pulled out, he kept adding more instructions to the list of what to do if they needed anything.

Sara had her own ways of seeking or rejecting help and ideas would simmer in her mind for a long time before she decided to put them to a test. To her daughters, however, each move their mother made seemed spontaneous. One such thought materialized that first Saturday the men folks were away.

After breakfast she laid out their best school clothes, crisp skirts and blouses, ankle socks, and freshly polished oxfords. While they got dressed, Sara tossed three pairs of rubbers, three lightweight sweaters, and an umbrella into a huge burlap shopping bag.

"We're going into town," she said cheerfully. "For the whole day. What do you think of that?"

"We love you, Mamacita," they said as they smothered her with kisses.

"Why do we have to take all that stuff?" asked Juanete. "It's not going to rain."

"You don't know that, and being prepared for the worst doesn't cost you anything." Sara smiled. "Your grandmother Jessica often said, 'When locks turn damp in the soap house surely it will rain'."

"What does it mean?"

"It means. . . . well, here I'll show you. Here, feel this doorknob.

"Now let's go outside and feel the latch on our front door. Feel the difference?"

"It's wet!" shrieked Espe.

"The Indians knew that the same humidity that dampened all their stolen hair, was capable of bringing showers or downpours, or worse."

"I'm scared!" said Espe, reaching for her mother's hand.

"No need to be afraid. We're going to have a good time in town today, and we can get those new coloring books you've been waiting."

"Are we going with Mis' Mattie?" asked Juanete.

"No, we won't impose on those dear ladies this time. They've done enough for this family. Now it's time to do for ourselves. We're going to hoof it."

"Good! We're going to ride the horses," said Espe.

"I think she means with our feet," Juanete said. "We're going to walk. Are we going to walk all ten miles, Mama?" She tugged uncomfortably at her own plaid skirt as it bunched up in front when she took a step forward.

"Not all at once, children. It's only five miles each way and we'll stop at Mis' Mattie's, which is the half-way point. We'll take a short-cut from there."

"Mama, I'm going to change my skirt," said Juanete. "It'll only take a minute."

At Mis' Mattie's general store they left their walking sticks propped against the front steps and walked briskly down a graveled road into the rich residential section of Riverton. The time flew by as they paced themselves to admire the manicured lawns where every flower was in its place, and the spacious houses looked as if they belonged in fairyland.

While in the car with their father they had never bothered to look. There were too many other things to distract them. Now they wanted to run up and knock on someone's door but they kept in step with Sara and were soon crossing the bridge downstream and racing for the first empty park bench. A small nondescript puppy came from the honeysuckle bushes that lined the path and sniffed at their feet.

"We can't rest too long," Sara told them. "We'll get our purchases and come back here to eat our lunch."

"But we didn't bring any lunch," said Espe.

"That's my other surprise."

Sara smiled and led them across the street to a department store where she selected a basic print fabric to make new dresses, a bobbin for her sewing machine, and some sharp needles and thread. At the next stop, the five-and-ten, the girls picked coloring books and crayons while Sara ordered drinks and hot dogs to go from the soda fountain.

They ate at the same park bench and found the same puppy waiting for them. They all shared their hot dogs with the puppy. Espe drank her drink quickly and left a few drops in the paper cup for it. He entertained everyone in the park when he shook his head with the cup on the end of his nose.

"I'm going to call him R.C." Espe squealed with excitement. "Because he likes Royal Crown cola."

"Don't start putting claims on him, Baby." Sara explained. "He has his own family somewhere near."

"No, he doesn't," came the answer from an old man sitting on another bench. "He's here all the time, begging and scratching his fleas."

"Leave him be." Sara shook a stern finger at the children when they reached down to pet the puppy. "Get your things together. With luck we can be back home before it rains."

They stopped at the country store only long enough to thank Mis' Mattie for letting them use her washroom. The girls wanted to show the lady their coloring books, but Sara was still concerned about the rain. They grabbed their walking sticks and started down the clay packed road. There were less than three miles to go when the first drops began to fall, and Sara urged them to run for shelter.

A car approached and slowed to a crawl. The lone driver offered them a ride, but Sara waved him on when she saw the face was not a familiar one. Under a steady drizzle, they turned off onto a rocky path that led up hill to Faith Chapel. It was the only country church, combined with a school, that served the less fortunate in the county. The door was never locked, even when there were no services.

Sara soon had a fire going in the potbelly stove and was getting their wet things dry. A little later they heard the whimper at the door. When they opened it, their eyes sparkled with excitement as R.C. raced in between Espe's legs. He shook himself and splattered everyone with wet dog smell before settling down at Sara's feet.

"Sure looks like he's adopted us," she said.

"Can we keep him?" asked both girls at the same time. Then they linked the little finger of their right hand and made a wish.

"What did you wish for?"

"Can't tell, Mamacita, it won't come true!" answered Juanete.

"Is this a real school?" asked Espe.

"It's more a church school, that's why you see more hymnals than schoolbooks. The children that go here don't have all the finery that's in the city, but I'm thinking they probably learn just as well if they put their minds to it."

Within less than an hour they were dry and the sun was shining brilliantly, but Sara had them put on their rubbers and suggested they wrap their belongings securely. She doused the warm ashes in the stove and the sizzle startled a sleeping R.C.

"You better wake up," she said, "or we'll leave you here for Sunday services."

R.C. took to his new home like a weevil to a cotton boll and quickly earned the same affection given Ojito, for whom their hope of return never waivered. The children were in such a happy state of mind that they did not question their mother's motives when she had them dress up again the next week on a sunny September school day and walked them to the Faith Chapel church. They offered no objections when she introduced herself to the teacher, said hello to the other children and left them standing, staring into space, lunch pails in hand. The teacher distributed paper and pencils to every child from a paper sack Sara had given her, then they all sat in a circle around the potbelly stove to sing. It was their first day and last. Brimming with excitement they ran all the way home after school to tell their mother how their day had gone.

Bill George was seated on the front steps and Sara was in her rocker nearby, talking about the cost of needles and thread when she heard them giggling, dancing and swinging their empty lunch pails.

"They've had a good first day," she said.

"Maybe I should've had them attend there sooner, but it never crossed my mind."

"It could be you made the right decision, ma'am," Bill George said. "In any case you're going to find out soon enough."

"I'll go get the cookies and milk and we'll have it out here," she said. "Try to quiet them down for me."

They paused only long enough to eat cookies and drink milk. They spilled some milk by giggling and playing. They had had so much fun at school and were excited. They related how much they knew about the lessons and how little the other children could do. While their audience waited patiently for them to end, R.C. came staggering out from under the porch.

"Now?" asked Espe, looking her sister in the eye and laughing.

"Now."

They each took one of R.C.'s front paws and stood him up between them on the garden path and began to sing.

Oh, Mary, don't you weep!
don't you moan!
Oh, Mary, don't you weep!
don't you moan!
Pharoah's army got drowned
Oh, Mary, don't you weep!

"Stop it! Stop it!" Sara yelled uncontrollably. "Don't you ever let me hear you sing that song again. Do you hear me?" She upset the sewing basket as she stumbled into the house banging the door behind her.

"We're sorry, Mamacita," they cried turning to Bill George for some kind of explanation.

"What did we do, Bill George?" Juanete asked. "Why is our mommie so mad?" Espe shook his arm frantically.

"That song's not a happy song, not when your Mom's still hurting inside 'cause she lost her children just a short while ago. You oughta be ashamed of yourselves."

"The teacher sang it at school," said Juanete, stammering over the words. "The other children said it was what we should sing to her, Bill George," said Espe, wiping away the tears. "What should we do now?"

"You can start by cleaning up these dishes without being asked. Then go in there and tell your mother how much you love her."

The grief and anger, inside Sara, still raged behind the closed door, and the children were too frightened to enter or knock. Keeping their voices as low as they could, they plotted a way to communicate their feelings of sorrow to her.

"She likes the Mounds candy bars," whispered Espe. "I wish we had one to give to her."

"Well, we don't," her sister snapped, "so we might as well stop wishing and start thinking."

"We could make her something for Villa Sara."

"Like what?"

"I don't know. I'm thinking, though."

"We could tear out a picture from our coloring book, and color it the best ever."

They thought that was a good idea and the whispers outside of Sara's door ceased for a while. Then they came back and the whispers started again. A thin piece of paper fluttered across the floor and Sara picked it up. Warmth and love flowed out from the hastily colored picture of a sunset over a field of sunflowers. She quickly splashed her face with cold water from the large porcelain wash basin, dabbed on some powder and rouge, and made a face at the image in the mirror. Her silent anger at her own rash actions was now somewhat curbed and she walked proudly out to find her daughters.

The relationship between the three that evening was cast in cement so strong that nothing any less severe than an earthquake could ever shatter it. They talked of many of the things they had done together and wanted to share with their father when he returned.

Everything but Sara's outburst and its cause. That would be their secret forever, with Bill George's help.

Sara continued to donate school supplies to Faith Chapel, but the children never returned for classes. Everything would have gone well if time stood still. They had not counted on another kind of war raging inside the heart of the Nation as a whole. Because they still had no electricity or radio, any news reaching them came secondhand and often fragmented.

One extremist group used the radio to preach isolationism and hatred or distrust of foreign nations. Intolerance had sprouted in strange and terrifying form to include hostility to foreigners and to foreign ideas in general. It reached the city of Riverton with the fervent opponents of Roosevelt's sweeping policy measures fanning the fears of coming change.

The Farm Relief Act, passed by Congress, provided that the government would make money payments to farmers who would devote part of their land to "soil-conserving" crops.

Earl became one of the six million to join in this program. He received subsidies that averaged more than a hundred dollars for each farmer.

Sara helped Bill George apply for benefit payments to the blind under one of a series of Social Security Acts.

These programs were generous to the recipients, but they created widespread opposition from the employers and workers who had to finance them. What should have been a joyful reunion of family when Earl returned from Cuba became a highly charged venture in human suffering.

That morning when he saddled Trader and rode off to his thinking place by the creek, he was thinking of his family's rights and liberties in a free society: The right to worship as they will, to speak and to write in freedom, to go about their own business, to choose their own work, to marry whom they will, and to rear their families as they wanted. He hoped his family would not become involved in a situation where he couldn't take some protective action. More important, he wanted to keep informed of rapidly moving events. There was only one place he could do that and not leave his land.

He turned Trader around at the creek and headed in another direction, off the clay-packed road and to a log structure nestled in a grove of pines, the country club for poor folks now affectionately referred to as "Rosalie's Hideaway."

The atmosphere was heavy with tobacco smoke and perspiration as he entered unobserved. The grating laughter, mingled with high voices, competed with the metallic clatter of the overhead rotating fan. He pushed through the milling customers and moved toward an empty stool at the bar. At that precise moment a roughly dressed, middle-aged drunk, with frizzled, pale hair, climbed on a table and started railing at the group of patrons nearby, who were also in varying states of intoxication.

"I'm quickly getting sick of these foreigners giving my old lady all them school supplies and spreading their fancy foreign ideas," he yelled. He threw a broken bottle down that smashed on the floor at Earl's feet. He jumped from the table, bellowing like a raging bull, and stamped toward the bar.

A tall, thin, older man stepped in front of him, hauled back his arm and let loose a wild swing that sent the drunken man sprawling. The jostling, noisy men nearby roared with laughter.

"I told you to keep your fool trap shut or I'd do it for you," the older man said.

"You taking up for the likes of him — a half breed?"

The drunk staggered to his feet and wiped away a mouth full of blood. He snarled deeply and raised one hand.

Earl glimpsed the hairy fist in time to dodge.

"I have no quarrel with you, you blowhard," he said as he moved forward with his hands clinched.

"His name's Bo," someone shouted.

Bo backhanded Earl hard, spinning him into the bar. Then he followed that up with a right to the stomach which doubled him over. Earl went to his knees, holding his stomach and moaning. He struggled to get up and fight back, but his feet buckled beneath him.

"Them little brats of his is too good to go to our school," the drunk shouted. "We oughta run them all the way back to where they came from."

Another bottle smashed somewhere in the room, a woman's voice cried out in anger and a man bellowed in pain, and then nursed a bloody scalp. The woman moved toward the bar and leaned over Earl. His soft hazel eyes had never seemed sadder.

"Your Sara isn't going to like this."

"My wife's a good woman, Rosalie. Same as my mother was before her."

"I know that, and you know that. It's these slinky companions of Bo that's gotta be made to see that." She looked deep into Bo's red, spiderwebbed eyes.

"You listen and listen good," she snarled. "That man's father built this place so all of us would have a place to relax when we weren't welcome at any other, excepting for a carryout from the back entrance. I happen to know that Mr. Earl here could have sold the property and for a good price. He had plenty of offers, but he didn't." She paused only long enough to get her breath.

"As for his children, they were all born right here in this county, and they have more right to be here than some of you. By the way, where are you from, Bo? I don't remember seeing you around these parts when Earl or his father were babies."

Bo grunted something and jerked his head at two slinky companions who followed him out of the building. Rosalie gave orders to the bartender that the next round of drinks was on the house. Earl looked deep into her sympathetic eyes and thanked her.

"You going to be fine," she said.

"As long as I have friends like you, Rosalie, I have no doubts at all that we'll be fine." He kissed her meshed gloved hand and slipped out, unobserved, through the side door.

Later that night, when Sara saw her husband doubled over in pain and vomiting into the wash basin, she realized that it would take a thousand Rosalies to corral the misinformers and curb the insults her family must bear.

For some time she had been studying the literature from a number of private schools. Maybe now Earl would be more receptive to the idea of sending them away to school in another year. But Earl's feelings remained unchanged, despite her arguments.

"Any successful reforms take time," he explained, "especially in the early stages. But in subsequent years the programs will have universal support. Your bigots will either accept those people different from themselves or they become the losers."

"Our children can't wait for subsequent years." Sara's dark eyes pleaded with him for understanding.

"Why don't you take them to Cuba to finish this year?" he suggested. "It would help us to know if your father is still in good health and I wouldn't have to worry about you three doing anything foolish."

"We would miss you," she said and smiled, "but we would never do anything foolish."

"Can I depend on that?"

"What could go wrong in Cuba? We would get the same respect that's given to my father."

"If they were boys I'd keep them right here with me but girls, I don't know if I'll ever understand them, especially the strong willed ones like you three."

"Some day they'll make you proud of them," she told him.

"With you as their mother, how could they do otherwise? Now you'd better let them know our plans before I change my mind."

"You knew I'd have gone without your consent, didn't you?" she said. "My girls are going to get a good education and I don't care what it takes."

"As long as your father's willing to accept the responsibility, I'm not going to look a gift horse in the mouth."

Pondering on the situation as he saw it, Earl had no intention of changing his mind. He had several new business ventures that would progress nicely with the lessening of family duties for a year. Then, too, there were the small farmers he had loaned money to when no banks would. Some were reneging on their promise to pay back and he planned to make good on his investment. He hoped to achieve his goal without antagonism, but if the situation got out of hand, at least his family would not be harmed. He kissed them and sent them on their way without reservations of any kind.

CUBA 1939–40

Sara, remembering her own education had been specifically directed toward the development of her many talents, placed total confidence in the island schools for her daughters. They would know her friends and their children. They would learn about the country's heroes and their accomplishments. They would understand the charms of the elite British and American landowners, and they would come to know the intelligence of some of the *campesinos*. Most of all, they would learn that all of this rich human potential could become a part of their lives as well.

As she again experienced these comforts from her past through her children, she added a glow and vitality to her own life. She was one of them, yet she had that certain sophistication travel had given her that made her more appealing. Her father was happy to see her spirited behavior return and encouraged her to accept more invitations from the people they knew. The girls would be safe with him when not in school.

On the surface then, all seemed to go well for some time. The duality of their loyalties, that would later surface, was not apparent to any of them, yet. If Sara was aware of this, there was no indication of that awareness in her daily life.

The Cuban schools could not keep pace with the fertile minds of the Grantley sisters. Accustomed to the freedom and flexibility of their home training, the restrictive silences and seating arrangements at times became too much for them. When their studies were quickly completed, they used the time to sketch pictures of the professors or to pretend to take notes. This distracted the most obedient students. They spent the siesta hour plotting pranks to play on the domestic help and they often roamed the streets freely without a chaperon. In America they had not been accepted as Americans, here they were being referred to as *"las Americanos."* Sara had to dedicate all her strength to blurring this dividing line.

They began music lessons with a Cuban teacher and, although they never reached their mother's concert status, they did manage to get to the recital stage. At least one of her daughters finished the duet they were assigned to play.

Juanete's mind was distracted when she heard someone in the front row say, "She skipped a measure."

Too embarrassed to cry, and too frightened to walk off the stage, she repeated the last two measures and ended with a measure of her own invention. To perfect their language, they attended private diction classes. For French, they stayed in a Frenchwoman's home for a while, speaking, eating, and living like the host family. They attended American movies with Spanish subtitles and laughed at all the right places, they often being the only people audible. They attended the opera with Sara and her father and filled their weekends with church services or movies.

They would ride the bus with Abuelito to other villages as Sara had done on bicycle five decades before. They joined the other young people in the evenings at the park where they strolled around in a circle, dressed to attract attention from the wider circle of young men walking counterclockwise. If one showed any interest in an introduction, a Cuban girl would say, *"Es americano,"* and it would circulate as *"muerte por los americanos."* They spurned advances. They did acquire the habit of kicking in the shin, or whacking the side of an arm with their fans to encourage more affectionate teasing. Sometimes this would be directed at an attached male, to the extreme displeasure of his girlfriend. "*Son mariposas,*" one of them would shout, who had seen them earlier with their parasols. Espe had a pink one and Juanete's was yellow. They were much like butterflies enjoying the sun and flying free of chaperones.

More supervision did not prove to be the answer. It seemed the simplest event could have its repercussions that stemmed from their dual loyalties. Before the day of the parade for some national hero, Sara had encouraged the girls to pursue what they thought was a wonderful plan. They had labored for hours getting the lines straight, mixing the right colors, and shaping the stars, for two flags—one Cuban and one of the United States. They had the correct type of glue to hold them in place, just above the window, in full view of paraders as they marched pass. Sara could never have been more proud as their efforts coincided with hers to further blur the line that divided her children from the people of this country, her birth country. It took only one extremist to rain on her parade.

The largest portion of the paraders had already reached the plaza, and the second platoon of Batista's soldiers were at the rear, and just a few feet from the paper flags announcing their unity in friendship. A shabby, bearded individual came from nowhere, and broke into the ranks screaming for attention. He pointed a bony finger at the two flags above the window and shouted a few more words. Before they realized what was happening, a group of four soldiers were given their orders. They marched in unison, bayonets drawn, up to the window and ripped the American flag to shreds.

"What's the meaning of this?" Abuelito yelled at them, shaking his cane for emphasis. He searched the group of soldiers for one with some authority. Many knew Bocan and his work, and before long a group of sympathizers had pointed out the officer in charge. More loud words of exchange, more emphasis from the cane, more wild movement of hands, more apologies, and then a smile and a handshake.

"Papa, what happened?" asked Sara, putting her trembling hands on his when he returned. "The girls are too crushed and frightened to go near the window!"

"An unfortunate mistake," he said. "I should have supervised the placement of the two flags."

"What do you mean, Abuelito?" came faint voices from the rectory.

"Come out where I can see you," he said firmly. "That's more like it. Wipe your tears, everything's going to be all right. Just remember next time you display the two flags together, never place the American one even slightly higher than the Cuban one while on these shores."

"Is that it?" Sara questioned. "All that military display over a child's drawing?

"Our lives are governed by a lot of idiotic rules. Someone ought to over. . . ."

"Enough, Sarita."

"I'm sorry, Papa, it almost slipped out."

"You're not in America and tensions within a country mount quickly when war becomes the big question."

"Will America go to war, Abuelito?" asked Espe, as she tried to unravel some of the events mentioned in her history class the previous week.

"Not if President Roosevelt can hold to his promise to keep out of the war."

"Then why are the British people so worried?" Juanete asked. "I couldn't hear all that your church members were saying at sunset vespers."

"When Churchill took office this May," recalled Sara, "it was with a warning that the British people 'must be prepared for blood and toil and tears and sweat.' "

On the last words she did a fair imitation of the Prime Minister of England and her daughters laughed hilariously. Grandfather tried to stifle a chuckle.

"The world is seeing a different kind of army in Germany," continued her father. "From the latest reports it seems there have been more restrictive laws passed against the Jewish people since the Nazis assumed power. We should be thinking of their pain. More laws, rules, and decrees, to undermine the human potential that could build a better world." Sara sighed deeply.

"I hate what they're doing."

"That kind of talk would place you under 'protective custody' in Germany," he said seriously. "The intellectuals, teachers, and former community leaders, are prime suspects."

"What's 'protective custody'?" asked Espe.

"That means concentration camp; doesn't it, Grandpa?" asked her sister.

"According to some nonpolitical observers, that is correct," he answered. "Can you imagine what it might be like to be forbidden to own stores and to work at your profession as a teacher, doctor, or a laborer, and to have all your property confiscated?"

"Will they ever take your property or keep you from working, Abuelito?" asked Espe.

"You shouldn't be worrying about that now, child," he said. "If it should ever happen, then I hope I'm not here to see it!"

"Papa, they should be concerned. I am when I read about orders that make people assume names to clearly mark them as Jews, or that Germans and Jews may not intermarry. And things like, any person having at least one Jewish grandparent is defined as a Jew, and so is a non-Jew who is married to a Jew, it's all so depressing. I'm glad we live in free countries, and I want my daughters to be glad too." Sara took a deep breath and stood up.

"Now that we've had our history lesson for the day, I think we should all write to your father to let him know when we'll be returning."

"I wish you were going with us, Abuelito," Espe said. "We haven't been all together as a family since," Juanete began to stammer, "since the picnic." All were silent, remembering the pain and the absence.

"We'll be together again soon," he assured them. "You take care of each other and that sweet lemon tree." Then he turned to Sara and he broke into a laugh.

"And you. I'll pray that under your supervision, their independence and originality will continue to flourish."

"I'll do my best, Papa." She smiled, and put her hand on his with confidence.

She moved energetically, after a prolonged discussion later with him about further education for her children. If their combined plan succeeded they had only a reluctant Earl to convince.

GEORGIA 1940

The beginning of the following school year found Sara working on the plan she and her father had outlined. She was busy completing enrollment forms from a mid-eastern school with a religious affiliation. Listed in their catalog as a finishing school for girls, it achieved its most dramatic success in the production of young ladies trained to face the new future. She had underlined the words that helped her select this school: criticism is encouraged, and originality and independence command a premium. As she read the admission rules more carefully, she discovered that little had changed as far as planned management of the nation's human resources. The restriction this time was on age. The student must have reached her thirteenth birthday by September and must not have exceeded the age of fifteen.

Some options were granted but only to day students. She read the require-
ments several times before confronting Earl with her complaint.

"You know how I feel," he responded. "Why invest in a girl's education
anyway? Some guy comes along and reaps the benefits."

"It's not the money," Sara began. "Their grandfather has offered to pay
the tuition. It's just not fair to bar someone because of age. Why can't they
plan a curriculum around the abilities and needs of the students?"

"You could write them and explain your situation. Didn't you say they
encourage criticism?" Earl smiled teasingly. "Maybe some understanding
church official will make an exception."

"Rules, laws, and decrees," Sara fumed. "Once they're in print, it takes
a war to make any exceptions to them. I'll think of something."

"I'm sure you will." Earl lit a fresh cigar and returned to the financial
section of his newspaper.

While behavior under stress may not be complimentary, Sara felt justi-
fied to de-emphasize age. Both daughters were just outside the restricted
area of acceptance. Espe was just twelve in March and Juanete was sixteen
in June, but could easily be taken for fourteen when she was with other
children. Sara rationalized that if she followed the traditional conservative
method and submitted her request for an exception, the church founders
would be at it for a year. She took the shortest route with a dab of ink and
a pen. Should the admission officers uncover any discrepancies later, it
would not have hindered her daughter from getting a taste of what was
needed in a new future. There was no need to press her luck too far. Espe
could postpone becoming a lady a few more years, so Sara concentrated
fully on getting the items all labeled properly and instructing Juanete on
what to expect on her first trip away from home alone.

*   *   *

As the years passed, it became more and more clear to the girls that
what Sara had done was the correct thing. In the ten years from 1940 to
1950 they had achieved the goals she had set for them and were happy
doing it. With a diploma, and working skills beyond their father's highest
dreams, they joined that segment of American society that enjoyed unprec-
edented prosperity.

Their education in a mid-eastern school combined with proficiency in
a second language opened doors to greater services and facilities in industry
under government designed programs. Concentration was on war production. With full employment and generous overtime pay, their decision to

stay on rather than go home for a visit was in the nature of a compromise between them and their mother.

Since their father had patterned his life entirely on keeping occupied every minute of the day, and night, with one financial deal or other, Sara had decided to visit her daughters, if only for a few days.

Once she was satisfied they lived in a nice neighborhood, in a clean apartment, and their jobs were what they said they were, she would leave them to their own lives. She had not counted on her daughters' persuasiveness or her own attraction for the working world.

When the days expanded into weeks, she accepted a part-time job during the day planning the menu for a large hotel. In her off hours, she volunteered to work at the Red Cross and the local soup kitchen.

On a dare one day, she picked up the violin. It delighted her daughters to see how well she still could play.

In her fifties, she glowed with the charms of a big sister while yet demanding a more lasting respect.

She was a mother first, but displayed the rapport of a trusted friend. Her daughters were very proud of her and they introduced her to their supervisors at the defense plant. She was also encouraged to join them at the USO functions, the parks, the music concerts, and dinners in the best restaurants. When invited to perform with the city symphony, she hesitated only momentarily. The three were finally being accepted for themselves and for what they could contribute to a new world.

The weeks turned into months and she charged her energy up to greet the first inch of snow that dusted parts of the state. That first taste of wintry weather was enough to send her packing for the warmer climate of home, for Earl, and for another dream not yet completed, Villa Sara.

Well into the sixties and mid-seventies, from rented one room dwellings to long, low, one story ranch houses to the buying of older homes to remodel, Sara played an active part in her daughters' lives. As their careers and families grew, their needs became her needs. On each visit to their homes she would bring a new cutting from the sweet lemon tree but every attempt to transplant failed even in the scientifically tested atmosphere of a grandchild's glass-enclosed experiment.

It also seemed that just when a new position brought a raise in pay earmarked for construction of Villa Sara, personal responsibilities, job demands, or a health matter intervened.

*   *   *

In 1960, when Castro seized all US property, Sara's dream faded even more. She had returned to Santiago to settle her father's estate. Events at the time dictated the disposition of his things. She kept articles associated with pleasant or significant memories: important documents, family pictures, his cane and gold cross, a painting, and her favorite, the brass ornate knocker from the front door.

When she returned to the States, she found her home struck by another tornado, and partly demolished again. Earl had moved into what he considered of value, a mobile home anchored beneath the walnut tress.

As the nation moved gradually into a period of prosperity to some, Sara found the following years relatively tranquil in comparison. With diplomatic relations broken by the United States in 1961, she felt less pain, knowing her father was spared a confrontation with the conquering ideology.

She continued her daily mile-and-a-half walk to the sweet lemon tree until a motorcycle group moved into the isolated spot. They found it to be an ideal haunt for their practice jumps and parties and her father's cane did not impress them. She was weakening and this aided in the decision to limit her space to the mobile home and its surroundings.

In her mid-seventies, she made what she said would be her last trip to visit her daughters and grandchildren. She told them then what she wanted after she died. She wanted to be disposed of with quiet respectability and with the minimum of fuss and publicity.

"Make it decent and quiet," she said firmly. She apologized about not leaving more material wealth other than the contents of an antique trunk.

Realizing that both parents were not getting any younger, Elaine made arrangements to transfer to a hospital staff near the family home. In this way the hours, days, and years passed.

Sara had seen the world at large recognize women as equals and she regularly clipped news events to send away to Juanete, who was now called Jayne, for research purposes. A twinkle came into her dark eyes each time Esperar, who was now called Elaine, advanced in the health field or when a grandchild achieved some honor in music or art.

In 1978, when Castro agreed to allow Cubans living in the United States to visit their families on the island, the sisters planned for a joyful reunion with a surprise holiday trip for their mother's birthday.

The only thing that worried Sara now was that she might become a burden to those who cared for her. As fate would decree, the reunion was not to be as planned and Sara's concerns were unwarranted.

In a brief memo on the blank side of some bank deposit slips Earl made this notation:

> I returned from town and found my wife Sara on the kitchen floor, unable to move, no one was near. She could not bear to be lifted. I later got her on a rug and slid her to the bed. She said she would be all right after a while. Next day, Friday, I saw no hope of our delay. Elaine and the grandchildren and also our first great grandson had planned to visit us that coming Sunday, before the grandchildren returned home to Wisconsin. I decided to phone them of the condition of their grandma. In about two hours they were here by auto—quick action. My granddaughter, Morene, also a nurse, found a piece of lumber under the house to make a quick splint—placed her in car (much pain suffered by effort) and decided to have an X-ray. Returned that same night by ambulance to the medical center. More X-rays and after some two weeks she was released to reside in convalescent home—best place under the conditions. We were informed while visiting her last that she could be released the following day. She is to be back within thirty days to check on the healing. Expenses "WOW". But nothing too good for her. A wonderful wife and mother—who was proud of her children. Sober thought: Where would you two sisters have been without her?"

For Sara, whose quotient of delight in her children had had no limitations, it seemed death was not an escape from pain but a chance to move to a higher plane of existence. The people who mourned her passing did so in different ways. Some relatives and friends just slipped quietly in at the church door later that week and walked slowly up to the solid mahogany casket to see her one more time. Sharing the light with a bed of fresh cut flowers was an ornate brass bell. Never again would someone answer its summons.

Some went down on their knees, said a prayer and blessed the souls of all the good dead as they prayed. Others, in their own special way showed their feelings of grief, loss, anger, guilt, or fear. Sara was dead. She had lived a full life and that knowledge flowed around the group as a Catholic priest and a Protestant minister shared the service.

"In Christian faith, the body is only the outworn shell of a spirit which continues to live eternally," said one. "It is the soul that matters."

" 'Tis but the casket that lies here, the gem that fills it sparkles yet," quoted the other.

A black vocalist from Timms Conservatory in Atlanta provided the music which was something sweet and sincere. The procession followed the seven-passenger, black, Cadillac limousine on the long, roundabout way to the grave site, through the heavily trafficked city streets. Then the talk began, first in low whispers and changing to quiet voices as they spoke about Sara and the kind of woman she had been.

"She never held back and was always ready with the right words and help," said one relative, wiping the tears from her eyes.

"Many's the time she'd get me up in the middle of the night and insist I get the doctor for some tenant farmer's wife about to give birth," added Earl.

"Is this limousine like the one Nana rode to the concert in as a violinist in Manhattan?" asked a grandchild as beautiful and sincere as Sara.

"You shouldn't be thinking materialistically," snapped another.

"And why not? She wouldn't want us to be sad, would she?"

"That's true, that's true. God bless her soul."

"And wasn't she beautiful?" Jayne said, smiling as she thought of her mother's face at the window.

"She must've been eighteen or. . . ."

"Twenty," corrected Elaine.

"You sure?"

"Positive, but you can ask Papa if you don't believe me."

"We married in 1918," Earl was saying as he puffed thoughtfully on a cigar. "A finer woman never there was, strong-willed to boot. Had no enemies that I know of. You would do well to follow her example. When your time comes, it comes, you know. Oughta make everything right. . . ."

"I'm remembering the time she stored her money in her shoes at the immigration office when she escaped the last revolution."

"Or the time she wouldn't let go the lead rope on that milk cow that broke its tethers and she was dragged across the lawn. . . ."

"Or the time we got caught in the rainstorm."

The voices rose and fell as the line of vehicles moved down a dusty road to a rural countryside. On a graveled footpath, widened to accommodate the funeral limousine, they passed an exhausted jogger, possibly returning from a lengthy workout. He crossed himself and walked on.

Even the winds in the oak trees, wearing their fall shades of yellow and red, that lined the cemetery served as an example that there is no misfortune not followed by a better day. As was her wish, an aging Curtiss Timms recited a final farewell from the Aztec "Anonimo de Tenochtitlan".

We come only to sleep,
We come only to dream.
It is not true, it is not true
That to the earth we come to live.

We are to become as the weeds in every spring.
Our heart has greened and sprouted
Some flowers will our body give,
And then it shall forever wilt.

As the coffin was lowered gently into the mother earth, to give new life to the dead, one by one and in small groups the people left. It was time to go back to their regular lives, to a new future. Overhead, a swallow flew, chirping sweetly. Higher than that, blue skies, white clouds, and a warm sun glowed. Had anyone in the procession taken even a moment to look back or glance in the rearview mirror, a small child stumbling over the soft red earth to place a crumpled sunflower on a new grave. That would have been something they could each share in any recounting of the day's events.

Earl, for one, forgot some of his sorrow with the good rememberings and the company of his family. His grief was a silent one. He would work through his sorrow and loss in his own way. He found strength in his own mother's Indian customs that said

"You must feel calm and peaceful, not sad or angry."

The past felt more comfortable than the present so he again chose to express himself on the blank side of three bank deposit slips:

"TO WHOM IT MAY CONCERN: This is Earl L. Grantley and my wife, Sara, residing on our farm, where we have for past sixty years, as man and wife. During that period, we have been seen the incoming tide, that brought joy and happiness; and also the ebb tide that took it away. The Depression of the thirties brought on by a little bug—called the boll weevil—that played havoc with the Agriculture set up—no profits—no jobs—no hopes—no nothing. Landlords broke—some committed suicide. Day & monthly laborers called so many HANDS—(Employees). Tenants—share-croppers, were helpless—without a guiding hand; sought relief from their dilemmas. So their eyes were focused on the north. Esp Detroit, Mich. Highly industrialized—so one by one the migration started looking for greener pastures. All was needed was strong backs and weak minds to fill the gaps that the restrictions on foreign labor had created.

"I was told, that no income taxes after certain age & no limits on income after same. So I didn't file any tax return; after no notice of Delinquency, I took it for granted that at age eighty-five, I was free from that chore. So if I was delinquent— so was the Revenue Dept—for not notifying me of same. Both erred in that case and to Err is human—but to Forgive is Divine. The line county surveyed few years ago, cut thro my farm of 800 acres for 384 acres—ab 1/2. So I pay Taxes in two counties. Taxes due 15th Nov.'78—$1287.12. Taxes due Dec. 20, '78— $1871.20. Total $3,158.32. Some people say—(They are laying up their treasures in Heaven). I bet lots of them haven't got enough layed up to make a down payment on their Harps."

He was always thinking, always figuring, and hoping others would understand his position. Old purposes somehow had to be incorporated into a new version of purposes and beginnings. Within a few weeks, his thoughts were interrupted by necessity and he became physically dependent on his daughter, Elaine. Diagnosis: Chronic Organic Brain Syndrome.

A new beginning was starting for him with one who was adept at coping with the Social Security bureaucracy, insurance companies, wills, and the probate processes. Now in his nineties, his struggle and dealings became a long and complicated process, and a source of continued friction within the family.

Chapter 9

WINTER 1984

*E*arl W. Grantley smacked his weathered palms against the aluminum chair arms. After several attempts, he pulled himself up, reached for his cane, stiffened, and then sat back down.

"Hell, you not listenin' to a thing I say," he grumbled. "Still got your face buried in a book as usual. Better be a good one. Life ain't worth living ain't worth writing about."

From across the recreation room his daughter, Jayne, took a deep breath. She tried to shift her attention to the wet, shadowy tree branches brushing against the picture window behind her father. She wished the sun would come out to take away some of the winter chill, and then they could go on a walk. There was never any need for words when they were walking.

"You hear me?" he snapped.

"I hear you, Papa." Her dark eyes flashed behind tinted designer frames.

"You were saying the young people today don't have any respect for the elderly and that we're spending too much money, cluttering our brains with nonsense."

She knew before she spoke that he had not heard a word. His glazed, grey eyes were submerged in yesteryear's simpler ways.

He made a ritual of unwrapping a cigar, lighting a match, and letting three of them burn out to his finger tips before he put the fourth one to the end of the cigar. He puffed quietly for awhile. Then he looked up and his eyes moved from one framed picture on the wall to another.

They finally came to rest on a collection of antique tools, a Civil War weapon or two, and an old tennis racket near the exit door. His eyes looked as if they had a cushion of tears in them.

"Which you'd rather have, Baby? Three square meals a day or two square meals and your cigar?" He did not wait for an answer, but told about the time when he had asked that same question of his old cronies back in 1934.

"It's like a survey, don't you see. You can guess what their answer was, can't you?"

"I have a feeling you're going to tell me, Papa."

"Yep," he chuckled. "They all said two square meals a day. A man gotta have his tobacco. You know if I had saved all the money I spent on my smoking, I'd be rich today."

Those last two words sent sharp arrows through her nervous system. He was rich. With his holdings he could own a tobacco plantation. She began to sense some of the frustration her sister, Elaine, had had to endure as caretaker since their mother's death.

Money tucked away in hidden accounts did not pay today's bills, she wanted to tell him. She wanted him to loosen the purse strings and share in the added expense of running a home on a single family's meager income. She also wanted so much to let him know that her reading only enhanced her living.

She wanted to tell him the origin of that cigar band he'd just removed, folded, and put on the end table. She wanted him to know how, back in history, the noblemen would soil their white gloves from the nicotine stain. Then some brilliant young lad designed the band for advertising, and it solved the problem and made the company a fortune. If it made money, he'd like that. But he was already asleep.

The banging door startled him awake. The half lit cigar fell from his hand, dumping two inches of ashes on the new green carpet.

"That your mom?"

"No, Papa. It's only Denice coming from work."

"Who?"

"Denice. Your granddaughter."

"Now there's a good woman for you. Your mom. She's always thinkin' of what's best for her family. An angel, that woman, if ever there was one."

Denice breezed in, grabbed the mail on the entrance counter ledge, and ran furiously past the seated figures, trailing a fragrance of Estee

Lauder perfume that blended nauseously with the cigar smell. Over her shoulder she threw some words in their direction.

"Hell, Grandpa. Mom's going to kill me when she gets back from Emory. You keep dropping your smelly old cigar ashes on our carpet."

Grandpa sank deeper into the chair, his thin, bent shoulders slumped forward, and his hands holding tight to his hickory cane. The voice bounced back through the vents of the heating system.

"And don't think your smearing them around with your feet is going to fool me."

He continued to do the ol' soft shoe to imaginary music and began to tap his cane in rhythm. He spoke softer this time.

"Ashes don't hurt nothin'. Your Aunt Nell used to say when I'd apologize. 'Never mind,' she'd say. 'Ashes kills any moths hidin' there.' You get that, baby girl?" He flashed a toothless grin across the room.

"Can't tear yourself away from that book long enough to listen, can you? Little rabbit mouth, that's what we called you when you were small. Remember that? That Denice is a pretty little thing. Not so little, but she's got nice legs."

Denice sailed back into the room, flipped to a late soap opera, and, balancing a tray of snacks, slid into a super recliner. Her ample figure was clad in T-shirt and cutoff jeans. Fizzing pop and crunching chips, added new sounds to grandfather's endless chatter.

After a moment he got up, stretched, shook each leg slowly, and the planted himself in front of the TV, and addressed the soap character.

"Pretty girl, what you cryin' about? Better dry those tears. I'm ninety years old and I can tell you what true sorrow is. You hear?"

Denice weaved her head left, then right of the standing figure as long as her patience would allow, then she asked him to move or sit down.

"He's being stubborn," she said. "Look at him. Hasn't shaved since Mom left two weeks ago. Those old pants have frayed cuffs, and I bet underneath that knit blue sport jacket he's still in filthy old flannel p.j.s.

"Can't you make him move, Auntie Jayne?"

"You've got the remote control, Denice. Switch channels and let's see what happens."

Another crying female appeared on the screen in an almost identical setting. Denice turned to her aunt in desperation. Jayne put the book down.

"I'll get him something to eat. Something light. I've somehow lost my appetite," she sighed. "I'm not your classic nursing home attendant."

"He can afford to buy a dozen barber shops but look at that hair. It's a stringy white, and down to his shoulders." Denice stopped only long enough to swallow some pop.

"Come on, Papa," Jayne touched him lightly on the arm.

He brushed her hand away, mumbling.

"Oh to be in Paree, now that Spring is here." He blinked his eyes a few times at the TV image and looked down at his worn over-sized jogging shoes.

"Those are my shoes, too," Denice said, looking up. "Says they are his." She put her fingers back into the dip and coughed on a chip.

"You better put some clothes on," he said. "Sounds like you're getting a cold."

He moved his cane ahead and let his right foot follow. This was going to take him some time, but damn it, people were always rushing and getting nowhere. His left foot caught up to his right, and then he moved the cane ahead again as he passed Denice's chair.

When he reached the kitchen archway, he spun playfully around and looked back at her.

"Good-bye, pretty lady. Talk to you later."

"Is he always like this?" her aunt asked, and reached over to grab the last chip from Denice's plate.

"You ought to hear him when there's a football game on, but what scares me is when he lights the kerosene lamp during the night to save electricity. Then when Mom hid the lamp, he found the candles."

"He never sleeps in his bed anymore," Denice said as she flipped back to her favorite program.

"I was going to ask when he visited the farm last or if he ever talks about the place, but you go ahead, finish your program."

"Mom'll take you out there when she gets back, but not him. Not after what happened last Thanksgiving. But she can tell you all about that, too."

SPRING 1985

As the new Mediterranean blue compact kept pace with the fast-moving traffic down the Georgia freeway, the sisters' thoughts were drawn back in time. They were two of five small, dirt clad children scrambling toward the river. They had cane poles over their shoulders and dangled a rusty tin can of worms. An earth-colored hound dog was weaving itself in and out among them.

They both could feel the drowsy warmth of that long-ago sun on their cheeks and, breathing deeply, they tried to summon back that damp, earthly smell of the bait can. They looked out the car windows at the freshness of the recent rain. To the right some distance from the road stood a crumbling stone chimney of a tenant shack. The twisting brush concealed any other rotten remains. The fragrance of the pine, the wild honeysuckle, and the dogwood blossoms tranquilized them to silence.

The reflector lights at the junction pulled them from their reverie. The mileage gauge indicated they should be near Red Hill, the dividing line between the Grantley land and the neighbors. Elaine, the driver, spoke first.

"Jayne, do you know where we are?" she asked as she shifted into second to make the next sharp turn and then drove under the arc of a beautiful rainbow.

"How can I ever forget? Red Hill. Red Hill, a symbol of Papa's solitude and seclusion at one time."

Jayne looked at the narrow hill squeezed between two other hills of oozing, reddish-yellow clay coming down to the highway.

"Remember how it was on rainy days? It was slippery, like the glass mountain in the fairy tales," said Elaine.

"And on dry days, its deep ruts kept us from going to school," added Jayne.

They laughed as if they were six and ten again, riding in the back end of their father's 1927 Ford pickup, hitting every bump with a screech.

"Just think, we use to eat that clay like candy."

Elaine signaled a left toward a wider adjoining gravel road which showed evidence of recent construction and pulled over to the side. She turned off the engine and spoke again.

"That clay was gum to our little black friends. Chewing and swallowing it was what made us 'hale and hearty.'"

"Are you thinking what I'm thinking?"

"No, you wouldn't dare."

Jayne had already opened the door on her side and had started up the embankment.

"Well, what the heck? There's still little traffic. I'll run some clay through my fingers, but nothing's going to get me to eat that."

She could imagine Jayne trying it, then regurgitating it all over her new seat covers. Hadn't she jabbered all the way here about being glad to get away from kids and looking forward to retirement in another year. How her nerves were shot and she felt like a computer in overload. She breathed deeply and joined her sister. How wonderfully relaxing to be just digging your toes in the red clay.

It started to rain and, though it was only twelve-thirty, the sky was a dark menacing color. They could barely see what was left of the old farmhouse nestled in the clearing.

"We'll wait in the car for Rick," Elaine said. "He has the only keys."

"I brought a snack for us. You can never be sure of the time with Rick."

"When was the last time Papa was out here?" Jayne asked.

"I saw 'FOR SALE' signs along the edge of the property coming in. Papa wrote about having some big deal with The Lincoln Loggers of America"

"Papa's always got some plan going in his head," Elaine said as she poured coffee from a thermos and handed a sandwich to Jayne.

"That's our problem. Papa can write such fluent letters and is quite lucid when he is talking to Rick about financial matters. Neither you or Rick have seen him at his worst with his sporadic escapes into the past, and his increasing tendency to drift off. Denice tells me you got a generous sampling of it yourself now."

"Do you think he's putting on an act?"

"At ninety-three? Naw, but you can imagine what would happen if Papa were left to wander these thousands of acres. He'd set fire to the place or scare off any buyers with his stories.

"He won't admit to the fact that he doesn't own it anymore." She tilted her head to one side, all the color had drained from her face.

"I've been trying to keep the ol' blood pressure down and keep the weight down too. At times I wish Papa hadn't made me his administratrix. All that legal jargon gives me a headache."

"Yeah, Papa wrote me. You live here and you're a nurse. It was a logical choice." Jayne reached over to give her sister a friendly nudge and smiled.

"What is he like? This Rick?"

"Some people mistake him for Omar Sharif and it causes quite a stir when they ask for his autograph in Atlanta or Florida where he often goes on business."

"Omar Sharif? You kidding?" Jayne's brown eyes narrowed, and squinted against the glare of the sun as she stared at her sister.

"You're not kidding."

"He's like Papa in many ways. Holds on tightly to the almighty dollar. Long term investments they call it. But Rick Steele's a financial wizard. He was educated in this country, but as a child, he lived in Israel and Beirut."

Just as quickly as it had started, the rain stopped and the sun burst from the sky, bathing the surrounding area. They moved to sit on a pile of lumber where part of the porch still existed.

"Papa said in his letter that God sent him Rick just at the right time. What did he mean?"

"Some business deal Papa had going. Some developer was ripping him off and feigning friendship, which Papa thrives on. Rick recovered part of the losses when he took over the accounts."

The sun left little dry spots here and there on the porch, but they found a place to sit. They were two lone figures hugging their knees, childlike, as though waiting for their father to come home from work. They watched the cream colored Lincoln Continental ease its way up the low incline onto the massive front lawn, coming to a stop under the row of walnut trees.

Rick looked like a golf pro who had just made a hole-in-one. He leaped from the car, grinning with enthusiasm.

"Don't move!" he said. "What a sight you two make. Norman Rockwell would envy such a painting. Let me get my camera." Even as he adjusted the lens, squinting to bring the image into view, he spoke rapidly.

"Have you been filling Jayne in on what's happening here at the Grantley Estate, Elaine?

"Sorry, Jayne, about meeting secretly like this. We don't want to see your father hurt. Bless his heart. He's a lot like my dad. Saving his money for his two daughters' future. Ain't he something?"

He put the camera back in the glove compartment and removed a folded blueprint from an attaché case on the seat.

The two human statues waited patiently for permission to move.

He walked back toward them, firmly shook Elaine's hand and wrapped a strong arm around Jayne's slumped shoulders, and planted an affectionate kiss on one freckled cheek.

"So, what do you think? Did Elaine show you your Lookout Point yet?"

"We're coming back next weekend," Elaine said. "Give us more time to explore. We gotta get back to Papa. I hate to impose on my friend, Rita, to father-sit for long."

"Ain't she sweet though? I must say Jayne, your sister's been loyal to both your parents. She's doing right by them and now making a home for him. That trailer was no place for him alone.

"Elaine tell you I found him passed out on the floor one day. Just like we found your mother, even in the same spot. Let's go inside."

The sagging porch shifted slightly on its unsure pillars as they entered, Rick taking bold strides ahead to caution them about the loose boards. The air was full of the mustiness of age. There was no light and the lack of life made the place smaller than it really was. Rick rushed past locked rooms that seemed to cry out to the intruders.

Elaine followed at a distance. She had been here many times. She had been in charge of the transfer of some furniture to the mobile home, when living in this house was no longer safe. She was responsible for the salvaging of a few antiques, some money, and some documents from a safe, after the first vandalism when her mother died. She had also come out here when they were restoring it, their own first dream house, as a young couple, before the birth of her grandson. She had also been out here many times before moving Dad in with them for safety.

Jayne felt drawn to the closed rooms as they continued down the long corridors but she looked to Rick for direction. He finally stopped at the big ballroom piano with its carvings and pushed aside the paint drip cloth to spread out the blueprint.

"You haven't seen this portion of the subdivision yet, Elaine. Here's your property, Jayne. Right next to Grand Lodge of Georgia. That's one side of your villa you won't have to fence in. They have one of those expensive aluminum cyclone jobs surrounding their property.

"Have you told your father you've invested money back into the estate yet?"

"Papa rambles on in his own secret world," Elaine explained. The muscles of her face were drawn down introspectively. "You're the only one who can get that close to him and actually carry on a conversation."

"I'd rather wait until I have something built before I tell him. Let it be a surprise. Lookout Point was one of his favorite spots. I want to set this up right." Jayne pulled the blueprint closer as she spoke.

"We've got two new houses going up on the north river now." Rick turned to Elaine.

"One owner, a lawyer, just brought in his cabin cruiser. They're working on the docks. Get offers all the time for your piece of land, Jayne. Any time you decide to sell, name your price."

"That wouldn't go well with Papa. Buy and sell," Jayne struggled for the right words. "After all we're from that generation when the women left big business and financial dealings alone."

" 'Takes a real man to make land like this pay off,' " Elaine mimicked Papa.

"If you'd save your money and stop spending foolishly for all these repairs, you might amount to something yet," Rick said and laughed with them.

"That's your father all right. Ain't he something else? Say, I'm planning to stop over to see him some evening soon. Think he can use a new pair of slippers and some cigars?"

"And something to wash it down with?" Jayne added. She and Elaine tried to stifle a snicker.

"You know what you two look like?" Rick smiled. "Two retired wealthy eccentrics. You'll be able to name your price someday. Play your cards right."

Chapter 10

Early the next Saturday, Elaine parked the car at the farmhouse, indicated the trail Rick had pointed out the week before, and headed toward Lookout Point. It was about two miles away as the crow flies and deep into the rich, timbered countryside. There was no need to hurry. Just follow the orange ribbon markers at the end of the logging trail.

Jayne lagged behind, stopping occasionally to catch her breath. She had not taken a walk in the woods since that nature hike with the third graders back in Michigan last winter.

Her students had been amazed that an old lady could keep up the pace in the snow while they searched for tracks and winter creatures. Some of the classmates had to turn back halfway and stay in the cabin with one of the scouts. Their physical weakness only gave her the strength to push on.

Now in the cool of this late August morning she watched her sister swinging one of those virtually indestructible polypropylene workmen's thermos jugs in one hand and testing the ground before her with a hickory stick in the other.

She marvelled at Elaine's stamina in her mid-fifties. She carried her short and stocky frame with such assurance that she looked much taller than her actual five foot, one inch height. The bounce and energy she projected, and happy gleam in her eyes, gave her a more youthful look. Even though the hair was silver white, cut short and permed curly for easy care, every strand was in place and framed a pretty, blemish-free face. The eyes were definitely Irish like her father's, but the face was a legacy from her Spanish mother.

She was finding herself analyzing others more and more as she approached retirement age, but she had yet to achieve her greatest ambition and felt at times there was a missing link in her own self awareness. She was glad when Elaine stopped to pick up an arrowhead.

"We'll cut through the old Bill George place," she said. "It's closer. The logging trail means walking an extra mile, and my feet still hurt from midnight duty at the VA. Besides, I know where we might find more Creek relics, and make this trip profitable."

"You sound like Papa now," Jayne reminded her.

"Naw, 'be prudent' is his favorite expression."

They moved carefully through the underbrush, feeling the surface with their long sticks. Soon they were out of the denser area and near a clearing.

"Can't we rest a few minutes?" Jayne asked. "How long before we spot one of the markers? I'm starting to get tired."

"Shouldn't we be smelling the sweet lemon blossoms by now?" she asked as she settled herself against the gnarled root of a large oak.

Elaine chuckled. She was too cautious to sit down, so she squatted on her heels nearby.

"Better watch where you sit. There are wasps' nests, snakes, and ticks."

"Nothing you say can disrupt this untouched paradise. Just smell that honeysuckle." She drew a deep breath of cool, pine and flower scented air and watched a hummingbird, like a tiny helicopter, hover over a low hanging limb of a honeysuckle bush.

"Just let me savor this moment."

"While waiting, we might as well leave a few crumbs for the army ants."

Elaine joined her sister and offered her a cookie from the lunch kit.

"Sorry I can't offer you a drink. We'll pass a spring soon, I'm sure. Right now I could use a cigarette. I didn't pack any because I didn't want to take the chance of starting a forest fire."

"Oughta be some berries around here. We picked enough of them as kids. Even a persimmon tree would be a welcome sight," said Jayne.

"Where there's berries, there's bears. And don't think I'm saying this to scare you. Hunters have reported seeing a black bear in here last season. A motorist spotted one crossing the highway not long ago."

"Now you have me worried. The faintest rustle's going to sound like a bear sneaking up on us." Jayne jumped up, dumping crumbs among the branches and dry twigs. "What time is it anyway? Where are those land markers?"

Elaine removed a wristwatch from the lunch kit and looked at the dial. Puzzled, she gave it a few shakes and put it to her ear. First one then the other. "It's almost two o'clock. Poor Papa, he'll probably be wondering where we are." Concern showed in her childlike voice.

"We can't stay long at Lookout Point, just inspect the property, and try another cutting from the lemon tree maybe?"

"I understand. I brought the camera along to take a few pictures, then we can leave. I'd feel much better if we could find one of the orange ribbons, or get a whiff of sweet lemon blossoms."

An hour later they still had not seen a marker as Elaine forged deeper through a tangle of pathless undergrowth and untouched thickets. She stopped once to get her bearings and Jayne almost bumped into her.

"We'll stay along the creek bed," she said. "That should lead us to the river. Water flows downstream. Sooner or later we'll end up at the farmhouse."

They eased themselves into the sticky mud, only to find one end blocked by the rotting stumps of fallen trees. Elaine reversed directions and climbed toward the ridge. She slipped on some wet leaves and her lunch kit landed near the creek. Both knees of her jeans were ripped but she forced herself to get up. She grabbed a low branch and moved on, not stopping for words or inspection. Jayne retrieved the lunch kit, trying hard to suppress an urge to break the silence.

The snapping of dry twigs and the swooshing of their shoes were the only sound they were aware of for another hour. They had lost all sense of direction now and simply walked because to stop would admit defeat.

Two weary women scrutinized the thick shrubbery for some sign, any sign, of civilization.

When they came to the next clearing, they dropped down into the thick grass.

"John wanted me to pack his pistol," Elaine said. "It fits so neatly in the lunch kit. He thinks it's too isolated to go around here unarmed. Now I'm beginning to think he was right."

"I could use a cigarette too." She was trembling so much her fingers were all thumbs as she reached for her stick to get up again.

"I remember sitting over there," said Jayne. "I think we have been going in circles. Do you think this could be our reparation for getting the Latin teacher lost that summer when he was hired to tutor us?"

Despite hunger and fatigue, Elaine laughed at remembering how all the girls had a crush on Réné Ryan, who had eyes only for pretty Miss Ingrid Cunningham, the first year English teacher.

"Boy do I remember how we led them around in circles when Mom and Dad, having invited them out for a picnic, asked us to show them around. They were panic stricken when we said they would have to cross the creek on that fallen log in order to get back to the house."

"I remember Ryan threatened to flunk you in Latin and you said. . . ."

"Let me see if I can remember. 'You can take away my grade, but you can't take away what's already in my brain."

"Close enough, but this isn't getting us to Lookout Point or back to the car."

Her usual springy gait was now slowed. Elaine thought of how often, jokingly, she had remarked that she needed bilateral foot transplants.

"I never realized this place was so enormous. One creek is very much like another and no telephone wires or anything to guide us."

Toward evening they came upon a small path and followed it. Somewhere in the tangle of scrub oaks beside the road, they heard a twig snap. Terror gripped them and held them rooted to the ground. A buck deer darted from a strip of woods, came to a sudden stop, flicked its tail, and vanished back into the underbrush.

A little later, had they not been still watching hopefully for an orange marker, they would have never seen the man's body lying near a fallen log.

"Is he dead?" asked Jayne, as they slowly paced around the prone figure, pausing only long enough to nudge it, their sticks poised for any quick reaction.

"He must've tripped over that stump and fallen against this sharp edge," Elaine said and pointed to the first rock they'd seen that day. They must be near Lookout Point. There would be lots of rocks in that area.

"What'll we do with him?"

"Here, take my lunch kit and get some water from the creek. I'll keep an eye on him."

Jayne hurriedly filled the kit, spilling most of the water as she ran back to help.

"How is he?" She watched Elaine inspect a three inch gash on his left temple. The bleeding had almost stopped.

"It's only a superficial wound, not deep enough to need stitches," she said as she cleansed the wound and placed a paper napkin from her jacket pocket on it. She secured it with her head scarf, Willie Nelson style.

Jayne smiled and all her freckles seemed to come into focus. She closed the lunch kit slowly, shaking her head. Protective Elaine, dependable as the sun and quick to take charge in any emergency. If only she had some of that assurance.

The man opened deep blue eyes that stared out from a ruddy, bearded face, masked by heavy, black curly hair. He groaned and closed his eyes again.

"He must be in his mid-forties. He's not dressed for a hike or a hunting trip," Jayne said.

"Don't let appearances fool you. He could be an escaped convict." The concern in Elaine's voice was unmistakable. "Or even into drugs," she added.

The man groaned and tried to speak. He attempted to lift himself on one arm, then slumped back and passed out.

"He's gone now," Jayne whispered. "Help me with his shirtsleeve. He may have a broken arm."

"Know what I was thinking?"

"What?" Elaine worked rapidly and skillfully. "Nothing broken, just badly bruised. He passed out from loss of blood. What were you going to say?"

"Papa was telling me how you saved your pet chicken's life when you were five. He had stepped on it by accident and it would have been chicken pie if you hadn't breathed into its open beak. He would be really proud to hear about this."

Her eyes flashed with pride, but to protect her father, she could not even share this moment with him.

"There's no way we can explain this and not complicate the situation even more. He doesn't even own this land any more, yet he'll say he's got to get out here and tend to business."

"Look. He's coming around again."

As his expressive eyes began to focus, he made another attempt to sit up. Elaine reached over to help him.

"Abram Littlejohn here." He extended a hand in greeting. "Are you my angel of mercy? What's your name?"

"I'm Elaine Langstrom and this is my sister, Ja.. . ."

"We're just out looking for arrowheads," Jayne said, interrupting so quickly it startled them. For some reason he had an unsettling effect on her. That, not yet divulged secret, look. That name, Littlejohn. Salesman? Politician? I know it from someplace, but where?

"I'm here to look over some riverfront property." He directed his remarks to Elaine. He was slurring his words somewhat, and ignoring Jayne's questioning gaze.

"There are plenty of choice lots here. You have your pick," Elaine said.

"That clap of thunder was my cue to get back to my jeep in a hurry. A person could get lost in here. Damn, I must've been out for hours." He looked at his broken wristwatch as if studying it to determine why time flies.

"It's almost 4:30," Elaine volunteered. "John would be sending a helicopter search for us if we hadn't run into you."

"John?"

"My son. We. . . ."

"We need a ride to the main road," Jayne snapped, interrupting her sister again.

"We'll help you to your jeep."

His travel-soiled shirt was wet with sweat against their cotton blouses and soaking them as each supported an arm.

Along the way Jayne tried desperately to get her sister's attention, but all her clues went undetected. Her dread deepened as the jeep bounced over each rut in the corrugated road, leaving farther behind all hopes of seeing Lookout Point this trip. Her heart leaped when she saw the little country store in the distance as they exited onto the main highway. Although Elaine and Littlejohn were in the midst of an exchange about the financial prospects in real estate, Jayne leaped from the jeep as it slowed and pulled Elaine with her.

"You sure you'll be safe?" Littlejohn asked "I'd gladly drive you home."

"We have a ride at that store, thanks."

Jayne waved good-bye from the highway, with her arm linked with Elaine's. They watched him drive off toward town. Jayne smiled, watching her sister as she was trying to erase the scowl from her puzzled face.

"What got into you?" Elaine felt queasy. "He could've taken us to the car. My feet are killing me. And if I don't get a cigarette soon, I. . . ." She was too exhausted to argue. Arguing would use what little energy she could muster and she needed that energy to try to sort out the day's mishaps.

"You can get cigarettes at the store," Jayne said and turned to her. "We'll get a ride, too. There's a pickup and a car parked at the pumps." Keeping her eyes on Elaine, she was remembering, from the old days when they rode their bikes to this very same store. It must have been at least three miles from the Grantley Estates.

"What was that all about?" Elaine asked belligerently, once they were safe in their own car headed for Hillside.

"Did you really believe Littlejohn?" Jayne inquired quickly. "I found this orange streamer under his body as you were helping him. There was another peeking out his hip pocket, but I was afraid to pull it out, even when we had him so close getting him to the jeep."

"Damn. Now it's all coming back," Elaine said, after a pause as she accelerated to pass a slower moving vehicle. "He mentioned hearing a clap of thunder. It's been sunny and clear all day."

"Yeah." Jayne nodded and leaned toward her, grinning. "I've got his license plate number." She unwrapped a pack of gum and passed over a stick to Elaine. "I have this strange feeling we haven't seen the last of Mr. Littlejohn."

"Why would he remove all the markers?" Elaine asked.

"Maybe John can help me unravel this mystery."

"What about Rick? You gonna tell him?"

"What? And let him know we got lost. Let'em find out about the markers the next time he brings out a client." She pulled her lips into a thin, hard smile.

"Yeah, guess he would think we were irresponsible. Not an ounce of business sense between us. Just two eccentrics out bird-watching."

She reached in the glove compartment for a small notebook and pencil and began copying the license number she had scratched on the camera case with a stick while in the jeep.

"Looking at a map to see how to get to Lookout Point?" Elaine teased.

"Very funny," she snorted back at her sister. More than anything, she wanted to build a monument high against a hillside and facing a body of water. Just as her grandfather had hoped to do for his wife in Cuba before the Spanish-American War. Just as her mother dreamed of before World War II.

Underneath the surface there was always anxiety, but Jayne would never let others know about this lifelong ambition. Only Elaine would understand the reason for her intense longing. She could not imagine any man in the family responding favorably to investing in a villa with Spanish and Creek influences, and in timber country? Timber is worth a lot.

As though reading her thoughts, Elaine apologized and smiled shyly when Jayne caught her eye.

"John still thinks you'd best build something rustic, a. . . ."

"I know," Jayne interrupted her sister again. "That's why I'm not leaving this dream for another generation. Rick says he'll put in a road for me."

"You're talking about retirement next year. You know Papa and Rick have this estate money all tied up until five years after his death. What do you plan to use for money? Mortgage rates are higher than ever."

"We could pan the gold in my half of the river," Jayne said, trying to hide her disappointment. "I know the gold is there."

"It would take a fortune to extract it. But rumor is that where the water is clear, near your plot, you can see gold dust." She looked at Jayne for approval. "We'll find a way."

"Then we'll write a book." Jayne looked at Elaine for a long time. The words possessed a contagious kind of joy. "We have the characters and the situation for a winner," she went on to say.

"Oh what tangled webs we weave, when we practice to keep an old man happy." Elaine smiled.

"Is that our theme?"

"Sure. Jot it down." She punched the right-turn indicator and pulled into a paved driveway.

"Papa's goin' to be fussin' something awful. I hate to go in." They found Earl glued to the TV set, oblivious of their presence until they tapped him gently on the shoulder as they passed through the recreation room.

The smell of chocolate cookies and sweet, spicy pumpkin pies filled the house. Denice had spent her day off baking.

"I know where you've been," he called after them, his eyes still fixed on the TV commentator. Elaine and Jayne felt more at ease now, mainly because he'd talk endlessly if they stayed in the room and responded to him even a little. He usually answered his own questions anyway. There was little need to pay close attention.

"You went to see John. How did you find the old place? I've got to get back out there one of these days. There's so much work to do. I've imposed on my baby daughter now on. . . ." He had fallen asleep before completing the sentence.

"He's always saying 'he's got work to do.' Do you see him doing any work?" asked Denice.

"Only brain work," sighed Elaine.

"I wonder if he ever thinks of Villa Sara, or the sweet lemon tree, when he speaks of the old place?" asked Jayne.

"You'll have to ask him," they both said in unison.

"He'll ignore your question though and go on to something else," Denice continued.

"If Villa Sara is to exist, I'm afraid it's left up to us now. Can't expect any help from Papa then," Jayne said, reaching for the fresh baked cookie offered to her.

"Think we'll live to see it happen?" asked Elaine, filling the coffee cups again.

"Don't hold your breath, but at least you guys have the land, so I guess anything is possible," Denice assured them.

"A lot of questions to ask and problems to solve before anything can be made possible." Jayne breathed deeply. "Maybe we just should leave it all to the next generation."

"And why not," smiled Elaine. "It would make it a lot simpler for us."

That next summer a boy of seven sprinted ahead of his Grand-mother and vanished into the underbrush and overhanging pines. He had not had any luck finding arrowheads like Elaine and her nurse friend, Rita Alton. No luck at all!

He followed the creek bed until he could no longer hear their voices. He continued walking in a determined manner and looking straight ahead.

"Now where'd Chris go?" Elaine asked. "Honest, you've got to have your eyes on children every minute these days."

"He can't be far," Rita assured her. "I won't say don't worry either, not after the adventure you and your sister had in these same woods last year. Your concern is understandable."

"I didn't know my fear was that obvious, and my sister still doesn't completely trust Abram Littlejohn."

"Why did he remove the markers?"

"He wanted to protect the Creeks' burial grounds and make it hard for prospective buyers to find the site."

Elaine stopped in the clearing to shake some gravel from her canvas shoe and picked up another arrowhead.

"But when he learned that a Creek descendant had purchased the land, he even offered his services to my sister as a caretaker."

"There's certainly enough land here to build Villa Sara," Rita said enthusiastically, "and still allow the burial grounds to remain sacred. Knowing what I do now, I'll treasure my arrowheads even more."

When they reached the spot Elaine wanted to show her friend, she paused only a moment to get her bearings, and very quickly they were at the lemon tree.

A cluster of white blossoms hit the visor of Rita's sun cap and a small voice called down from high up in the sweet lemon tree. Looking up she could see a maroon football jersey, but couldn't see the concealed silky blond head.

"Look at me, Grandma." He hung like a monkey, upside down, on one of the thick branches that reached out over the creek.

"This is the neatest place for my tree house, I'm thinkin'."

"Kids," groaned Miss Alton. "Someday I hope he's in our shoes, trembling under a tree that holds one of his sons."

"Yes, and sprouting his own grey hairs," Elaine said, attempting to laugh off her fear for his safety.

"I can almost see Chris doing just that."

The boy straddled one of the limbs like a giant walking stick, and pulled a clump of blossoms and leaves with him as he bounced to the ground.

"Grandma, you almost freaked out, didn't you?" Chris said breathlessly.

Then not waiting for an answer, he scooted over to a big boulder and spread out a crumpled piece of paper he took from his hip pocket.

"Look at this!" he said beaming with pride.

Elaine gasped when she saw the crude drawing of a boy's first attempt at designing his own dream house. The seedlings of conservation and preservation had already been planted deeply into the next generation. She could barely make out the scribbled words under the sketch. Then, by straining her eyes with the effort, she noticed something that was perhaps as significant as the sweet lemon tree itself.

"The Indians," he had scrawled underneath his crude drawing of a house, "built their houses on high ground, and where there wasn't any, they raised mounds by hand and there they took refuge from the great flood."

Project Seek

Epigram

The pleasures of the senses pass quickly; those of the heart become sorrow; but those of the mind are with us even to the end of our journey.

Spanish Proverb

Chapter 1

The award-winning jeep spat fresh gravel as it screeched to a halt. Elaine Langstrom was driving much too fast on the country road, but did manage to stop an arm's length from the blockade:

Road Closed
To Through Traffic

"You reckon that sign includes jeeps, too?" asked her sister, Jayne Reeder.

"You reckon correctly." Elaine jerked the gear shift into park and looked frantically at her watch for the second time in the past five minutes. "Papa will be furious that we're not back for supper," she sighed, glancing at the mound of legal pad pages sailing from Jayne's unsteady hands.

"Poor J, can you ever get that mess the way the editors want it by October? Since we don't seem to be making any progress in getting Villa Sara built, it would be so wonderful to have the story put in writing."

"No problem. I'm depending on your analytical mind to help me with the structure." Still jittery from the abrupt stop, Jayne jabbed the dull pencil lead into her faded, jean-covered knee as she stooped to pick up the yellow sheets. After letting out a scream, she crammed the pages back into the worn manila folder.

Elaine Langston and Jayne Reeder, daughters of Earl Grantley and Sara Bocan Grantley, were united now at Elaine's home in Georgia for a special purpose: to assess the possibility of building Villa Sara, a place in honor of their mother where creativity could flourish. Villa Sara had

125

been a long-standing dream of their parents but had never come to reality during their lifetime. Now the two sisters hoped to find a way to make the dream come true.

While together, Elaine and Jayne also hoped to resolve the problem of what to do with their elderly father who now resided with Elaine in her home. Senility was slowly creeping up on the elderly gentleman, and his thoughts were mostly those of the past.

*   *   *

"Just a quick look at the old fishing hole to refresh my memory and add that touch of realism," Jayne told her sister once she had the papers reorganized and back on her lap. "Then we can be on our way to serve our father, the First Earl of Creek." She paused briefly to assist Elaine in concealing their day's rations and some tools under a canvas tarp. "Nice of your son John to loan us his jeep. Most twenty-year-olds wouldn't trust anyone over fifty even touching their customized wheels."

"With all this construction, I wasn't about to drive my new Imperial. And you couldn't have forgotten our adventure of two summers ago."

"No way. Getting lost trying to find Lookout Point, the mysterious Littlejohn found hurt and pretending to be a prospective buyer and you saving his life. Whatever happened to him?" Jayne asked, referring to the longtime caretaker of the Grantley estate.

"He's connected with the flood control project that's responsible for the work going on here now. John tells me that six-foot diameter outlet pipe is being laid to divert water from the creek to the river. This portion of the land where the pipe is being laid is owned by the historical society."

"Wow, quite a project. How much is this costing us tax payers?"

"Now who's sounding like papa? The project is funded mainly by a grant from the Army Corps of Engineers. Other phases—"

"How much in dollars?"

"Other phases of the two point six million dollar project include work near papa's old sawmill and dam north of here. Only it's not papa's land anymore—most of the estate's been sold to developers. You can't tell him that, though. His mind is often in the olden days."

"I'm glad we came prepared to hoof it this time," Jayne said, looking at the terrain ahead.

"It's only a little. . . ."

". . . a little piece down the road, right?"

They both laughed as two children might share a secret on a playground. Some of the rural southern dialect still held a certain charm they could not easily explain.

A few short strides off the expanding gravel road, the two sisters searched for the quiet sands that once led to the creek. The road and path were deserted, even though they now crossed the public easement to the river. The scent of honeysuckle and dogwood competed with their "Deepwoods Off" insect repellant.

As they continued along the way, a silence they had lost touch with now mesmerized their voices to a whisper.

"Do you ever wish we could go back in time and be kids again?" asked Jayne. "Swinging our lunch pails and avoiding the creek because Mamacita said so?"

"No way would I want to go back," Elaine did not hesitate to add, "but I'd want Mamacita here."

"Everyone misses Sara Bocan Grantley. I think she'd be proud of what her two daughters are trying to accomplish. It would be great if our book could hit the book stores in time for her birthday, since we haven't done anything yet toward building her Villa Sara."

"It's quite a challenge to build something like that. But I still think that by some stroke of fate we'll have a Villa Sara on our land."

The sudden rustle of branches and breaking dry twigs startled them. A young couple, hands joined, darted out from the underbrush and headed up a cleared embankment. Their shyless giggles permeated the air. When they reached the top of the incline where a steel-gray chopper sat propped on its mud-covered appendage, they turned, still grumbling, and waved.

"Who are they?" Jayne asked, inhaling deeply.

"How should I know?" sputtered Elaine. "I'm as much a stranger in these parts now as you are. But, look there," she said, pointing, "ahead is the atmosphere you seek for inspiration."

The creek, muddy and stagnant in places, trickled slowly below them. The honeysuckle and dogwood scents were now masked by the stench of decaying catfish remains. A soggy rowboat that served as a seat wobbled under the weight of a wrinkled man old enough to be their father. He wore the ever-present fisherman's cap and laced-up boots on giant feet. His hands were large and restless.

"That old-timer could probably tell us enough to fill volumes," Jayne said excitedly, putting a brisker stride in her walk.

"Don't forget," explained Elaine, "you're still in rural Georgia. People out here stay pretty much to themselves. They like it that way, and I can't say that I blame them."

"Just a couple of questions, then we can be on our way."

Jayne swayed slightly as she eased down the embankment, the loose soil she kicked up becoming imbedded in her Reekon sneakers. Feeling the need for support, she reached out for Elaine's outstretched hand.

Hands still trembling, Jayne cautiously approached the fisherman from behind. Still out of view, she watched him curse his meager catch, and with bony fingers, peel off a generous piece of wasp nest as fish bait for still another useless try at supper.

"It's after five!" Elaine called from a distance, disturbing the peaceful scene.

The old man's head lifted, his brows knotted together.

"How goes it?" Jayne managed cheerfully.

Then she saw his eyes and wished she had been less forward. Those eyes. Two deep pools glaring through tobacco clouds.

"Damnit, woman. Can't ya see I'm fishin'?"

Jayne chewed nervously on the inside of her lip. No use opening up any kind of dialogue with this one. But before she could think of an appropriate apology, he just as abruptly dropped his pole and did a nervous search for something in the boat. Spasms of fear swept through her body, freezing it to the ninety-degree sand. Her imagination took hold; she feared he was reaching for a gun. The old fisherman pulled out his chewing tobacco and bit off a big chunk.

"What the hell." The words came softer now from his parched, tobacco-stained lips. "Ain't had a decent catch since them government people put in this new road." He spat a graded curve that landed at her feet.

Jayne watched the sand drink the dark brown liquid and felt sick.

"More outsiders than kinfolks muddying the waters these days." He made an attempt to get to his feet but failed.

Jayne felt Elaine's presence close behind her, but still could not make her legs move, nor could she think of what to say.

The old fisherman continued, half talking to himself. "Ain't been the same since old man Grantley got moved out of his place. Nobody dared come near this creek when he was around, less'n they had a gun more powerful than that old Winchester of his."

Once he began talking, there was no desire on either sister's part to stop him.

"You two'd never got past that foothill yonder if'n Earl Grantley was still hereabouts." He stopped and spat again, this time into the water. "A body can't even fish over across the way. All them waterfront houses on stilts and their high-fired speed boats. Then there's talk of condos. Condos, fondos. Punk gangs at night. No peace a'tall lest you get here in the early or morning."

"The best success is always early in the day," Elaine whispered to her sister.

"According to District DNR Fishery Chief Cliff Packson, the fish just seem to 'shut off' in the afternoon," Jayne quoted from the travel brochure she brought from Michigan. "He believes the water just gets too warm because there's not enough leaf canopy to shield it from the sun's rays."

"Yeah, reckon it must be around suppertime or thereabouts," the old man continued.

"You reckon correctly," replied Jayne, thinking for a moment that the stranger's eyes loomed less menacingly. She could see a weak crinkle spread across his jutting chin.

"Reckon yer all here for the Grantley auction." He addressed them directly, stopping short of being too accepting, yet not waiting for an answer. "Got some mighty expensive stuff, I hear tell. Course I never been in that house. I hear it's haunted. Some Creek Indian curse. You see all these other new places built up?" he asked, sweeping his arm in a gesture to include the newly-build homes in the distance. "Pilfered, they say, during the last three months at the rate of two a day. But not the Grantley Estate. Strangest thing. All them valuable antiques and all. I hear tell the old miser had a fortune stashed away in mattresses . . . and somewheres else they never found."

Elaine could stand silent no longer. She pushed furiously forward. "Listen you . . . that old miser happens to be. . . ." She spun around quickly when Jayne took a firm grasp on the arm raised in defiance.

"Earl Grantley happens to be most respected where he is now," Jayne completed the sentence. "We'll be sure to tell him when we see him again that he's still thought of around the creek area."

The sisters' eyes met in mild understanding.

"You'd think we were the cause of his not catching any fish," Elaine sputtered, her face framed in disappointment at not being able to defend her father. "Let's get out of here before I throw up."

"Y'all come back soon now!" the old fisherman called as they turned their backs to depart.

"That was no time to be diplomatic," Elaine fumed as they headed for the jeep. "I realize that we say things about papa sometimes when he irritates us, but it just burns me up when I hear criticisms from strangers." She slammed the jeep in reverse, still cursing under her breath.

*   *   *

The two women drove ten miles down the freeway before either dared say more. Elaine's eyes remained riveted to the fast-moving traffic ahead while Jayne, drained of any original thoughts, shuffled through the yellow sheets of her manuscript. As her sister's eyes stopped looking harsh, she ventured a question.

"Well, are you going to do it?"

"Do what?"

"Go to the auction?"

"The only auction here was two years ago when Rick Steele, papa's advisor, had that land auction. I sent you the brochure. That old fisherman's brain is sun-damaged. But then again, he just might know something about those stolen antiques. Haunted house, indeed!"

"I did learn something while talking to the old coot, though," Jayne interrupted, nudging the jeep armrest. She studied her sister's face for approval. "I know now why the Lookout Point is so valuable—why Rick Steel has so many offers to buy it. Condos looming against the final glow of the sun—can you imagine?"

"I know," added Elaine. "When Rick calls with another offer, I always tell him it's reserved for something very special. A memorial of some kind. Leave them all in suspense."

"Mamacita would have been so proud of us."

"Indeed."

*   *   *

Fifty miles out from the Grantley Estate, a dense fog had forced many motorists off the freeway. The two women could barely see the lights of Hillside ahead. Elaine steered the jeep as close to the shoulder as possible, anticipating the three-car pileup ahead moments before the sirens sounded. She reached expertly for the emergency kit under the canvas tarp and slid from the driver's seat without a word.

And off she goes on a mission of mercy, thought Jayne, more in a manner of admiration and respect for her sister's assertiveness and skills than of total self-helplessness on her own part.

Struggling desperately to catch her breath, Jayne searched for a Kleenix or paper napkin to hold over her face. Then she pocketed the keys left in the ignition. Being stranded in an open jeep exposed to all types of pollutants was no way to comply with her doctor's orders to take the trip south and breathe some pure country air.

She removed her tinted bifocals to see better, but the smoke and smell made everything more blurred. She tried to make sense of it all. It seemed that every visit to the Grantley Estate had turned into a catastrophe. Coincidence? Hardly. Then why did she suddenly feel the icy chill of last winter's most severe blizzard that left her stranded for hours in a damaged pickup while her husband wandered off to assist another motorist? Was she destined to spend valuable time waiting at the brink of disaster, letting others rush full-force into its midst? And what of papa? Wouldn't he be just as worried for their safety when he saw the evening news? How could he not know of their whereabouts?

"Papa's got to be worried sick," came Elaine's voice through the diminishing fog.

She took her place behind the wheel as calmly as though time had stood still. No greeting. No accounting of casualties or extent of injuries. No fog cloud update. Nothing. She put the jeep keys back in the ignition, and off they drove in silence. There would be plenty of time later for particulars.

*   *   *

Within the hour, Elaine braked the jeep in the spacious driveway of her modern, four-bedroom brick home. "Rita's been here," she said.

"How can you tell?"

"My two dogs would be attacking the French windows by now if she weren't. She must have come over to feed them and take care of Papa, too. I better call her right away."

"Go ahead. I'll unload and secure the jeep," Jayne volunteered.

"No need to do that in this neighborhood. I never lock my car."

"That'll take some getting used to for me. Where I live, the hubcaps and hood ornament would be gone by morning, even in the more affluent districts. Kids use the ornaments for belt buckles. Get a good price for them, too."

"You needn't worry here," assured Elaine. "That's one of the good things you can get used to. But wait until you've been here a few days with Papa—that's another story."

"I know. It may be an odd story, but that doesn't make it any easier to deal with. I hate to be at odds with Papa, and not only on the subject of money."

* * *

Earl Grantley was seated in his favorite collapsible lawn chair blocking the TV when they entered the recreation room. He never looked up.

"You two go skedaddling off without a word," he mumbled. "You know, your friend Rita's been here and gone."

"I can see Rita's been here, Papa."

Elaine, undaunted by her father's unwarranted remark, raised her voice above the loud commercial showing a young acrobat leaping for energized batteries. She retreated to the kitchen and picked up the wall phone, punching in her best friend's number.

"I know where you've been," Earl said, looking in Jayne's direction, then back at the TV. "Hot dawg. Look at that pretty girl, would you! You guys never talk to me. Time was. . . ."

"So what do you want to talk about, Papa?" Jayne asked listlessly, sinking into a second lounge chair.

"Ever since. Well, how did you find the old place?" he grinned, but didn't wait for an answer. "I tell you, I've got to get out there one of these days when I'm not so busy. Gotta check things out."

He paused to laugh and took a long puff on the half-lit cigar, then waited for its ashes to hang precariously over the rug. He gave the arms of the wobbly chair a vigorous slap.

"So what'll we talk about, Papa?" Jayne found herself raising her voice so her father could hear her. Then she heard Elaine call from the kitchen.

"Jayne, see if you can get Papa to lower the volume."

She reached for the remote control and switched channels to the news and waited.

"Just let Rick or one of us know when you want to go, Papa. Papa? Maybe some other time we'll talk. You sleep now."

She waited then for Elaine to join her. They needed to plot their next move where their aging father was concerned.

It has survival value, she thought, *the kind of good that lies in Papa's cynicism.*

*   *   *

Later that night, weary from lack of disciplined sleep, Earl Grantley drank a full canister of Piña Colada and turned the TV on full volume.

Chapter 2

*T*he efforts of the Grantley sisters were not without their reward. Through their determination, they had combined the efforts of the family members, and a six-week summer vacation was scheduled for the construction of Villa Sara. Elaine's children, Wayne, Denice, Susan, John, and Bill, along with Jayne and two of her children, Donald and Alex, had united at Elaine's home in Georgia, sixty miles from the Grantley estate, to fulfill the long-standing dream.

In recent years, the Grantley descendants had become less involved in their own affairs and had focused more attention on issues governing the rapid changes taking place in the rural South. In its heyday, each member would visit occasionally, but as the economy changed, some could no longer afford to take even a few days off to make a trip. Sara's funeral had brought the immediate family together only the one time. Thus, several ambitious plans to build Villa Sara had been advanced over that time, but none had materialized.

Now, however, with interest rates at their lowest level in the nearly eight years since their mother's death, which in turn lowered gas prices and air travel discounts, plus a renewed interest in Americana pursuits, getting together was no longer a pocketbook thing. And it just so happened that Sara Bocan Grantley's birthday coincided with this peak of interest in ancestral preservation.

Upon its completion, the family planned to offer Villa Sara as a place where foreign exchange students could experience creativity and, at the same time, learn about the cultural backgrounds and language barriers that sometimes separated them.

It was a cool, early April morning when the long-awaited briefing sessions began. Promptly at seven o'clock, five fourth-generation male

135

Grantleys, the three Langstroms and two Reeders, gathered in the screened-in Florida Room. John Langstrom stood militantly in T-shirt and denims at the far seam of the forty-two-inch, elliptical, drop-leaf table. He looked pensively at his relatives who had left behind them the bitter cold winds howling across the northern states, while here in their midst, spring burst forth with a vengeance.

The air, still fresh from the newly-mowed lawn, came wrapped in a song of birds. The deep fragrance from Elaine's hybrid tea roses hugged the east wall. Hyacinths, purple iris, and clusters of apple blossoms burst into flower, their leaves shimmering in the sun's rays.

"I feel a great deal of responsibility since you made me chairperson," John began, "but your personal commitment is rare. Very rare. Here's what we have so far."

He pointed to two blueprints on a child-size easel to the left of the sliding glass doors, one marked "Interior" and the other "Exterior." Both sketches were very simplified versions of the Villa Sara model now safely protected in a plastic cocoon on a shelf in Elaine's storage closet. When John unveiled a revised model on the card table nearby, however, the room fell silent – a noticeably awkward silence until Bill Langstrom broke it.

"Taking my cue from Sara's love for space," he said, "I've designed some improvements while still keeping the Spanish theme."

"You can see he's utilized every inch," continued John. "I've made copies of the modifications he sent me earlier. They're all itemized for you."

"Good work, Bill." Alex Reeder clasped his hands in front of him and offered his best blue-blazer and striped-tie smile, diverting attention from eyes red-rimmed from lack of sleep.

"I think of all the things our parents went through and their parents before them to fulfil this dream. All their talk and no action. It's all up to us if it's ever to get done."

"Well, I certainly needed this trip," added Donald Reeder, Alex's younger brother. "It hasn't been exactly easy rearranging our schedule, but it'll be nice to be able to drill something other than teeth for awhile."

"I'm even looking forward to six weeks of roughing it," Wayne, the oldest Langstrom son, added, pounding the table with massive fists, his head sunk in giant shoulders. "We can work together – no doubt about that. Guns and guts made America free. And, oh yes, God, too. We mustn't forget Him."

"How's that?" asked John.

"Wayne's quoting a bumper sticker we saw while driving down here," volunteered Bill. "Wayne and his guns. Get him talking and we'll be here another six years still dreaming."

"I'd like to be sitting right here to see the final results," Donald said, tapping the list of papers in front of him. "If this consulting fee is more than fifty dollars an hour, we don't need it," he said.

"These figures are estimates I threw together while at law school," John answered. "Bill's quotes are on the highest quality building materials. We're ordering two by six exterior wall studs instead of two by fours."

"That's to provide premium insulation along with insulated wood casement for the arch windows," Bill explained. "And thermal-crafted for energy efficiency, I might add."

"We didn't want to go the full route with sub-contractors because you get into the problem of coordinating the work," said John. "However, Rick Steele arranged for the backhoe and bulldozer crew, and the spade work, you might say, is completed. The foundation and first floor awaits us."

"Damn!" exclaimed Donald. "And I was hoping to learn something about pouring cement." He threw his long arms out to dramatize, and in the process, upset the tray of drinks and sandwiches. He had not seen the young boy enter the room with the tray balanced precariously on one hand.

"I'll get that," John leaped to steady the coffee and lemonade.

"He's Susan's kid—no doubt about that," Donald snapped, dusting the crumbs from charcoal trousers that had lost their press somewhere near Atlanta. "Look at that face!" he added.

Ten-year-old Chris threw the bluest of eyes in his direction. He stifled a sob as he looked at John for rescue from his uncle's unwanted teases.

"All of you may not know this," said John, "but Chris is the one who rekindled this project when it was doomed two years ago." John ran strong muscular fingers through the boy's corn-silk hair. "Isn't that right, Christopher Michael Wright? You've got a lot more invested in this— don't you agree, my boy?" But John didn't give the child time to answer. "Where are all the women folks?"

"Left you behind as 'gofer,' son?" whistled Donald through near-perfect teeth. He tilted back temptingly on the unsteady folding chair.

Chris ignored the uncalled-for remark and addressed his Uncle John. "Grandma and Auntie J went with Aunt Tina to an estate auction," he blurted out, "and Aunt Denice and my mom are off to the vintage fashion show at the mall. But I heard Mom say they were on a fact-finding tour, whatever that is. Grandma left me in charge of eats. You need anything else?" he said proudly.

"Just as I figured. They go skedaddling off without a word," John fumed.

"You sound like Grandpa Grantley." Chris muffled a giggle.

"Did they say when they'd be back?" John asked.

"Grandma said they trust you with the dream. That's all she said," Chris answered, busying himself restacking the fallen sandwiches.

"Back to our plans then, gentlemen," John said, sounding faint. He then began to chuckle, dark eyes flashing. "Auntie J keeps specifying the arched windows as though we'll seal up the whole structure and forget in our foolish behavior."

"Yeah. And Mom wants to make sure we have lots of closet and storage space—and a separate entranceway for dirty feet," added Bill. "To Auntie J, sandstone, Masonite, and cement block are interchangeable."

They all laughed.

"I don't think any of the women really know what effort it takes," frowned Wayne. "Are we going to have them fussing over every little item on this list?"

"They'll be too busy thinking and planning for the things that go inside the finished villa," assured John. "And Littlejohn will keep them busy with the patio and landscaping. We've got a lot of hard work ahead. I don't think you guys will need those golf clubs you brought along."

"Let's not make this too painful, John," grimaced Wayne, pouring himself a fourth cup of coffee.

"Right on," added Donald. "The bottom line is 'If you're not having fun, you're paying too high a price.' I'll take some more of that lemonade, Chris, my friend."

"I'm not your friend. Get it yourself!" snapped Chris, looking to John for a reprimand that didn't come.

"I love the challenge," Alex said, rubbing his hands together. "Can hardly wait to install the computer-operated layouts in the underground level."

"Let's skedaddle then," said Chris.

"We'll take the jeep," said John. "You'd better leave a note for your grandma."

"I'm a step ahead of you, Uncle John," said Chris. "I put a note on the refrigerator under the Miz Piggy magnet. Grandma is sure to see it first thing."

"We're going to pull this off, you guys," Wayne said as John headed the jeep in the direction of the construction site.

Chapter 3

As Denice Langstrom and her sister, Susan Wright, entered the poolside atrium at Z-Inn, an usher in '20s attire handed them the Vintage Fashion Show program and a pair of antique opera glasses with a modern zoom lens attachment.

"It's such a romantic idea," Susan said, dreamy-eyed. "Villa Sara does have some hope now that our brothers want to be involved."

"If it actually gets built, you can bet your sombrero it'll be the best retreat this family ever had," Denice said in hushed tones. "You think they'll ever find the right person to stay way out there full-time to guard things?"

"I hope so. That Littlejohn gives me the willies. I keep remembering how he snooped around and peered in on us when the old farmhouse was still nearby."

"I do like the idea of planning our own housing units. Just imagine yourself relaxing in a whirlpool set into a redwood deck that's bathed with the heady perfume of eucalyptus trees."

"Eucalyptus? Better think pine. You sound like one of your travel brochures," teased Denice. "I bet none of our ideas so far compares with the plush resorts you've handled for your clients. Anyway, the gazebo will be my project. I can see my boyfriend with me under that southern moonlight."

"Romance or not, this weather is too hot today to think of winter coats," Susan nudged Denice. "Take in that nineteen twenty-four style. Do you believe this fashion trend?"

"I could live with that one," Denice said. She paused to locate the description in the brochure. " 'That lustrous, soft Bolivia with a small percentage of cotton for additional strength. The popular loose-back model with convertible collar and a tied-at-the-side closing. . . .' "

" 'Heavy twist stitching,' " read Susan softly, " 'and two large buttons trim the back. The loose sleeves have stitching to match. Two welt pockets. Coat is full-lined with twill sateen.' "

"I'll take two in reindeer color," laughed Denice.

"Just what I need for those chilly evenings at the travel agency," sighed Susan. "Okay, so we got carried away for awhile, but be realistic. Do we have to sit through more of this?"

"Shhh! They've just glided into the thirties. And you know my boss expects me to be here. After all, she gave me the morning off from Latest Fashion Boutique so I could attend this career development function. If I snuck out, it could mean my job. What else did you have in mind?"

"We could see what the fellows are up to at 'Tech Talk' down the hall."

"Don't tempt me. Put your glasses on and get a load of those shoes on that model."

"We might learn something," insisted Susan. "Could help us be more literate when our brothers get on their high-tech lingo."

"Oh, why not. So you've twisted my arm. But this had better be worth the risk I'm taking. Let's at least wait until the set changes for the forties."

"Remind me to buy one of those Plan-A-Flex Designer Kits for planning my unit. It's got vinyl peel-and-stick. Makes your diagrams look professional."

"We'll never tell your blueprints weren't done freehand. Count to three now, and let's go."

*   *   *

"Going, going, gone," the words echoed across acres and acres populated with antiques and not-so-valuable household goods. Elaine scanned her copy of "Kivel's Price Guide" as she moved quietly from lot to lot. Jayne and John's wife Tina followed closely behind.

"It helps to judge values and make other bidders think you've got some expertise," Elaine explained.

"Ironic, isn't it?" said Jayne, examining an odd piece of ceramic sculpture. "We've got just as much talent and skills as the men, but we just never got around to building Villa Sara. Now we're stuck at an auction while our sons have all the fun."

"Your father never expected to see boys, especially a fourth generation of Grantleys, carry out the dream," said Tina. "Does he still feel the creek may have a curse on boys?" Tina was referring to the fact that Earl Grantley's only three sons had drowned many years ago in the river that ran through the Grantley Estate. Since that time, he believed that the property was possessed by a Creek Indian curse.

"Yes, he does," answered Elaine, "but I thought we raised our boys differently. Now I find they think just like Dad—that women don't know the first thing about hammering a nail."

"Our daughters could prove them otherwise," said Jayne. "And we, too, may have a chance to show our expertise at architecture."

At the mention of their daughters, Jayne's thoughts wandered to her daughter who was at the time attending an International Music Festival in France. "Do you think Morene would like this piece of sculpture?" she asked. "I know I promised myself I wouldn't buy anything. I came just to observe."

"Go on, buy it," urged Tina. "Think how happy it'll make her feel when she returns home. But listen, has Morene made her statement to the Villa Sara project yet?"

"She made some suggestions. Says to use an abundance of whites, ivories, and neutrals to create a soothing atmosphere that makes coming in from the heat and humidity a welcome experience. And use lots of purples, pinks, peaches, and reds as accents."

"Doesn't she remind you of Sara, our mother?" asked Elaine. "We'll be able to use a lot of her suggestions, I'm sure."

"Look at that sign," said Tina. "Can you believe some of the language today?" She consulted the auction guide. " 'Intelligent windows'? Men must compose these catalogs thinking we women will swallow anything."

"The bidding is what scares me," admitted Jayne. "My palms sweat and my heart pounds every time I hear the auctioneer shout. I could be spending my time more profitably writing our book."

"I find it exciting just watching," said Tina, "but I know better than to leave my checkbook at home."

"You won't have to do the actual bidding today," explained Elaine. "If you see something you like, just circle it in the brochure. I'll register for us and get the bidding number before the next sale begins."

"Do you believe some of this junk?" whispered Jayne. "Should we buy this box of broken tile? Might come in handy to fill the path to the patio of Villa Sara."

"If not, Chris will love to aid it to his stone collection." Elaine sifted through the broken pieces of glass, plastic, stones, and minerals, and a broad smile crossed her lips. Another bidder peered over her shoulders and said they were phony.

"Circle that lot," she told the others.

"But you heard what he said," Jayne objected.

"Trust me. I'll let you in on a little secret later," Elaine said.

"Now there's something I definitely have to have!" Jayne's eyes moved over a painted cut-away of an ancient Aztec building.

"I like the ornate frame around it," said Tina. "How much do you think it's worth, Elaine?"

"Just circle the item on the page, Tina. We'll discuss value later."

"Tina's getting the fever, I'm thinking," Jayne said. "I sure like the earth tones in that piece of tapestry. The inner-woven quote is a perfect contrast."

She read the script:

> To select well among old things
> is almost equal to
> inventing new ones.
>
> Trublet

"Trublet. Nicolas Charles Trublet, sixteen ninety-seven to seventeen seventy. French clergyman and essayist," volunteered a bearded observer, "but it's a fake." He lowered his voice. "Take my word for it."

"Trublet?" Jayne repeated softly as the bidder moved on. "It's priceless!" She observed Elaine with affection twinkling in one eye and calculation in the other.

"Fever's got her for sure this time," teased Tina. "Isn't it time for us to think about eating?"

"I was hoping to find a display case of some kind for the Villa Sara models," said Elaine. "I'd like to see both versions under glass in a prominent place."

"I can't picture roping a display case to the roof of your Imperial, but we could look at other auctions," Jayne suggested.

"Tina's right. We should get something to eat." Elaine led the way to the parking lot.

"Are we going for coffee and sandwiches under the great circus tent out front," Jayne asked, "or are we planning to eat lunch at home?"

"Since that son of yours, Donald, sanded down the rough edges and adjusted the partial, my tongue's ready for something better than junk food," Elaine continued. "Tell you what. We're halfway between home and the construction site. What say we skedaddle over to that little restaurant on the highway near the Mason Lodge? Then afterwards, we could pay our sons a secret visit."

"Excellent idea!" shouted Tina. "Maybe I can find an arrowhead or two or pick up a piece of that ancient wood John says they dug up. It's just what I need to lend contrast to the table centerpiece I'm working on."

"Is she talking about wood from the old barn?" asked Jayne.

"No. There wasn't much left when the old barn burned. What there was got bulldozed long ago. Tina means the wood found forty feet down when the work crew dug the well at the site of Villa Sara. John brought me a few pieces. The rest of it's under concrete by now."

"Think of that," said Jayne thoughtfully. "Forty feet down. What significant historical value. Must be priceless. One sliver of that wood encased in acrylic with a little research added to a brochure. . . . We could make a fortune!"

"She does have money fever, Tina," said Elaine. "Think we can get her attention long enough to divulge our plan?"

"Did you bring your grandfather's binoculars?" asked Tina.

"I keep them in the trunk of the car all the time now that construction has actually begun. Those binoculars are a priceless heirloom. They served during the Spanish-American War. Our *abuelito* watched the Rough Riders from a balcony in Santiago as they charged up that hill. The magnitude of its lenses is still as powerful today."

"I reckon that means we're not eating here then." Jayne quickened her step to keep up with the younger two-some.

"You reckon correctly," said her sister. Then she and Tina both let loose with a playful giggle.

Chapter 4

The do-it-yourselfers found Littlejohn with his broad back against the wall of his lean-to. From there, he could watch the entrance to the Villa Sara construction site without having to move. Littlejohn was a slightly stooped, likable-looking sort, tanned to a deep earth-brown. For two years as guardian of the Grantley Estate, he had gotten away with supplementing his income growing a certain plant he called "Nature's Joy." To others, the plant was known as marijuana.

Littlejohn had all the skills to reroute water from the pipeline to his secret plot and would have succeeded indefinitely, or spent some time behind bars, if John Langstrom had not stumbled onto him while hunting with a friend. Since that time, a special bond had formed between the two men.

Littlejohn greeted his benefactor with a genuine smile. The man hid a deformed right hand behind him as he extended the left to each of the visitors. When he got to Chris, he lifted the excited boy high above his head with the good arm before releasing the squirming, squealing, delightful mass of muscles.

"You've grown ripe-corn high since two summer's ago, ma'boy." Littlejohn beamed a toothsome grin. "What's your mama feedin' you these days?"

Chris returned the grin breathlessly. He ignored the question and posed a rapid one in response.

"Did you take good care of my sweet lemon tree like you promised?"

Littlejohn's smile faded with the thought of the tree that had been started from a twig brought to the Grantley Estate from Cuba in the early 1900's. In an effort to prolong the truth, he said, "What's this? No hello or how've you been? No small talk. It's been a long time. Things change, son. Let me hear about your school and the traveling you've been doing." Receiving only a burning stare from the boy in return, the old man looked helplessly toward John. "Haven't you told him?"

"I thought it best you explain things to him," said John. "I haven't found just the right time to break the news."

"Well?" persisted Chris, still looking the man straight in the eyes. "Did you?"

"Better come right out with it," advised John. "Chris is a Grantley. He can take a lot of disappointments."

"It's this way, ma'boy," Littlejohn began slowly, eyes filled with compassion. "With no markers of any kind, the loggers got a few trees from the plot not designated for clearance. I was gone into town most of the day. My day off." He paused only to plead with John. "I don't think this is going down too well," he said.

"You're doing just fine," John assured him.

"Anyway," began Littlejohn again, "the sweet lemon tree was . . . did you ever see how loggers work nowadays? All that big equipment. Logs on one truck and another machine to grind up branches, leaves, and all into pulp right on the site. I tried my best, honest I did. But I had no way of knowing the lumber company would clear the land so fast. I couldn't be in two places at once, could I?"

"What's done is done," John said, gritting his teeth. "Littlejohn did inform me as soon as he could. He did his best, Chris. There might still be a cutting left. We'll start another."

"It won't be the same," Chris cried. "You can't climb a cutting. I'll be too old to hang from its branches when it gets tree size." He swung at Littlejohn before John could stop him. "I hate you! I hate you!" He kicked and pounded his small fists against the big man's chest until exhausted. Then he collapsed in a heap beside the heavy combat boots.

John lifted the boy calmly and started toward the army cot in the lean-to. He assured Chris all the time with promises of replacing the sweet lemon tree.

"We'll get you another, Chris," he said, "even if it takes making a trip to Cuba when diplomatic relations are resumed. Meanwhile. . . ."

"Meanwhile we fellows need you, too, Chris," came voices from outside. "Remember, we have another promise to keep. That dream we're building."

"They're right, son," said John. "So what say we wipe away the tears and skedaddle while we've still got some daylight. I don't like the looks of that sky."

"You promise?" Chris rubbed his eyes on his uncle's T-shirt.
"Promise," said John.

*   *   *

A hundred feet or more down the steep embankment from the
building site, three female figures bedecked in a plethora of jungle prints,
bellied down like skilled commandos scanning the terrain before a surprise attack. Through her grandfather's binoculars, Elaine sized up the
skeleton crew of sons in a battle scene between nails and thumbs.

"This is like filming an event for a movie about another generation,"
she said. "I've got Chris in focus. He looks so in control."

"And why wouldn't he be? He's in boy heaven," added Tina, squinting against the sun. "He'll learn a lot about construction this summer."

"And a few words I'm sure his mother would rather he didn't," said
Jayne. "I wonder what they could be talking about?"

"Probably yelling for socket wrenches or a speed drill," laughed
Elaine.

" 'Sander, curved-claw hammer, chisels over here, Christopher
Michael Wright,' " said Jayne, imitating one of her sons.

"I can just hear Chris asking, 'You want standard or metric?' " Tina
said, lowering her voice.

"No need to whisper," Elaine told her daughter-in-law. "They'd
never hear us with all that noise."

"Your Wayne might," volunteered Jayne. "He has ears like a fine-
tuned radar detector. Let me see if I can find my son Donald."

She reached for the binoculars and started fumbling with the adjust-
ment. She tried squinting with and without her bifocals, gave the lens of
both eye pieces a thorough cleansing, then tried again to focus.

"You keep up that ritual," admonished Elaine, "and you're going to
set the woods on fire. All that reflected sun on this bone-dry pine."

"But I can hardly make out Donald," Jayne complained. "He's found
a shady spot under a pine tree. I think he's fanning himself with a fly
swatter. He's allergic to bees, you know, and if there are any around,
they'll find him."

"You're both worrying needlessly," Tina said. "Let me have a look."
She immediately began to shade the lens with one hand to focus in on
her husband John. "I'm glad they can't see us," she said. "John is hanging
up-side-down from the rafters. Hope they hold. He's gained weight now
that he's stopped coaching the high school wrestling team part-time.

Wish I knew what they're really saying. Their mouths are moving like programmed gears on a toy robot. 'Mechanical heads switched to expression mode,' they call it. 'Nose and brow levers functioning at maximum capacity.'"

" 'Get me this. Get me that. I need more nails, Chris,' "Elaine mimicked. "Here's another nail for Sara. Another rivet for *Abuelito*."

"What's Littlejohn doing?" asked Jayne. "Can you see where they parked the jeep?"

"Wait a minute," said Tina. "I don't see Chris now."

Elaine reached frantically for the binoculars. "They had the poor kid running circles," she said. "He's probably taken off to the creek where it's peaceful and quiet."

"I hope he put things back in their proper place first," said Tina. "What irks John most is to find any tools missing."

"Now who's worrying," teased Jayne. "Can you see Chris yet, Elaine?"

"Not yet. Something's wrong—I can feel it," she said. "And look at those guys. Not even aware the child's not with them."

"I just knew they'd get too involved in their work to supervise a ten-year-old for long," sighed Jayne.

"Here, Tina, you take the binoculars for awhile," Elaine rubbed her eyes. "Search around the creek area. Your eyes are the youngest here. There goes my blood pressure up another twenty points!"

"Don't panic yet," Tina advised. "He could be hidden in the bushes taking a leak."

"If you don't spot him soon," said Elaine, "we'll have to go up there."

"What—and make a scene?" Jayne made a face. "The guys would love that!"

"Love it or not," added Elaine, "it's either that or sit down here and stew our guts to a boil."

"You two hush now," Tina whispered. "I've got something."

A lone puppy darted from the underbrush across the lens and wagged his tail about where Chris should have been.

"Well, don't that beat all!" Tina said.

"What?" the two sisters asked in unison, both reaching for the binoculars.

Tina cautiously pulled them away. "Not yet. I've got to get a better view. It's a puppy for sure. A puppy with only three legs!" she yelled excitedly. "If there's a dog within a few feet, there's surely a boy close by. And there's Chris, zipping up his pants, happy as a flea."

Tina relinquished the binoculars to Elaine, who, with a sigh of relief, murmured, "He'd better not bring that dog home. I hope John can refrain from encouraging him to."

"Haven't we seen enough?" asked Jayne. "If we don't get back to our planning, we won't have a staff to meet our first foreign visitors. Or had you forgotten that pile of applications and resumés we have to sort through for that August opening of Villa Sara?"

"I haven't forgotten," said Elaine. "That's reason enough to hurry this construction so it can pass the building code well in advance of our first guests' arrival. It's that part of the dream Sara would wish for most. And you're right, there's nothing we can do here but worry."

"And we can do that just as well in the comfort of the Florida room while categorizing the applicants," Tina said.

*   *   *

When the three women arrived back at Elaine's house, they found Denice and Susan at the elliptical drop-leaf table deep in high-tech brochures and leaflets. Plan-A-Flex vinyl peel-and-stick for interior designing was strewn in every available space.

"What in heaven's name is all this?" Elaine questioned while entering the Florida room from the outside.

"High-tech, Mom," Denice said. "Isn't it exciting?"

"It's time now for low-tech," said Elaine, "and we need that table. Where's the mail?"

"Villa Sara will be big enough for both high-tech and low-tech, Mom," Susan added.

"What happened at that fashion show anyway?" Jayne asked.

"Wait until you three see what Denice brought home," Susan said excitedly.

"Go look in the living room," Denice beamed. "We took the liberty of moving grandpa's overstuffed lounging chair since he won't be needing it anymore."

Facing a macramé wall hanging and occupying a good one-third of the large living room sat an enormous octagonal glass display case. Its brass edging reflected the gleams in all eyes focused on it.

"I'm almost afraid to ask where you got it," said Elaine.

"Or how much it cost?" added Jayne.

"It's incredible!" Tina breathed deeply. "See how the glass picks up the brilliant lilac and yellow from the macramé wall hanging? We love it!"

"Okay, girls, where did you get it?" asked Elaine.

"Susan unwittingly flashed provocative glances at the right person," teased Denice, nudging her sister playfully.

"You're going to get me in trouble," said Susan. "Mom knows better. They're remodeling Sports Aware at the mall, and all older furniture and fixtures were on sale. Call this our donation to Villa Sara."

"It's in two parts," explained Denice. "You can divide the unit into two corner display cases if you want. I'm anxious to see the two Villa Sara models displayed properly, aren't you?"

"Looks like a perfect fit," said Jayne, sizing up the flexible sectional and visualizing the 1890 model of Villa Sara and its improved 1980's design. "I think I'd like them better in two separate corners myself."

"I agree," Tina said.

"Let's leave it for now and see what the boys think when they return," said Elaine. "In the meantime, it makes an excellent table for us to spread out the mail and get busy categorizing those resumés."

It took the women a good two hours to sort the candidates into three piles using the criteria set up previously by the participating southern university named in Sara's will. As trustees of a fund to promote a ten-day intercultural exchange for younger precocious children, the university had, for lack of a better name, labeled the project SEEK: Social Exchange Expands Knowledge. Dr. T. Andrew Skillsworth, professor of Clinical Services and named as liaison between the international division and host family, went so far as to advocate in one of his speeches that the acronym SEEK could well be: Sara Expects Every Kid to reach that level of potential where he or she becomes a contributing member of society.

Acknowledging kids who could mastermind solutions to the problems of today and set the stage for tomorrow was the primary goal from the university's standpoint. However, as Sara's only immediate heirs, Elaine and Jayne had the authority to screen applicants for staff and foreign interns. They would also supervise the overall program and be supportive where needed.

Since SEEK would be the first experimental program to honor early teens, it would have ready access to Dr. Anita Calden, an authority on leadership, and Keith Nessman, creativity consultant and an authority on program planning.

Elaine had suggested they divide up the fifty qualified applicants selected from the two hundred and one responses among the five of them. Each was to take ten to examine with the purpose of finding that specific skill, background, or characteristic that would set that individual apart from the others. With only four positions to fill, it would not be an easy task to select the best. They all seemed relieved when they heard the dogs barking frantically, indicating the male family members' return. At least for now they would not have to make that critical decision.

Chris entered first, swerving in to avoid the dogs while deftly holding high above his head a small terrarium of some sort. After setting his catch-of-the-day to one edge of the display case, he spouted nonstop, "You just gotta see my puppy, Mom. I named him One-less because he's got only three legs. Littlejohn says he's got one less chance of getting a paw in a bear trap. And Littlejohn's keeping One-less for me." He took a deep breath. "Uncle John says my puppy is part Doberman and part pit bull."

"Why couldn't it have been a kitten?" interrupted Susan, admiring her son nonetheless.

Chris continued. "And . . . and . . . Littlejohn gave me this tank and what's inside. Can I keep it? One-less treed him. Uncle John says it's a guilt gift from Littlejohn. What's a guilt gift, Mom?"

"Slow down, son," said Susan, putting a rubber band around the stack of papers she was reviewing.

The others did likewise after hearing sounds coming from the kitchen indicating the older sons were raiding the refrigerator.

"Yes, start from the beginning," added Elaine. "But let's go in the recreation room where pizza should arrive any minute. Garbage pail pizza, California style. The way you all like it."

After the pizza had been eaten and the events of the day elaborated on, Susan gave her son another special hug.

"I'm so proud of you, Chris, for forgiving Littlejohn about the loss of the sweet lemon tree. It shows me how reliable you've become. However," she added, "I hope you won't strike anyone again when you get angry with them. There are a lot better ways to handle a situation."

"As soon as we find a better place to keep your iguana out of everyone's way," said Elaine, "you can help us put the Villa Sara models in the showcase. We'll think of a way to get another sweet lemon tree planted."

*   *   *

The next day, after hearing the forecast for thunderstorms, work at the construction site was called off at the break of dawn. That left a flat-truck trailer loaded with materials under the protecting eye of Little-john. More pressing still, however, was the fact that there had been no word from Savannah about the special Spanish tiles needed to complete the roof once everything else was in place.

It was decided that the men should go to Savannah and find out firsthand what they could do to speed delivery. As designers of Villa Sara, it was decided they had to create a closer relationship between the craftsman and the manufacturer. None of them could be absent if things were to get done promptly and with fewer mistakes and more harmony.

Chris pleaded to tag along, but when he found out he couldn't take the iguana, he gave the problem more serious thought. He watched the minute palpitation of the yet-nameless lizard's breathing and the jerky flicker of its translucent golden eyes. He wondered if it glowed at all in the dark. It looked as though it might.

As he observed more closely, a red, gill-like skin puffed out on the wet leaf of grass, subsided, and flicked out of sight.

"I guess you'll be safer with my mom than in Savannah," he said hesitantly. Then he raced toward the van, half submerged under a yellow raincoat.

"Use your persuasiveness effectively," Jayne called after them.

"And concentrate on the person with the most clout," added Elaine. "But don't forget to stop off to see Grandpa Grantley on your way out of town. As for us, we'll tackle our paperwork while we've still got current. Some weather!"

"Damn! It *would* rain the day Steve promised to take Susan and me swimming," said Denice, frustrated at not being able to fulfill the plans she and her boyfriend had made. "Maybe there's a good movie showing. I'd hate to spend the whole morning debating over who's best for this or that job."

"You two go on with Steve if you want to," Jayne said. "Elaine and I will do what we can—with Tina's help, of course."

"Of course," said Tina. She had already removed the rubber band from her ten applications.

*   *   *

When Steve Goldstein, personnel manager of Future Plastics, drove up in his Mercedes an hour later, he became intrigued with Project SEEK and volunteered to help in the selection process. Denice and Susan quickly concealed their disappointment and divided their share of names with him.,

"I know what this project means to all of you," Steve said. "And although I'm a newcomer to this area and didn't know Denice's grandmother Sara, I admire what you're all doing."

"He always knows the right thing to say," commented Elaine. "Steve, you make all of us proud to have you here as a vital part of this ten-day intercultural exchange."

"So what do I do first?" he asked.

"We're selecting the best four candidates from the fifty you see on paper. These have been screened by background and skills mostly. Now we're taking a second look at the written paragraph required with the basic data," explained Jayne. "Keep in mind as you read any references to social justice and fairness or specific notations about children with these special talents."

"Wish they'd had something like this program when I was in school," Steve commented. "I was in an advanced class, but whenever we students inquired about something, we were told we were there to absorb all we could, not to ask questions. I was bored out of my skull, as were ninety percent of the other guys. It must cost a fortune to organize and carry through something like this, but I think it's fantastic."

"The sponsoring countries will pay for their English-speaking candidates, including airfare, supervision, insurance, and pocket money," said Denice, surprising everyone with her concealed knowledge. "Villa Sara's trust fund covers other expenses, books, and equipment. I don't know about the staff's salary."

"These are all student interns on staff," added Elaine. "The university pays them a small stipend from a global grant given the Department of Educational Psychology. They get class credit, also."

"I think I've got the gist of what you're after," Steve said, examining the third resumé in his pile. "Is this what you're looking for? This person writes: 'Children of promise must have someone to turn to when dealing with unhappy circumstances. I hope to share my own feelings with them and offer lots of meaningful opportunities for them to express their feelings.'"

"That individual sounds right for our 'Most-Desirable' list, Steve," said Elaine. "Put it over here near Chris's iguana's terrarium for now."

"I hate to be the one to tell you ladies, or Chris," volunteered Steve, "but that's not an iguana. It's a green anole or Anolis carclinensis, more falsely and commonly called American chameleon."

"And since when did you become an authority on lizards?" Denice teased.

"Since I majored in biology among other things, such as ignoring a beautiful girl's hasty barbs."

"John is going to buy Chris a book on lizards when they finish their business in Savannah. Part of a guilt gift," interrupted Elaine. "We'll let him make the discovery himself. We do appreciate your comment though, Steve."

"Yeah," said Susan. "Now that you've told us, we can all say to Chris, 'I knew that.'"

"Here's a live one," said Jayne. "Listen to this." She wiped her glasses on the seam of her jungle print blouse, blinked her eyes several times, and began to read: " 'The capacity to negotiate, say many psychologists, emerges in most children between the ages of eight and eleven, and includes the ability to step out of a situation and look at others' points of view. I look forward to examining current issues with these leaders of tomorrow.'"

"If I didn't know the high quality of student interns you're dealing with here, I'd be inclined to believe some of these resumé paragraphs are commercially written," Steve commented.

"It remains to be seen if the action measures up to the wordage," Elaine said. "But that's a chance any profession must take where staffing is concerned."

"I'm only glad we don't have to end up fighting educators and labelers," commented Jayne. "I've gone that route and don't care to again."

"Anyone else have something to share?" asked Elaine. I'm not sure," said Tina. "But this one interests me. Probably because John is studying Law. 'I must anticipate anger—lots of it—directed to every adult involved in the program by some of these brilliant children. And some of the older ones may want to confer with attorneys and demand that their wishes be considered. As their mentor and facilitator, I would provide a foundation for workable interactions and seek guidance from a professional in the community to get the job done.'"

"Wow," sighed Susan. "I'm sure glad I don't have to compete with this group. But I'm thrilled that my son Chris can be the American host to SEEK's very first enrollees."

*   *   *

The screening continued until the committee had ten outstanding candidates, all with the versatility required to fill any one of the four positions: Biology/Science, Music/Art, Nutrition/Recreation, and Problem-Solving/Global.

It was finally decided among them to leave things as they were for now and meet later with other members of the family to make a final decision. The sooner the selections were made the better, so they could meet the finalists in person and still have plenty of time to make any changes if replacements became necessary.

"I'd say this work session went well, wouldn't you, Denice?" asked Steve, giving her an affectionate light punch to the left side of her nodding head.

"Huh!" sputtered Denice. "Now can we please leave so we can catch the early show?"

"Or are you taking us to eat someplace first?" asked Susan.

"Susan Wright!" admonished Elaine. "Where're your manners?"

"I'm sorry, Mom. The words just slipped out."

"It's a splendid idea," agreed Steve. "I'm glad I thought of it. And I insist you all be my guests. How does pan pizza California-style sound to you?"

"Anything but pizza!" They all groaned in unison.

Elaine's two dogs barked their approval.

"Steve, I'll drive my car, too," volunteered Elaine. "Then you three younguns can leave right after eating. The rest of us can spend a leisurely afternoon at the mall."

"Don't take Auntie J anywhere near a book store, Mom," Denice warned from the driver's side of the creme-colored Mercedes. "If she wants a book, tell her to get busy on that novel she's writing."

"Steve," called Jayne from the front passenger side of the Imperial, "do you trust Denice with your Mercedes? I want all of you alive so you can read that novel."

Chapter 5

*E*arl W. Grantley moved with a spring in his step down the long corridor at the Flunsa Rest Center. He wanted to show how well he could walk without a cane if he had a mind to. In clothes fresh and clean, there was a kind of youth surrounding his ninety-four-year-old, frail, stooped body.

"What kept you so long?" he greeted no one in particular. "My calendar has ten o'clock circled. Did I ever tell you how I got my watch?" He looked at the black-band Bulova given to him by the bank for a minimum deposit.

Director Amelia Akright met Earl at the reception desk. Placing a matronly hand on his wrist, she cooed enthusiastically, "Why don't you give your grandsons the grand tour of our facilities while I speak with John?"

She extended one hand from under the clipboard to gesture to John to follow. Then she quickly scanned the sheet of paper and made a few notations, returning the clipboard to a volunteer aide.

Earl pushed her hand away and grunted. "Huh! Grandsons? Shows how little she knows."

When Mrs. Akright and John had disappeared into the main office and the door was closed behind them, Earl led his grandsons down the south wing. By the time he had shown them through the smoking lounge and kitchen area, Earl felt comfortable enough to ask another question.

"Did you bring me some beer?" he asked.

"Grandpa, you know they don't allow alcoholic beverages on the premises," said Wayne. "How's everything otherwise?"

159

"Thought we might slip out for a little nip," Earl whispered. "No harm in askin', is there?" But he didn't wait for an answer and hurriedly ushered them into the entertainment center.

In the middle of the room, his mind snapped as though on cue. The grandchildren were no longer relatives—they became in his memory lapse performers from the tour group that sang at the Veterans' Hospital. Earl lifted the lid of the upright piano. He gave its swivel stool a whirl and turned to Wayne with a big grin.

*   *   *

Wayne, always ready to face any challenge, decided to play along to see just how far his grandfather would lead. He rolled up imaginary sleeves and sat down on the swivel stool.

"What'll it be, partner?" he asked.

Earl beamed and pulled from a plaid flannel hip pocket his prized Hammond harmonica. "Let's make it 'Buffalo Gals Won't You Come Out Tonight.'"

He juiced out a few chords, rubbed the excess saliva off against one knee, and prepared his lips for the next rendition.

The other grandsons joined in to harmonize 'Waltzing With Matilda,' and while Chris had no point of reference to these oldies, he soon found his own place. He sidled up to Wayne and shuffled imaginary sheet music, deftly wetting a finger as he turned each page.

The impromptu musicians had attracted quite an audience by the time Mrs. Akright weaved through the congested wheelchairs blocking the entranceway. Over the roar of applause, she ordered attendants to bring things back to their original order. She then looked to John for support.

"I hate to break up this audition, fellows," John said, pointing to the wall clock and then to the dial of his digital gold watch, "but we've got that appointment in Savannah, and it's almost noon."

"They're going to play in Savannah next," Earl announced to his captive audience. "You heard 'em!"

With her staff's help, Mrs. Akright finally calmed the disappointed group with promises of a terrific lunch.

Before leaving, Chris whispered in his great grandfather's ear, "Next time I come, I'll have a surprise for you."

*   *   *

En route to Savannah, Donald tried to interpret John's expression. "Okay, don't keep us in suspense any longer. What did grandpa do this time to stir up action at Flunsa?"

John cleared his throat and opened the driver's side window vent. "We might as well get some of this natural breeze and save the air conditioner for the real hot stuff."

"Quit your stalling. We know Akright didn't call you aside just to discuss the weather," Donald said.

"Akright says grandpa has been wandering off from the premises again. The last time they couldn't find him until one of the other tenants remembered that he liked to sit in the van. There he was, sound asleep. Grandpa told them he only wanted to find a quiet place where he could do some thinking."

"Sometimes I think it's us normals who are all screwed up," added Donald. "Grandpa seems totally at home there."

"It's the best thing for him under the circumstances," Alex said. "I worked once with a recreation crew at a veterans' hospital. I know what your mom must have gone through struggling with grandpa to take his bath or to get him to bed at a decent hour."

"At least grandpa gets more supervision from the staff at Flunsa," Bill added. "But I'm afraid he'll get around to conning some unsuspecting volunteer to drive him out to the old place one of these days."

"He wouldn't dare," Donald said feebly. "Would he?"

"He may just fool us all one day," John said firmly.

At that moment, a honey bee flew through the open vent, buzzed in a spiral above Chris's head, then dived toward Donald's frantically moving hands and came to rest under the right cuff of his white shirt.

Just then, John swerved the van to avoid collision with an oncoming pickup and scattered his passengers in all directions.

"Everyone in one piece?" he asked. But he didn't wait for a reply. "Did you see that joker? His rear wheels hit the traffic cones at the intersection. He crossed two lanes and almost struck that road crew. I hope somebody got his license number and reports it."

"And all along I thought it was the bee," said Wayne.

"I won't relax now until we're safely back in Hillside," Alex mourned. He turned to face Chris in the back seat. "You okay?"

"Uh huh," answered Chris. "But Uncle Donald don't look so good. He smashed that bee, and now his fist is all swollen."

"Oh my God," said John. "He's allergic to bee stings. We've got to get him some help fast."

"Any of you have a plug of tobacco or some snuff on you?" asked Donald's brother Alex. "Pull over to the side of the road when you can, John. Some of that red clay will serve as a poultice until we get him to the doctor. There's an exit just ahead. Hang in there, Donald. Keep talking to him, Chris, and check that seat belt for landing soon."

Chapter 6

Company officials in Savannah had said their truck would be able to deliver the Spanish tile in three to five weeks. Apparently a problem had arisen regarding some clearance dispute at the docks. Within that time frame, the Grantley clan hoped to take advantage of the temporary lull in activity to reassess their goals and analyze the methods they must use to obtain them.

There was still a good chance that Villa Sara would be ready to welcome its first foreign guests in August; that is, if all concerned could hold to their realistic goals. They hoped to meet the university staff, complete their selection of student interns, and inspect wiring and plumbing within the next few days. All fixtures, flooring, furniture, and interior paint had to be ordered and held in storage. Each member of the family was able to make a good impression as they promoted their special ideas.

Activities at the construction intensified well into the long hot afternoons, and as the time drew closer, the volunteers pushed harder, worked a little faster, and fought distractions and occasional moments of panic with the assurance that they were masterminding a global complex.

The arrival of the special Spanish tile on the twenty-sixth day called for a celebration, even though delivery was made shortly after midnight—and fifty miles from the building location. The travel-weary cherubic driver, hands moving nonstop, apologized when he aroused the dogs, then John, at the Hillside address.

"I've been driving all over the State of Georgia since noon, trying to find this Villa Sara," he said. "I knowed how much you wanted these tiles—you waited so long and all. I just thought I'd bring the load to the only other address I had. Y'all tell me where to put it, and I can be on my way."

"Put it?" asked John. He rubbed his eyes in disbelief. "Wait just a second. I'll wake my brothers, and we'll have you follow us to the construction site."

"That's one thing you can say about these Southerners," commented Bill later, "what they lack in speediness is more than compensated for in courtesies. The driver could have parked somewhere and dozed off until who knows how long."

It's a welcome sight all right, even when courtesy comes under a past-midnight shadow," someone voiced from the darkness. "Littlejohn is going to be spitting nails!"

Littlejohn was busy installing outdoor showers so "his" boy John and relatives could change into fresh clothing each day rather than sweat it out fifty miles one way back to Elaine's place. He had also cordoned off the location from unscrupulous "collectors" (better known as thieves) using an assortment of tin cans filled with gravel tied to rope. The dog One-less had just treed a coon when the jeep and truck swung into their allotted space.

"I've been expecting you," Littlejohn said with a big grin. "I just knew it would be today. Just knew it."

One-less hobbled in view and rubbed himself against Littlejohn's high-top leather boots. The big man leaned over and scratched the small mixed breed gently behind the ears.

"Don't get too attached to One-less," John warned, "or Chris will send you on another guilt trip."

"I know what you mean," Littlejohn answered. "Let's get that tile unloaded while I'm still awake. And while you're here, you might as well have an early breakfast with me."

"Now, Mister, that sounds mighty inviting," accepted the travel-weary driver without hesitation. "No wonder I couldn't find this place; it's so secluded. A perfect place to raise kids these days. What you might call a little boy's heaven. Can't wait to see what it looks like in the daylight." He extended his hand. "The name's Bryan, Sir. Bryan Tipton."

Littlejohn hesitated a moment, then clamped down hard with his good grip. He was surprised to meet a strong resistance.

"You ain't much to look at, young feller," he said, "but you got a working man's lock. Let's keep him here a few days, boys. We can back that truck up close enough so we can reach the tile. No need to unload."

They all looked at each other dumbfounded, shrugged their shoulders, and followed Littlejohn into the lean-to. They looked like boy scouts with a secret sneaking back into camp pass the sentry after curfew.

*　　　*　　　*

"Something wrong, Wayne?" John asked when they were midway on the completion of the tile roof.

"Yeah, I have this strange disturbing feeling. Like we're being watched."

"Wouldn't surprise me any," added Alex. "As much as we've tried to keep this all a secret and avoided publicity, some curious soul is bound to step over the line for a closer look."

"They'd have to be on foot," Littlejohn said, "because I've got heavy logs blocking the entrance for now. We'd hear any other jeep or truck using the old logging trail."

"No cause to fret," said a beaming Bryan Tipton. "No one's getting near this place. It's sealed on three sides by a deep forest of pine. Only other approach I can see is that river yonder."

"Well, Wayne, you satisfied?" asked Donald.

His answer, however, was muffled by the sound above them. From the Spanish tiled roof, all eyes turned skyward to watch a Marine Corps helicopter hover a brief second, then gently lower itself to the clearing staked off for the gazebo.

Rick Steele, family advisor, business partner, and Realtor, sprang from the still vibrating machine. Dressed casually, he had just zipped by Lear jet to Atlanta, pulled some military strings, and now grinning excessively at his unexpecting audience, began to speak.

"Y'all seem surprised," he beamed. "Told you if you needed anything to just give me a call, and within twenty-four hours I'd deliver."

"Rick, you're always doing things with style," said John, rushing over to greet him. "But Mom never called you."

"I know," Rick answered. "But look who did."

When the rotor blade clicked to silence, Rick turned to assist a young woman also dressed in casual attire. She wore a smile that spread full-length across a golden-tanned model's face.

A strained grin crept across Donald's still bee-swollen face. He leaped forward to embrace her.

"My God. It's you, Morene. We didn't expect you for two more weeks," he said to his beaming sister. "We thought you'd be coming with the student from France."

"Christina won't be coming," Morene said. "But I'll explain all that later. I want a hug from all these handsome men before the heat gets to me and I slip right from their arms. Where's Mom and the others?"

"They're opening gifts and reading mail in the comfort of the Florida room," answered John. "You wouldn't believe all the correspondence from families we never even heard of. People from all over the world. They all remember Sara Bocan Grantley. How they learned about Project SEEK is anyone's guess."

Taking them all in with her affectionate gaze, Morene continued to speak. "I have a crate at the freight office. Who's going with me in the jeep to get it? It's something special from my French 'family' with regrets that their daughter couldn't come this year."

"John, why don't you volunteer?" offered Rick. "You've seen this land from the sky. I was hoping the others might like a spin above. I've got another couple of hours with the pilot and his craft, so what say we do it?"

"You'll never regret it. *C'est magnifique,*" Morene cooed, purring her lips in her best French imitation. "I speak of the aerial view, John, not the jeep trip."

"Ain't she a sight to wake up anyone's sluggish morning?" Bryan Tipton said, nudging Littlejohn. "I ain't never seen the likes of her."

"Stick around a little longer, and you'll be meeting another just as pretty," said Littlejohn. "In fact, some say the Langstrom sister studying accounting in Atlanta could be a twin to Morene. They're about the same age, too."

"You know a lot about this family, don't you?"

"Oughta, I've been around here from the beginning. So was my father before me. My father was Grantley's doctor. Lost his life trying to save Sara's three sons. They all drowned in this very river you see yonder. It kind of turned things around to see her grandsons make something productive of his place in her honor. Sara Bocan Grantley. Now there was a beautiful woman."

"Well, I can't stay any longer, as much as I'd like to," Bryan apologized. "I'm due to haul another load of tile to the Carolinas by noon tomorrow. Sure hope to come back this way again, though."

"You will, my lad," Littlejohn yelled above the roar of the helicopter as it departed with its first load of passengers. "You can count on it!"

Chapter 7

The large crate from Paris held a Steinway piano. Morene provided information about the French family's many prior commitments and again expressed their regrets. Elaine wired a speedy thank you and invited them another year if it could be arranged.

"All the pieces are beginning to fit together, it seems," Morene said to the group gathered around her at Quincy's for their victory celebration—victory over the completion of the Spanish tiled roof and celebration over her safe journey.

"I hope our foreign students have as easy a flight as you did," Jayne addressed her daughter. "By the way, has Denice shown you her idea for the gazebo?"

"Not yet, but I hope to see it soon. I've got much to share with you, too," she said, "but it can wait. What's high on the priority list at the moment?"

"Painting the interior now that we have a roof over our heads," Denice explained. "Decorating has a low priority because we can do that on a rainy Saturday."

"Is that the forecast for the weekend?" someone asked.

"Don't we wish," said Elaine. "We need rain. Everything is so dry. One carelessly lighted match and all our efforts could go up in smoke."

"No sweat, Mom," Bill assured her. "Littlejohn has the best irrigation system rigged up of any I've seen. We're lucky Villa Sara has access to a creek and a river."

"Did you ask Littlejohn to water the place down good—just in case?" asked Jayne, fidgeting with anxiety.

"Time to change the subject I see," said Wayne, detecting his aunt's nervousness. "Morene, how did you like Paris? Any news in the romance department?"

"Wrong subject," piped Morene. "I'd rather hear more about your Project SEEK. What's the staff like, and what's your agenda for tomorrow?"

"In two days, your mother and I will be meeting with the four finalists for the staff positions," explained Elaine. "You can sit in on the briefing, if you'd like."

"We have other plans that day, Mom," reminded Denice. "We're going to take Morene to the mall to look at some art work."

"Art work? Sure," teased John. "You know what that means? If you desert us on the job, you'll have to double your output the next day."

"We can more than double our efforts if you stay out of our way," Susan hastened to add.

"I have a feeling that tensions are going to be higher from now on than at any other time," said Donald, exercising his bee-stung arm.

"No tensions that a good night's sleep couldn't nip in the bud," Alex told them while midway out of his seat. "Unless we're expecting one of those past midnight deliveries."

"No way," answered John. "Our job is practically finished. We may even get that round of golf in by early afternoon."

*   *   *

They made it through the first hour of the next day without a quarrel, even though the matte, linen-white walls were not completely dry. The moving of heavy furniture, Chris's unexpected regression to talking about the sweet lemon tree, and the various sounds vibrating from stereos in different sections of the building, however, soon put a strain on the once cooperative hive of workers.

"There's too much confusion here," admitted John after the second hour. "This isn't working. Too many hands and feet. Three of the ten acres don't give space enough to hold three generations at once."

Irritations and arguments followed as to whom he might be addressing, so the boys finally walked off in a fury to play golf. This threw their sisters off balance, making concerted efforts even more difficult.

"Who moved the display case?" asked Elaine. "Denice, did you have John move it from the center of the room?"

"No, Mom," answered Susan for her. "We moved it ourselves. Is something wrong?"

"Just didn't want scratches on the floor," said Elaine, inspecting the creamy beige floor tiles. "Keep everything away from the walls. Let's give them plenty of time to dry."

"It's quick drying paint, Mom," reminded Denice, spreading one hand fanlike across the wall. "See."

"I see a few ceiling spots missed," volunteered Jayne. "But then again, maybe it's only the natural lighting."

"Can't you two go somewhere else?" asked Susan. "You're making us nervous."

"We'll work for awhile in the basement then," said Elaine. "Let me know if you need anything."

"Not 'basement,' Mom. That's so gross," corrected Susan. "Try saying, 'lower tier.' It's a more classy term for a classic establishment such as this."

Jayne fought off a rebuttal the best way she knew—by ignoring it.

"Just go . . . go. Skedaddle," Morene teased. "Go to the creek and compose something for me."

"Good idea," said Jayne. "A few minutes in the wilds could reduce my coronary risk factors or whatever else has me feeling so sluggish. Coming, Elaine?"

"May as well. You girls send Chris for us if you find you need anything. Anything at all."

"Not me!" snapped Chris. "I'm going with you, Grandma." He dashed out the door before anyone could object. Under one arm he carried his book about lizards.

"I feel recovered," admitted Jayne a few hours later when they returned for lunch, their first eats in the Villa Sara dining room.

A mirror elegantly framed on the one partial wall was set off with a rounded, cantilevered shelf. A painted canvas hung on a trolley track which slid like a door to close off the dining room from the adjacent living room.

Morene's creation was a color wheel, red, yellow and blue (more precisely, magenta, yellow, and cyan) super-imposed on an abstract equilateral triangle. Different shades, tones, and tints were artistically arranged to blend with the surroundings, picking up the color variation from square to square of the creamy beige floor tiles.

The room was flooded with natural light filtering through matchstick blinds from the floor-to-ceiling arched windows. The antique walnut round table and caned chairs, salvaged by Elaine and John from Sara's collection before the old farmhouse was destroyed, now cast a silhouette against the matte, linen-white wall.

Denice had placed a small palm tree near the window closest to the living room, and other symbols of warm climates were scattered about the room. Every object was chosen for its shape and texture. None of the contributors felt afraid to break some decorative code, but created what pleased them most of all.

They sat in silence for some time munching chips dipped in their favorite guacamole from a hand-painted earthenware sombrero and drinking Diet Pepsi from paper cups.

"This isn't a table setting for stylish dining," said Denice, "but we can't use the kitchen isle with the drop-leafs until John or someone can sand down the drawer above the storage space. It's either warped or poorly constructed."

"Everything is just fine," said Elaine.

"We wanted to use the cherry hardwood end table ensemble," continued Denice, "but there are only four of them." She cast a glance across the room at the sixteen-inch-high cabinet that doubled as an end table, its four tables ready to be pulled from a frame supported on cabriole legs.

"Will you stop fretting," said Jayne. "The atmosphere sparkles with your workmanship. I'm impressed. Does our daughter's enthusiasm spur our vigor, Elaine? Are you ready to arrange some of the rooms downstairs?"

"I'm ready if you are," she answered. "But it's 'lower tier,' remember?"

"Oh, Mom," Denice and Susan chorused.

*   *   *

At the end of the day, the descendants of the Grantley family were quite pleased with what had been accomplished once a brief separation of generations had taken place. One more day and Villa Sara would be at a stage to welcome the four staff members—or so everyone thought. Fate, however, had a way of altering the best laid plans.

Chapter 8

he tornado was spotted by state troopers as it traveled along County Road 170 just north of Villa Sara. The report of the touchdown, however, never reached the people because of damaged power and telephone lines. Lightning also struck the antenna tower at the home base for the county's radio system, leaving dispatchers without contact with patrol cars and other emergency vehicles.

The tornado moved houses off foundations and tore off roofs in its hour-long rampage—the same time the Grantley women were traveling from Villa Sara to Hillside. They now sat in the recreation room by candlelight worrying more about the boys out on the golf course than about any damage to Villa Sara.

Shortly after ten o'clock, John dashed in, dripping wet, trailed immediately by the other four. All were sputtering nonstop about their close call with death. Despite repeated warnings from the clubhouse loudspeakers, two golfers were struck by lightning only moments after the Grantley males had taken cover.

No one got much sleep that night, but by morning, the sun, dressed in fluid yellow, splashed the countryside with a welcomed coolness.

*   *   *

The tornado damage to Villa Sara was not as serious as it might have been had not such skillful hands put it together. A tall pine had demolished Littlejohn's lean-to, but he had already moved his belongings into a spare room. Some Spanish tile had loosened and were broken when blown to the ground, but nothing they couldn't repair with spares stored in the workroom on the lower tier south wing.

171

So, once again, luck smiled on the fourth generation of Grantley sons. And once again, it was time to get some unbiased reaction to their architecture.

*   *   *

Elaine and Jayne met with the four student interns in the Florida room at Hillside. They faced one another at the elliptical drop-leaf table, awed by Project SEEK and what it had to offer them and what they could offer each other.

"Thank you for coming," Elaine began, giving them a big smile that approved of what she saw. "We thought it best to go over our objectives away from the confusion and distractions that might mar a meeting at Villa Sara at this stage. We'll take you there later."

"Well, now," said the apparent spokesman for the group. He returned the smile, and from the pocket of his imported Henley shirt, took out his note pad and pen. He was slender, not very tall, and wore wire-rimmed glasses—a casualness that seemed calculated when one noticed the grease stains under his fingernails. His voice was soft and low.

"I speak for the rest of us, Missus Langstrom," he began. "We're all looking forward to this assignment. I'm Victor Griffith, your naturalist. You have the position listed as Biology/Sciences. All of us have just completed pre-training at the University. You might say we're programmed to start next Monday as planned."

"Yes," said Jayne. "We're impressed with your credentials—all of you." She leaned forward to make a notation in her legal pad. "We want to make sure our team selection is the very best possible on such short notice. In brief, we're proud to have you. Should there be any problems during your stay at Villa Sara, you are to report directly to my sister Elaine."

"Have you as a team made any plans other than the ones we've talked about?" asked Elaine. "Any equipment or supplies you need other than what you use from the University?"

"That's Jasmine's responsibility," answered Victor, turning to Jasmine Singh, a tall, slim young lady with dark hair braided in a French twist down the back. Her dark almond eyes shined from an Asian face. She was dressed in blue jeans and an over-sized white blouse splashed with geometric shapes.

"We have a list here of some things we thought were important," Jasmine said as she slid the typed sheet over to Elaine.

"The University vetoed some items, but we'll accept any challenge you hand us. We're prepared to create from what nature around us provides. And we expect the same creativity from the children when they arrive."

"That's what we like to hear." Jayne smiled broadly at her. "And what better way is there to teach problem-solving? We'll see that you get what you need. Wouldn't you agree, Elaine?"

"Absolutely," Elaine answered. "You want to involve the students in decision making. I'm reading from someone's resumé: 'Decision making builds respect, reduces stress, and contributes to the child's stability and well-being.' Would the writer please identify herself?"

Seneca Pontiac began rocking back and forth, then casually lifted her ad-for-fitness body—all five feet and ninety pounds. Without a word, she began a practice warm-up routine. She was dressed in blue jeans and a sleeveless T-shirt.

"Is that an invitation to join in?" asked Jayne, "or does she do this often before she speaks?"

"You would be pleasantly surprised at what Seneca can do," added Victor. "She is as much at home on a baseball diamond, too. And what she does to make any meal nutritious . . . well, you have to eat some of her food to believe it."

"Victor makes a good test subject," Seneca said in a hushed, confidential tone of voice. "You could feed him honey-suckle blossoms and he'd smack his lips."

"She's correct on that point," said the fourth intern, Cabot Nichols. He shoved a baseball cap back on a mop of long, neatly-styled red hair. "The truth about Victor I'll try to conceal from the students, but as for Seneca's quote, I plan to refer to it often in my problem-solving sessions."

They continued to share their thoughts until a gray haze covered the sun. Promise of rain for a hot, humid day, perhaps? They all hoped it was not a sign of another tornado.

At the first convenient pause, Elaine lifted one hand in a closing gesture. "You must see Villa Sara first in the daylight," she said.

And off they went.

Chapter 9

Once past the main highway and hardtop turnoff and about halfway up the gravel road, Elaine pulled the car over slightly to one shoulder. She signalled the other driver to do the same. The beauty of the red roof tile and its concrete block structure simulating ancient adobe bricks sprawled before them in all its three acres of hacienda charm.

"When you stand back and study a house," said Elaine, "you can inspect and make your own preliminary evaluation. Are you pleased with the view of Villa Sara from here?"

"It's old world charm and creative future both at the same time," Jasmine said. "No one would have expected to see a hacienda secluded by a pine forest."

"It's so peaceful and quiet," added Victor, "with nature's own sounds to welcome us."

In the distance, One-less howled agreement. "I really don't think you could get a totally impartial opinion from this group, Missus Langstrom," added Cabot. "The site is historically right for Project SEEK."

"And saturated with Creek Indian lore," cut in Seneca. "Look at this." She brushed the rich soil from an Indian arrowhead. "The Creek Indians built on high land, and where there was none, they built their own."

"I can see you and my grandson Chris are going to get along just fine," Elaine said. "Chris penciled similar words under one of his drawings of a dream house on a hill when he was eight."

"Seeing your facial approvals exceeds my expectations," added Jayne. "Much work still needs to be done to the surroundings, however. The area from the gazebo to the creek will provide picnic and recreation space. The flagpole awaits a banner. I see the flats of assorted flowers have arrived—they'll need to be planted."

While Littlejohn moved one of the lawn sprinklers to allow them a clear path up the stone-tile walk, the group passed through the wrought-iron gates under the main archway and into a flower-festooned garden.

"Some of these flower arrangements are a marvel to me," sighed Jasmine. "Unimagined even in the days of Claude Monet. Someone has a good eye for color."

"I think there's a little of all of us in that choice of colors," said Jayne, "but Littlejohn here has done most of the planting so far."

"We'll be glad to help," volunteered Victor. "We'll get the foreign students involved."

"Look," continued Seneca, "even the sunbrella and wrought-iron furniture coordinate with the shades of blossoms and greenery. The beauty invites you to sit and enjoy it."

Just as Elaine reached for the ornate knocker to announce the arrival, Denice called from the foyer entrance. "Time for that later," she said, and ushered them through glass doors into the main living area showered with light from above.

"I call this modular, hexagon grouping of seating 'a planning place.'" Denice pointed to an arrangement of LeCorbusier sofas of soft leather in cool neutrals resting in a central sunken area of the room. "My sister Susan thinks of it as a 'conversation pit.'"

At one end of the room was the fireplace, and at the other, a custom console under a pastel painting in abstract. The painting was designed to capture the textures of stone, wire, marble, or wood sculpture placed indiscriminately about the room.

"You'll notice that we've tried to depict the universalistic concept of citizenship in society. Whew! I didn't think I'd get it all out in one breath," Denice said, smiling.

Seneca moved ahead of the group into the kitchen/dining room area with the intensity of a food inspector before renewing a restaurant license. The wall plaque captured her attention:

> It is not the quantity of the meat, but
> the guests which make the feast.
> Edward Hyde Clarendon, 1609–74

"The first Earl of Clarendon, of course," said Cabot. "It's only appropriate to have the English contribution. Have you considered placing a royal picture above your fireplace?"

"That particular spot is reserved for a very special person," explained Elaine. "We should have the portrait mounted by the time of the house warming celebration. It's being restored and reframed at the moment. That coffee should be about ready though."

Fresh-ground coffee had just finished perking in a twelve-cup Toshiba programmed earlier to be ready when the tour broke for refreshments. Denice and Susan had set out silver trays piled high with elaborate foodstuff on the breakfast bar. The evening sun now spilled in through an overhead skylight.

They skipped the other living features when Chris came stumbling up the lower tier slopeway with his "iguana." John's warning to leave the terrarium in the study nook came too late. Chris couldn't wait until the staff came below; he had something he wanted to do right then. He went without any introduction directly up to Victor Griffith.

"You going to help me record my iguana's measurements?" he asked.

"You must be the herpetologist of this project," Victor said. "Then let's go below deck and see what you've discovered so far."

Chris led Victor to the lower entryway where a sleek console and mirrored wall provided a bright red contrast to the greens and browns of the lizard's glass environment. Behind the sliding red panels were lots of spacious shelves and storage space. He placed the terrarium on the pullout, natural wood shelf and selected the lower of the two saddle stools from Norway to sit on.

Victor had to raise his stool the full eight inches. They both swiveled the three hundred sixty degrees, just to get the feel of it.

"You have your Field Guide and checklist I see," said Victor proudly.

Chris had taken them from a wire basket and was now examining the point of his number-two pencil for sharpness.

"Herpetologists use a formula for noting the length of a lizard's digits," explained Victor. "The first number refers to the front foot. Then after the slash, the number refers to the hind foot. The digits in the number refer to the length of each toe reading from the inside to the outside and counting from the shortest to the longest."

"Take a look at this," said Chris. "I put down the numbers the way I thought they'd be in a human. Is this right?"

Victor took the pencil and began to check the notations against Chris's hands.

"Your thumb, number one, is shortest, and the pinkie, number two, is next shortest. These are followed by the index finger, number three; then the ring finger, number four; and finally in length of the middle finger, number five. So your figures should be one, three, five, four, two slash. So far, you're on target, Chris."

"The other numbers have got to be right, too," Chris said, beaming with confidence, "cause I'm not taking off my shoes."

"Let's be scientific and check the notation out anyway," urged Victor. "After the diagonal slash, the big toe is often the longest, and so on. Slash, five, four, three, two, one. Everything checks out. Now partner, let's glove up and do this for real with your Anolis carclinensis."

"That's Latin for my green anole, isn't it?" asked Chris, but he didn't wait for an answer. "I just like to call him an iguana because I named him Igu."

"Well it's a good name," said Victor, "and I wouldn't want you to change it."

The two herpetologists worked with measurements so intensely, they were unaware when the rest of the group reached the lower tier.

*   *   *

Wayne Langstrom sat behind the computer equipment deftly adjusting knobs that controlled an air-conditioning unit, obtained maximum illumination from lighting and heating, and programmed the acoustics to reduce noise neurosis.

The computer room, the second largest room on the lower tier, had on either side soft leather cushions for relaxing or thinking. It had a built-in desk and shelving for software and other accessories.

Between the computer room and one end of the gallery-like area and the hobby nook where Chris was working on the other, was the largest room, a huge recreation center with every piece of exercise equipment imaginable. It was carpeted for comfort while doing sit-ups. The room contained a massive fireplace, a sauna and spa, a stall shower, and glass doors which opened to a sequestered side yard.

The lower tier, with its entrance also from outside, faced the sun and river view. Since this section of the house was partially underground, natural daylight was admitted by a sloping bank of double-glazed windows the full width and to the ceiling. It was rumored by some that when the sun's rays hit the stone veneer beam that extended upward in the center of the room, it glistened like a flint arrowhead.

Panels of glass and cork partitioned the front view of rooms from the sleeping area in the back. Here there were two full-size bedrooms at each side with sliding doors, storage and closet space, and a shared bath.

Between the two sets of bedrooms was the library or conference room, fully equipped with built-in book shelves. One wall, to the surprise of many, had a hidden panel for maps.

The possibilities for utilization of space was as extensive as the imagination would allow, and as Bill would explain secretly to his business associates later, Villa Sara was all planned for easy conversion to office space by Realtors, attorneys, accountants, or anyone else needing a home office.

It was Jasmine who offered the next suggestion as the home inspection tour headed for one of the exits.

"I know just the wording to place at each of your exits," she exclaimed, about to burst with enthusiasm. "Every exit is an entry to somewhere. Linda Ellerbee quotes it in her interviews. Don't you think it's appropriate?"

"Who in heaven's name is Linda Ellerbee?" came the response from several males in the group.

"She's with NBC Network—or was. I'm not sure of all the details of her lawsuit," said John. "My wife Tina might know. She listens to a lot of talk shows."

"You're a big help, John," said Jasmine, smiling. "Let's just leave it at that. See who is curious enough to look up the information. Isn't that what we'd say to our gifted foreign students as bait?"

"Never volunteer the whole answer. Is that your strategy?" asked John. "Do you really expect these too-smart-for-their-own-good students to react as well as we have?"

"We'll soon find out," added Elaine. "Next week is staff orientation. Then next weekend, a little welcoming party. But for now, we'll have our refreshments in the screened-in gazebo. Lead the way, Denice. This is your project."

*   *   *

Built on a wooded site just beyond the house, the white octagonal gazebo was flooded with enchanting light. Electric fans had been hung from the ceiling to make eating out more comfortable. Only one event marred what could have been a pleasing finish to the staff's first visit.

Seneca was the first to notice it as she looked northward to verify the arrowhead vision under a setting sun. Someone had painted a four-letter word in bold glossy strokes across several glazed windows.

Elaine was visibly upset when she saw it. How could it have happened? And when? Would the blame be placed on Littlejohn, and would he again have to apologize for not being more alert? What other security measures must they consider to prevent a recurrence?

Victor Griffith suggested they get the scaffold out and try to remove the graffiti. John, however, felt it should be reported to Crime Stoppers, even though he was not looking forward to the publicity. He also accepted the responsibility for checking into liability insurance for vandalism and personal safety of the staff at Villa Sara.

Chapter 10

The restored portrait Elaine had mentioned to the staff earlier was delivered early that Monday morning. Littlejohn signed for it and had it installed over the fireplace in the living room before anyone was aware.

A wide grin stretched across his worn, tired face as he stepped back to view the epitome of elegance in its ornate mahogany frame. Slim and erect in a sunflower-yellow lace dress with ankle-length full skirt and soft grey leather buckled shoes, Sara Bocan Grantley posed with one hand resting on the back of a wicker rocking chair. The other hand held a single, long-stemmed sunflower. Her Dresden doll-like face had the hint of a smile, and dark eyes peered out under the hair style of the 1900s. It was as though she wanted to acknowledge the gift of fresh cut flowers Littlejohn had brought in from the patio.

"Well, pretty lady," said Littlejohn to the woman in the portrait, "are you pleased with what you see? Your two daughters and grandchildren have made your first dream come true. Now, if only your husband Earl could get over his grief and come to share this joy with us. But John thinks he'll only listen to Rick Steele, and Rick said he's waiting for the right time to bring Earl out here. Didn't want to make the move too stressful for him.

"You always liked Rick, didn't you?" Littlejohn continued. "Even when he teased you with his high-falutin' car phone and you were baffled that it rang and you could talk to him without telephone wires. You might say Rick was the son Grantley always wanted.

"We're hoping that, in time, Earl will come to realize that that Creek Indian curse hasn't surfaced in this generation. And you know something else? I hear that doctor's treatment with Jobst stockings has reduced the swelling in his legs and helped the blood circulation. Some days he's better than others. We're all glad they didn't have to amputate. You know Earl. He has astonishing recuperative powers. Wouldn't surprise me one bit if he made it out here on his own two feet one of these days—rules or no rules.

"Well, I be talking with you again later. I'd like to see what you think of these foreign students. If they're anything like the ones in the public schools today, I don't rightly know how to handle them. But I'll stand by John and your family as long as I'm able. Did you hear that? That's your grandson, Chris. He's always the first up and raring to go."

"Who you talking to, Littlejohn?" asked Chris. He scratched an insect bite on his arm from the night before.

"Just thinking out loud, ma'boy. Just thinking out loud."

"Is it fun—thinking out loud?"

"You better believe it is. You still want to go fishing?"

No answer.

"Did you hear me, Chris?"

"Did you really know my great-grandma Sara?"

"I'll tell you all about her on the way. Now get your fishing gear. And you'd better leave a—"

"I know. Leave a note telling where we're going," finished Chris. But he didn't move from the spot. He kept staring up at the portrait.

"She sure was pretty, wasn't she?"

"That she was, son. That she was."

Chapter 11

At the first session during staff orientation week, the four student interns were given a brochure that stated, in part, ways to be supportive:

> Your job is that of mentor and facilitator. You are to bolster the youngsters when they need it and provide a foundation for workable interactions among all concerned. They are brilliant, and in some ways, very mature, but they are still kids who need your guidance, affection, and encouragement. They can be uncooperative, snappy, hostile, and unforgiving.
>
> There are no definite time lines. Listen and learn with them during SEEK's first ten-day intercultural exchange.

Printed on salmon-colored paper of good stock, the brochure's cover sported an embossed arrowhead. Under the emblem in bold large letters were the words:

REALITY CAN BE MORE WONDERFUL THAN DREAMS

"Getting diverse groups to work jointly is so complicated," offered Cabot Nichols, the historian. "But I've found that the more intricate the situation, the more we begin to like it. You have to meet the youngsters in action to really know them and appreciate their contributions to our society, so let me introduce them to you in this way: After giving you each student's name, I would like to ask him or her to do or tell you something they consider special."

Looking out at the group of students gathered before him, Cabot said, "From China, we have Chang Han Sung."

With the introduction, an eleven year old boy stepped forward. He was small for his age, but what he lacked in inches, he more than made up for in cleverness. In his hand, Chang carried a reed basket of small white glass pieces similar to small buttons. He put a handful on the table and began removing them four at a time with a chopstick. He then asked the other students to bet on how many would be left after the last four were removed. After each game, Chang paid the winners, but he always had a three-to-one advantage.

"What's this game called?" someone wanted to know.

"Chinese fan-tan game," said Chang. He beamed as he counted out coins in Chinese currency and pushed them over to winners with a chopstick. "You must find out if I have cheated you by converting Hong Kong dollar to American money." He threw back his head and laughed jokingly. "Confucius say, 'It's the only way to play honest game.'"

There followed a mad rush through the various current newspapers conveniently placed about the room. A search for the New York exchange rates littered Villa Sara with enthusiastic squeals of discovery. The excitement dampened, however, when Stefi Grau put through a telephone call to a local bank.

"The New York exchange rate for the Hong Kong dollar at this very moment is seven point eight one four," she shouted above the clutter.

"That's not fair!" someone yelled.

"All's fair in getting the problem solved," she replied.

"Thank you, Chang," said Cabot. "Next we have Stefi Grau from West Germany."

Whimsical Stefi Grau, eleven and a half years of age, stepped to the front of the group dressed in a red-trim, USA Olympics knit T-shirt and cotton and polyester shorts. While the other students sat bewitched before a crackling fire, Stefi began telling castle tales. She told them that isolated as they were atop a steep hill with a sweeping view of the wild countryside, she felt the serenity and unhurried life similar to village life in her town east of Frankfurt where the famous Grimm brothers were born.

Stefi paused occasionally in her storytelling when a change in action and mood was needed. She conveyed these changes with her flute, possessing the ability to call up music on the spur of the moment. Her blonde braids bobbed in rhythm as she played.

"A stein of beer to Stefi," cheered another student, L. Travis Parrington, lifting an imaginary toast. "Better make it root beer, though," he added. "I'm in training."

Cabot's voice could be heard again as Stefi took her seat. "Next we have L. Travis Parrington from New Zealand."

A muscled twelve-year-old, Travis tipped a baseball cap back on curly brown hair. He proudly displayed the Major league team insignia screen-printed on his baseball jersey and athletic shorts.

L. Travis Parrington recalled for the group that in New Zealand where mountains seemed to stand guard over the fields where he lived, there was a celebrated hotel opened in 1884 by a proprietor who kept the mutton in a well and ordered his beer by carrier pigeon. The proprietor had somehow survived immense shingle slides caused when sheep devoured the fields of lilies that seemed to wire the landscape together.

The competence Travis displayed in his sharing helped his colleagues combat their shyness, and soon others began to share a few moments of their experiences.

After Travis's introduction came that of Nobuaki Kombura from Japan. Nobuaki, his eleven-year-old body decked out with a Masters of the Universe top of polyester-and-cotton knit, heat transfer on front, and Big Mac denim jeans, strutted to the center of the circle.

"The Japanese lanterns and plodding carts you still see in your American school films are Sonys and whizzing Toyotas now," Nobuaki said proudly.

"In Japan, you learn early in life that nothing is guaranteed, so we Japanese, for one hundred yen, can buy fortunes good for one year. When we don't like the fortune, we give it to the trees."

"To the trees?" asked Chris as he examined closely the stunning face of the visitor.

"Yeah!" came the surprised answer that stirred each listener's mind and heart. Then Nobauki continued welding the serenity of a temple garden with that of Villa Sara.

"The trees, practically white with folded-up paper, become common-place in the areas where there are many temples and shrines. And dozens of roof tiles with wishes inscribed on them are laid at the feet of the sacred Buddhas. The prayerful may buy a wish for three hundred yen and tack it to a board of wishes. Kiyomizu Temple is my favorite. It sprawls on a forested rise of Higashiyama Hill, much like this place, and gives an overview of the city."

"If I was in Japan," said Chris, "I'd buy a wish."

"And what would you wish for?" asked Nobuaki. "You seem to have everything here."

"I'd wish for a sprig of the sweet lemon tree," he said seriously. "How much is three hundred yen?"

"Aw, man, here we go again!" groaned Kareem Lamar Jefferson, still groggy from all the cultural confusion. "I knew I shoulda stayed at home," he continued. "When are we gonna eat?"

Streetwise Kareem, a black boy from the United States, remained seated in his chair. He had mellowed a great deal since his reluctant first arrival as a noisy, disruptive replacement for the student from France who had cancelled. Sponsored by the Big Brothers' Association to achieve a cultural balance, Kareem made it known in no uncertain terms that he was there only as a favor to his sponsor.

"My name's Lamar," he asserted. "My folks may have named me after Kareem-Abdul Jabar, the Los Angeles Laker, but you betta call me Lamar, or I won't answer."

"I can relate to what you've said about your name, Lamar," said Stefi Grau. "People, foreigners mostly, tease me about Steffi Graf, the tennis pro. Truth is, if they'd just think about it, Steffi Graf was a child herself when I was born. My parents couldn't have named me after her."

Lamar sneered, "Y'all talk funny!"

"Hey, man, so do you!" snapped Carlos.

Chris quickly intervened, hoping to stem any international conflict on their first meeting. "You want to see my iguana?" he asked timidly.

"Man, that's nothing but a ole lizard," Lamar said.

Then he turned to the nearest target for his next verbal assault. Andries was merely experiencing the fun of just watching the iguana when it came.

"Hey, man, you black?" Lamar snarled.

Olive-skinned Andries Pretorius from South Africa calmly explained that he was of Indian descent, and that he, too, had problems.

"At the airport," he said, "many travelers looked at me as though I were an Arab with a bomb in my backpack. You Americans are so quick to judge. But I forgive you because it is only natural for you to do everything very fast. It is more fun to experience. I came here not to take sides, but to be your friend. When we know each other better, then we talk politics, yes?"

"Bravo, *amigo!*" applauded Carlos, extending his hand and grinning excessively. "I understand, man."

Carlos Moreno de Cardenas, the young boy representing Ecuador, was dressed in a workwear shirt with knock-your-eyes-out yellow, blue, and hot pink accent and washed out jeans. He nudged Lamar affectionately.

"I'm sure you know a lot about things that we don't know, Lamar," he said. "If you'll let us, we can show you how very much alike we all are. That's what we're here for, isn't it?" When no answer came immediately, he continued. "Who can tell, man. Maybe before these ten days are over, we'll have pooled our talents in some spectacular way. Dig?" He glanced at Lamar quick enough to catch a faint smile push its way out the corner of his wide mouth.

*   *   *

Carlos's prediction could not have been more prophetic. The chance came during the second week of camp—the day before their Agrirama field trip. The occasion spurred their first cooperative efforts.

Chapter 12

*U*nobserved by the staff or other students, Chris sneaked out early the morning before the scheduled field trip to Agrirama. He wanted to make sure his "iguana" had its constant supply of nourishments, and he needed to remove any uneaten food from the terrarium before it began to decay.

"Don't plan to cure infections," Victor Griffith had taught him, "but rather practice hygiene to avoid them."

His dog snapped playfully at his heels every step he took down the wooded trail toward the creek.

"We've got to be quiet, One-less," he said. "We're doing this now so we won't miss any of the other things planned for today. We've got to find a special treat for Igu, because I'm going to be away all day tomorrow."

One-less whimpered faintly and began a series of exaggerated jumps and turns that only spurred Chris on in his search for just the right foliage. When he found what he liked, he put a goodly supply in a plastic bag and headed back as quickly as he could. He tried to ignore the dog's odd behavior since his own discomfort at the thought of leaving Igu for one whole day had subsided somewhat. He gave One-less an affectionate tap on the head as he entered the lower tier of Villa Sara.

Chris joined his companions in the morning activities and became so engrossed, he almost forgot about Igu until Lamar sidled secretly up to him during lunch. Lamar had already eaten his food hurriedly and had run off to explore Villa Sara, inside and out. Now he returned with news only for Chris's ears.

"Your lizard is acting funny, man," he said.

189

It was so unlike Lamar to whisper that Chris reacted quickly. His first thoughts were that Lamar had somehow taken the terrarium cover off and was teasing Igu with tweezers as he had been caught doing before. But when Chris hurried over to the terrarium and saw the gill-like area behind his pet's jawbone puffed out to double its size, he was frightened.

The reptile gave a shrill, shivering rattle which lasted for what seemed an incredible time. The small head moved like a speeded-up video tape. Its legs continued their robot motion for a short while; then the spine and gills subsided, and it lay motionless.

"He's flaked out," said Lamar. "I'm going to get Carlos."

"Not yet," pleaded Chris. He reached for his surgical gloves.

"Yeah, man," insisted Lamar. "Carlos will know what to do. Unless you're ready to admit you fed your own pet that weed. Put your lizard in something else for now and empty that terrarium in the garbage, you hear me?"

No answer.

When Carlos joined them in the study nook, Chris learned that the special treat was marijuana. Only Littlejohn could help them out of their predicament.

"Don't you two remember anything?" scolded Carlos. "At our first orientation session, we were told that if we ever faced a problem too big to solve on our own, we were to choose the one adult we felt best to advise us. I say this matter calls for Littlejohn."

"Littlejohn isn't staff," Chris reminded Carlos. "And the others are going to know something's up." All hope for his Igu's recovery drained from his expression.

"They said, 'any adult,'" Carlos assured him, "and I'm going to hold them to their promise."

*   *   *

It was unusual request, but a legitimate one, and none of the staff objected. Although time-wise the notice was abrupt, arrangements were quickly made for a problem-solving session with Littlejohn.

Littlejohn was overwhelmed that he should be so honored and hesitated at first. When told in confidence what the problem really was, he knew why they had chosen him.

Chris handed over the crumpled, brown paper bag with the evidence, confident that they had done the right thing.

*   *   *

"You youngsters have a safe field trip," Littlejohn said the next morning. "And don't you worry about a thing. Everything will be taken care of while you're gone. Igu'll be fine."

Chapter 13

When the Villa Sara van, its arrowhead logo brilliant in the mid-August morning sun, pulled out of the lot for Agrirama, the passengers were unusually quiet. The silence, due to the lack of noise from the two most boisterous members, was staggering. Lamar and Carlos were still mulling over with Chris the problem they had left with Littlejohn.

Elizabeth was the first to break the peaceful spell. She tried unsuccessfully to muffle a sneeze. Mikhail, seated ahead of her, turned around. His English failing him, he switched to Russian.

"*Zdrast vooyetye,*" he said.

Elizabeth looked up from her journal writing and returned Mikhail's smile. "And good health to you," she translated.

Elizabeth Frances Fairfield, a student from England, was dressed in a pull-over, cotton, color-spliced top and matching slacks. She was already a student of English history and was deeply interested in architecture of any period. She had taken the Oxford entrance exam as a joke when she was ten and tried to join a college at eleven. Now at twelve, she sat in a van musing at all her fellow travelers and being everywhere in her mind. She made another quick notation in her journal as her look took in her shy seat companion.

Julia Niemcewicz, timid in this strange land so far from her native Poland, seemed deeply disturbed.

"You see," said Elizabeth, "we're not that different from you, Julia. We have the same sneeze."

When Julia didn't return her smile, she tried another approach.

"Is something wrong?" she asked. "Can I help?"

193

"I'm worried about my presentation to the group since it's my turn tomorrow to give a . . . what is it the Americans call . . . a food bash." Julia took another deep breath before continuing. "I should have stayed at Villa Sara to prepare my notes and make better food selections. I do so want mine to be as successful as Carlos's Ecuadorian fiesta."

"We've all felt that pressure," assured Elizabeth. "Remember our leading-off session what we decided as a group to share in the food preparation under Miss Pontiac's supervision. I was really nervous as we democratically selected the date of our choice."

"Yes, I remember Lamar flipped a coin and Chang opted for chopsticks," Julia said smiling.

"Feel better?" Elizabeth asked.

"Much better," Julia replied, "but I'll still worry."

"Just remember that we're all your friends, and we're here to experience a new country," added Elizabeth. "Would it help to talk through your plans with me? I'm a good listener."

Their combined efforts soon became so mind-boggling, they both drifted off to imagining the event as actually taking place:

*　　　　*　　　　*

Dressed in their countries' traditional attire, Julia and Elizabeth were Polish friends entertaining their comrades at Villa Sara. Elizabeth sat at the Steinway piano with her original Polish composition displayed before her. Julia stood near the fireplace under the portrait of Sara Bocan Grantley.

"I was about to cop out on you," she began, "but that was yesterday. I had it in my mind that I'd rather be talking about my true love—to build my own sloop like the Polish captain Barbara Gajewska—but my friend Elizabeth has helped me bring order into my presentation, so this is what I have." She looked directly into the faces staring from the modular, hexagon grouping of seating.

"I have discovered in my research while here that one Joseph Barnanowski, a Pole and a member of Company F, the Second Michigan Cavalry, was given the title 'The Most Patriotic of the Polish Veterans' in the Civil War. He was in seventy major battles and had a thirty percent casualty list. And what intrigued me most is this regiment was not only well organized, but disciplined as well. I learned that after engaging in those seventy battles, they reached Macon, Georgia on May first, eighteen sixty-five when the war was practically ended.

"The regiment was broken up into companies to guard a number of towns and preserve order. They were all mustered out on August seventeenth, eighteen sixty-five here in Macon, Georgia. They were disbanded in August twenty-sixth the same year.

"Just imagine. Joseph Baranowski and his men might well have stood on this very spot. And if any young ladies here are interested, Baranowski was only fourteen in eighteen fifty-four when he came to America. He had gray eyes and was five feet six inches tall.

"Since by coincidence or divine intervention I happened to select this day, August seventeenth, to share my Polish food bash, I want to commemorate this brave, Polish, Civil War hero. Baranowski was also a farmer, and the food we are about to eat comes to us from a like source."

There followed cheers and applause she could not imagine, but she gave the cue to Elizabeth to begin the music.

"Because Barnanowski was appointed bugler for his company and also had re-enlisted, we felt he might have enjoyed an original song dedicated to the occasion. Then after our Polish dinner, I have two short stories to tell you. One the staff thought a bit risqué to share with you before you ate, and the other is a mystery."

She led them down the crushed stone path to the gazebo. Over the entrance hung a banner prepared for the occasion during one of their art sessions with Jasmine Singh. The banner read, "*LEPIEJ WYDAC DO PIEKARZA, NIZ NA APTEKARZA*," a Polish proverb noting that good and abundant food is required for good health.

"This proverb is still visible in kitchens of the Polish-American people today," said Julia. "So let's enjoy good food and good health."

*   *   *

"Hey, man," yelled Lamar and Carlos, who had been listening in on the girls' conversation, "When do we eat?"

The driver of the van picked up their image in his overhead mirror and smiled.

"You see, Julia," said Elizabeth, "really ravaged young men will eat anything."

They giggled uncontrollably until the van slowed to a crawl in the heavy highway traffic, and Chris let go with an ear-piercing shrill cry of joy.

"That's my great grandpa Grantley!" he beamed. "I wonder where he's going?"

Another similar van had eased up window-to-window with them but headed in the opposite direction. Earl Grantley, puzzled, peered back and blinked his eyes.

Chris started to lower the side window, then in time remembered his experience with his uncle Donald and the bee. He decided to wave his hands frantically instead.

By the time the face registered in the old man's mind, the vans had separated a car's length.

"That was him!" confirmed Chris. "Wait till I tell my mom."

"You don't know for sure that was your great grandfather," a voice came from somewhere near him. Chris was sure it had to be the skeptic Lamar.

"It was him all right," he said. "Didn't you see him grin and wave?"

"They were all grinning and yelling," added Lamar. "Them that were awake, that is. That's just old folks being kind."

Tears were beginning to well in Chris's soft blue eyes until Mikhail intervened. To the Russian member, nothing went unnoticed under his unblinking gaze.

"Oh, please excuse my interruption," Mikhail Doetoevski said, "but what means 'F-L-U-N-S-A'?"

At the same time, Mikhail unearthed a bilingual dictionary from the huge pocket of his sporting, gone-wild print shirt – the shirt he had exchanged at the airport with Andries of South Africa as a joke to confuse the curious onlookers. He searched for the word "Flunsa," balancing the dictionary over his bleached denim pants.

When English failed him, he again switched to Russian. When that failed, he resorted to smiles. For him, those came easier than words.

" 'Flunsa' is the name of the rest center where my great grandpa Grantley stays," volunteered Chris. "I told y'all it was him. I don't know what the name means though."

"I know what 'Flunsa' means," said Stefi Grau from the center of the van. "But I'm not going to tell you. You can look it up for yourselves."

"Man, that woman makes me sick," grunted Lamar. "She makes me thirsty, too. I'm headed for the first water spigot I see when we park."

"Hey, you can't drink that tap water. You could really get sick," cautioned Carlos.

"Says you and who else?" asked Lamar.

"In Ecuador, the tap water is unsafe even for brushing your teeth. You soon get used to controlling your thirst until you get home where your mom boils the water."

"This isn't Ecuador," the others chorused.

A series of giggles filled the van until the driver turned into the Agrirama parking area. A grade school band arrayed in patriotic color uniforms waited at attention to greet them.

Chapter 14

An exhausted, tour-weary group, filled with food and Agrirama information and loaded down with souvenirs, staggered into the van at the end of the long day. It would seem good to get back to Villa Sara while there was still some daylight. Provided, of course, that there were no mishaps or too much traffic on the way.

They all hoped to rush through their group discussion session where it was a custom to recap the day's activities, and then be free to pursue their own personal plans.

Julia had decided to go over once more all the items on her list for the Polish Bash the next day. Elizabeth would add a few more notes to her journal. Stefi had bought a travel guide she couldn't wait to study more carefully in her own room. Chang, Nobuaki, and Travis had met new friends while on the tour and were already composing secret codes to send them through the mail.

Chris had only one thought in mind—his pet Igu. Carlos and Lamar shared his concern, but were more anxious to hear from Littlejohn regarding his solution to the problem of the lizard's eating marijuana. Mikhail and Andries had their heads together searching the dictionary while examining the brochures distributed at Agrirama.

No one, with the exception of Julia perhaps, doubted for one moment that they would all have a restful, undisturbed night's sleep. But it was not to be.

Chris bounced out of his seat and reached the exit door before the van had come to a complete stop. "I don't see One-less. Something is wrong," he said. "My dog always knows when I'm back and is usually waiting."

He dashed ahead before any one could stop him, threw open the wrought iron gate, and rushed to the kitchen. Spotting a note, he ripped it from under Ms. Piggy's magnetized grasp.

"Grandma left a note!" he called out as he raced back to share its message with the others who had by now collapsed in the softness of the seating in the planning place.

"She says to 'stay put' and someone will be back soon." He turned the note over as though there might be more, all the while fighting back tears. "I don't get it," he said.

"Maybe it has something to do with your great grandpa," offered Lamar. "You said that was him heading this way. He coulda got lost."

"This is no time to tease," said Elizabeth.

"We shouldn't speculate, either," added Stefi. "Chris's grandmother would have given more information if it were that urgent."

"What should we do then?" asked Travis.

"Just what the note says—stay put," said Stefi.

"Hey, man. I'm not going to just sit here," groaned Carlos. Then he turned to Chris. "How's your lizard?"

In the excitement, Chris had forgotten the most important thing on his mind the whole day. What if that's where everyone was, in some laboratory having his Igu analyzed, or at the jail trying to get Littlejohn released?

Chris stood motionless until Carlos and Lamar each grabbed an arm and headed toward the lower tier, leaving the others with puzzled looks. They had just reached the slope when One-less barked—or rather howled. He howled painfully, in fact.

"One-less wants me to follow him," said Chris.

"But what about your lizard, man?"

"Let him go, Lamar," said Carlos. "You and I can take care of that lizard without him. That is if there is a lizard."

*   *   *

With Chris in pursuit, the dog's sensitive nose picked up a trail along the creek bed and up the other side into the dense pine area off the Grantley estate. They crossed miles of undeveloped land, and nothing seemed familiar to Chris after the first hour. It was getting dark, and he was beginning to wish he had thought to bring his flashlight. For comfort, he reached down and patted One-less.

"How much farther?"

Whimpering, One-less led him deeper into the underbrush over dry twigs, fallen logs, rotting leaves, and more clearings. When the moon went behind a cloud, Chris was about to give up the hopeless night hunt and return to Villa Sara. When he looked around, however, he wasn't sure in what direction to go. Finally he decided he was safer with his dog, even though it seemed an endless search for the unknown.

After hunting for many hours into the night, One-less came to a place in some briars where he had previously made a hole big enough for a boy to crawl through.

"You can't expect me to crawl down there without a light," he stammered.

Something moaned from deep within the briars.

"What you got there? Puppies?"

Chris lowered himself to all fours but held desperately to his dog's collar. One-less began to paw the ground violently.

"If it means that much to you," he said, "I'll poke around a bit with this old limb, but I'm not crawling down there for anyone. Now behave yourself."

He gave the loose branch a few shakes, then stopped to listen. His eyes widened when the groan came again, followed by a flash of light.

"Who's there?" came a voice from deep in the hole. A man's voice.

"Who are you?" Chris gasped.

"I asked first," said the man.

"If you want me to get you out of there, you better tell me who you are," said Chris. "And stop playing games."

"Promise you won't turn me in, and I'll tell you." The voice sounded frightened.

"What did you do?"

"Never you mind. Just promise me, and I'll give you my name. Not that it'd mean much to a young feller like you."

"Throw me your flashlight so I can see what I'm about to rescue," said Chris.

"My mama didn't raise no fool, young man," the voice sounded stronger.

One-less nudged Chris and whimpered.

"Okay, dog, I'll take a chance, but you'd better not race off and leave me." Then, almost blinded by the flashlight beam, Chris called down into the hole, "I promise, I promise."

"I'm Earl W. Grantley, and this is my land. Now get me out of this darned hell hole so I can go home. I always intended to fill in these old storage places but never got around to doing it.

"I'll have you out in no time, great grandpa. I'm Chris . . . Susan's son."

"I knew that all along," Earl sighed as he held tightly to the larger branch Chris had extended to lift the frail body to the surface.

"You sure you're all right?" Chris asked.

"Of course I'm all right. Why wouldn't I be?"

"Grandma is going to be worried sick—that's why I'm going to leave One-less here with you and go for help."

"You'd never find your way, even with my flashlight," the old man said flatly. "We'll send your dog here for help. He can do it if anyone can. Did you know that a dog's nose is three hundred thousand times more sensitive than a human's and can pick up a trail that is several days old? Why, a person's job is to protect. . . ." His voice trailed off.

"Great grandpa Grantley, you asleep?"

Chris listened for the old man's heavy breathing and picked up the flashlight from his trembling hand. He flashed a few beams across the sky, testing the power to guide One-less and his posse back to the right spot if they needed the light.

Chapter 15

Earl moved right in at Villa Sara and sat dejectedly on one edge of the modular seating. Words of concern and a battery of verbal assaults from his family did not seem to bring forth any satisfactory response.

"We scoured the area all evening for some sign of you," said Elaine. "According to Missus Akright, you left the Faith Chapel picnic right after lunch."

"A man in a wheelchair saw you wander off, Papa," added Jayne. "What possessed you to leave a church picnic?"

"You had us worried sick," continued Elaine. "Can't you understand that?"

"I had a house like this once," Earl said to no one in particular.

"It's possible he's so numb from his experience of the day that he doesn't even flinch anymore," whispered Elizabeth to Julia. "I know I'd be."

"*Ick!* You guys look like weirdos with all that gook on your faces," chided Lamar. Then he nudged Chris. "Man, your lizard wasn't nowhere to be found."

"We searched everywhere for him," said Carlos. "And we couldn't find Littlejohn either."

"Littlejohn got that lizard and burned rubber," Lamar grinned.

Chris's weary eyes glared back at the two boys. Then he edged closer to his great-grandfather and called to Elaine, "Grandma, where's Littlejohn?"

"One question at a time, Chris," came the reply. "We'll get Papa straightened out first."

"Let me handle him, Missus Langstrom," volunteered Victor.

203

Elaine nodded a faint approval.

"Come with me, Mister Grantley. You can bunk in our room," he said firmly, taking the old man by the arm. "You won't be beholden to me either. I don't mind using my sleeping bag."

"We're all staying here for the rest of the night, Papa," Elaine called after them as they made their way to Victor's room. "Get some rest now."

"I lived in a place like this once," Earl said again. He nudged Victor. "Who are you?"

"I'm Victor Griffith from Athens, Sir."

"That's in Greece. I know that."

"Yes, you're right. But I'm from Athens, Georgia. I'm a student at the university."

"I know that. But nobody's taking me to Greece. Did I tell you I lived in a place like this once? Can't rightly remember exactly where the outhouse is though."

"We'll have time tomorrow to look around," Victor assured him. "You're staying for our Polish Bash."

"Bath? I don't need no bath." He pushed Victor's hand away from his arm. "Just had one yesterday. They're trying to drown me."

"No bath, Mister Grantley," said Victor. "I only want to get you into some dry clothes, and then you can rest for a spell."

"Yeah, I really had quite a day, didn't I, Victor? But I didn't mean to give everybody such a scare."

"I know you were just testing your wings, as my papa used to say, but your family and friends at the Center really care about you. Don't try it again."

"You're a good son, Victor. Will you tell them at Flunsa Rest Center that I'll be back tomorrow when I find someone to take me?"

"Your daughter has already told them. John will be taking you back. From what I hear, he has a little surprise for you."

*   *   *

When Victor returned and related to the others that Earl Grantley gave little resistance and was asleep the minute his head hit the pillow, there was an audible sigh of ease.

"Thanks, Victor," said Elaine. "He'd never have been as cooperative with one of us women."

"He's a rebel all right," said Victor, "but a delightful rebel nonetheless."

"Well, now that that's taken care of," added Elaine, "it's time for the rest of us to 'hit the hay,' as Papa used to tell us."

"But Grandma, what about Littlejohn?" Chris asked.

"You sure this can't wait until morning?" She held out her arms for him.

"You promised. And I've got lots of witnesses."

"Okay, I'll tell you what we know so far, but you'll have to be patient and wait until tomorrow for anything definite." Elaine paused until Chris nodded his approval.

"We noticed, your Auntie J and I, that Littlejohn was busying himself most of the morning after the van pulled out for Agrirama. He poured cement around the octagonal wooden bench he had built to encircle that unplanted area. He came in the house only once for a cool drink we offered him. Then we left him to his work.

"He did say once, however, that he was making a surprise for you, Chris, so I'm sure he'll tell you all about it. Anyway, John drove up just before that call came from Missus Akright about Papa wandering off. He went to tell Littlejohn and found him doubled over. He said he was burning up. His good arm and shoulder were numb when John rushed him to emergency room."

"What happened to him?" they all chorused.

"John called from the hospital and said they had identified the poison. He said Littlejohn is still dizzy when he turns his head, but he's going to be all right."

"Do they know what caused the poison?" asked Victor.

"John says Littlejohn must have jabbed his finger on some sharp object in the creek bed when he tried to get a salamander to replace Chris's 'iguana.'"

"That would explain it," said Victor. "The back skin of the salamander is toxic. Authorities say there are an average of thirteen hundred and eighty poisonous granular glands."

"Wow!" came the response as the listeners moved to the edge of their seats, wide awake. "Tell us more," they urged.

"The way the arithmetic works out, only sixty-nine thousandths of one gland is enough to cause the death of a mouse. Between twelve hundred and twenty-five hundred mice could be killed with the poison extracted from the skin of just one such salamander."

"Lucky for us Littlejohn ain't no mouse," said Lamar.

"Why does the salamander have so much poison in him? someone asked.

"These toxins also help to keep the salamander free from infection. You see, they guard him against parasites and bacteria that's in the mud and water down by the creek."

"I think we should leave it at that for now, Victor," said Elaine. "They really should get some sleep. I promise to let all of you know the whole story in the morning."

"Grandma, if Igu is dead," said Chris, "Littlejohn won't have to hide it from me. I can handle it. I'm a Grantley, too, remember."

With that Chris followed Carlos and Lamar to their room, perhaps to speculate more as to what really happened at Villa Sara while they were away on a field trip.

*   *   *

At the Polish Bash, all went as Julia and Elizabeth had visualized it would—up to a point anyway. They had not anticipated Earl's impromptu contributions.

It all began while they were beginning to sample the *zajac zupa* and Julia was explaining that the rabbit soup was best when made with wild onions and that Littlejohn had helped by providing the delicacy. Most of the children made a face, but Earl smacked his lips.

"The onion works like magic," he interrupted. "I know that. Why, you can use half an onion on a bee or wasp sting. The pain stops at once and the swelling goes right down. I speak from experience. If old Bill George was here, he'd be able to tell you I'm right."

They heaped their plates with fresh *kielbasa*, roast goose, breakfast ham, apple sauce, and potatoes. The bagels went well dipped in the rabbit soup or eaten separately smeared with freshly churned butter.

Most of Julia's guests only tasted the asparagus sprinkled in bread crumbs and fried in butter, but Earl ate lavishly and added his commentary.

"Green food is good for the old folks—that's right," he said. "Those Polish farmers knew what they were talking about."

Then he was quiet during the serving of desserts. There was apple pie, baked apples, and pears in syrup to choose from or combine.

"Got any beer?" he started up again.

"I wanted to make some dandelion wine like my ancestors used to," said Julia, "but it would take at least five days just to remove the impurities. My relatives used the wine on the Fourth of July celebration. It was served also on August fifteenth, the day set aside for the flowers to be blessed in church. Have some more water," she offered.

"Yep," said Earl, sounding as though he had actually sampled the nonexistent dandelion wine. "That wine could cure any ailment. I'm telling you. Neuralgia, liver flare-up, gastric stomach. It could lead you into a ripe old age."

"Hush now," someone said.

Victor touched Earl's arm lightly. "I think Julia is ready to tell us a story," he said.

"This story is over one hundred years old," she began, "but it is one of my favorites because it illustrates the Polish humor at its best."

As she spoke, she pulled from an elaborately embroidered knitting bag a young lady's silk-laced corset. There followed a shower of laughter and suppressed giggles.

"This is called a *gorset* in Polish," she explained. "But in high Polish, it becomes *sznarowka*. The young woman in the story was getting ready for her ocean voyage to America. She was advised to remove every other *podpierac* so she would feel more comfortable." A vivacious Julia then removed every other stay to demonstrate.

"By removing every other stay, you notice there leaves a pocket. Every other stay pocket could then be filled by inserting a surplus of seeds of some kind. In this case, it was tomato seeds alleged to produce tomatos having a *kielbasa* flavor. *Kielbasa* is the Polish sausage you liked so much," she explained.

"I'm wondering what the young lady must have looked like who wore that *gorset*," added Earl, and he started to wander off on a tangent when he got another nudge from someone.

Julia asked Elizabeth to pass around the dish of sunflower seeds while she uncovered her next teaser.

"Them's nothing but mushrooms," Lamar sputtered. "What's so mysterious about them?"

"Never mind, Lamar," said Carlos. "Go on with your story, Julia."

Carlos muffled Lamar's mouth with one hand while his friend squirmed in protest.

"Many of the stories of mushrooms were brought to this country by the Polish foresters," commenced Julia. "In Poland, the button-type mushrooms would appear after the first frost in September. They were given the word *podpinki*. The people had many food-gathering, mushrooming parties.

"As each batch of mushrooms was ready to boil, they would place an onion and a silver dime in the huge kettle. It was a superstition that if the onion or dime turned black, then the mushrooms were poisonous and had to be thrown away. Why do you suppose the silver dime was really placed in the kettle?" she asked her audience.

"We don't know. Why?" asked the students, apparently not in the mood to think through the riddle.

When no one came up with an explanation, Julia continued her story.

"A silver dime meant a lot in those days to children, so one reason may have been that parents did it to get the younger family members to help in the washing, rinsing, boiling, and canning of the mushrooms. When the job was over, the kettle had to be scoured and cleaned. Whoever cleaned the kettle would get a dime as a reward."

"Hey, that was pretty sneaky," someone said.

"It was even rumored that after the first heavy frost, there was certain spacemen seen walking in the forest."

Now the whole group began to perk up and gave their complete attention.

"However," she said, "it was more than likely a Polish person in a black fur coat with a flashlight looking for these button mushrooms."

"You wouldn't catch me in the forest at night," added Lamar as he twisted free from Carlos.

"You'd probably scare–" Carlos started to chide him but was interrupted by the sound of a motorcycle.

All eyes turned toward John as he drove up on a restored nineteen thirty-six red Indian Chief.

"Man, that's some chopper," exclaimed Lamar. "I wonder what something like that costs?"

"Is that Lamar I'm hearing?" asked Stefi teasingly. "I hope John Langstrom quotes him a yen figure."

"I came for Grandpa," said John, moving quickly through the group of gaping faces up to the gazebo where Earl was just getting out of his chair at the table.

"Grandpa, you always wanted to ride a motorcycle," reminded John. 'Now's your chance. I even brought an extra helmet. Let's see how you look."

The helmet swallowed the frail white head, and if it had not been for the king-size, unlit cigar in his mouth, the face would also have been concealed. He grinned with delight and turned toward the waiting audience circling the motorcycle.

"Some old people are sure lucky," moaned Lamar. "I wouldn't mind spitting gravel with that baby."

They all laughed but Chris. He finally shoved his way up to John and faced him with the one question that had bothered him all day.

"Where's Littlejohn?" he wanted to know. "Grandma said you'd tell us."

"Littlejohn is still a bit dizzy when he turns his head," said John. "He'll be along shortly."

"Where is he now?" Chris insisted.

"He wanted a few moments to himself," John said, at the same time running his fingers gently through Chris's soft damp hair. "He isn't quite ready to face you. He blames himself."

"We gotta talk to him," Carlos and Lamar joined in. "It's urgent."

"Okay then. If you feel that way, you'll find him in the van. He needs some cheering up right now. There's plenty of food left. Why don't you take a generous serving over to him."

"Might do more good than a guilt gift, huh, Uncle John?" smiled Chris.

"Right you are. Now skedaddle before Littlejohn falls asleep on you and Grandpa chickens out on this motorcycle ride back to the rest center."

As the slowly fading sun cast its final rays against the arrowhead beam of Villa Sara, the two helmeted figures bobbed over the gravel road on a restored Indian Chief motorcycle into a new adventure—boys once again, faces glowing with the joy of flight.

*   *   *

"There goes the Geriatric Knight Rider," teased Elaine.

"I'm worried about Papa," said Jayne. "He's never done anything quite this risky."

"No sweat," assured Elaine. "I intend to follow—at a safe distance, of course."

"Of course," came a relieved answer.

"Care to burn some rubber with me then, Missus Reeder?" Elaine said playfully to her sister.

"Wouldn't miss the experience, Missus Langstrom, come hell or high water," Jayne answered. "Do you think Papa will be able to hang on for sixty miles without falling asleep?"

"John has him strapped in as securely as a baby," said Elaine. "I saw to that before they rode off. Now just relax, will you?"

"I'm as relaxed as any woman with a white couch would be," Jayne smiled.

"Where did you get that expression?"

"I read it somewhere. Just thought I'd try it out on you. Do you like it?"

"It'll do until you can think of something better. Why don't you try it out on the editor when you have that meeting next month?"

"I'll have to give that some thought. Something still puzzles me about that meeting. Could we have a rehearsal when we get back tonight?"

"Well, we sure can't do much heavy thinking in this traffic. I see John has turned off at the next exit. Glad to see he decided to take the old highway. Brace yourself for a few bumps."

Elaine cleverly and skillfully held her Imperial's pace behind the red Indian Chief motorcycle. Like a fish too elusive to catch, only a driver with radar vision could pick her up in their rear view mirror. She held it at a safe speed until she saw the motorcycle reach the entrance to Flunsa Rest Center. She made a U-turn at the left exit and headed west.

Chapter 16

eplacing the Polish banner of a previous celebration, a kaleidoscope of flags hung across the gazebo. The state flag of Georgia's field of blue blended with the three blue stripes of Cuba's flag. Its state seal and Battle Flag of the Confederacy with white against white, thirteen stars against one large star, four small red triangles against one larger triangle, hung as a measure of respect for Sara Bocan Grantley.

They waved briskly in the early morning breeze, snapping in rhythm with other flags, ballooning to touch China, Ecuador, England, Japan, New Zealand, Poland, Russia, South Africa, The United States of America, and West Germany.

From her portrait over the living room fireplace, Sara might well have looked out at the festive scene and smiled, knowing that no militiamen would disrupt this gesture of world friendships, no near disaster would occur as it had in Cuba when her daughters' display of patriotism was misinterpreted and their paper flags were ripped from their mountings. No flag would fly higher than another; the free air space would be shared equally.

Teeming with reluctant enthusiasm, all but three members of Project SEEK had gathered around the gazebo for their post-view session. They sat silently facing Victor Griffith as they had done many times during their ten-day cultural exchange, wondering how long they must wait for Carlos, Chris, and Lamar.

"They're still down by the creek," volunteered Mikhail in a more perfected English. "They sit on the wrap-around bench that Littlejohn mounted in concrete and kick at the loose dirt."

"Perhaps we should leave them alone a while longer," Jasmine said.

211

"We'll go get them," chorused Andries, Chang, and Nobuaki.

Everyone then wanted to get into the act, and some became very theatrical.

"If I sent you three, I'd lose half my audience," said Victor. "Better for you to go Mikhail."

"No need," Mikhail replied. "Here they come now."

"You're late, fellows," said Victor.

"Why—did we miss something?" Lamar grinned sheepishly as Victor and the others ignored his remark.

"I want to remind all of you once more that this session will be brief," he said. "We want to assure some degree of order for tonight's gathering of restrictive guests. The university officials will have one major question to ask each of you about Project SEEK. We want you to be honest in your appraisal, even if the press should lean toward a political response."

"Why must it be televised?" asked Elizabeth.

"Why don't they just leave us alone?" piped in Chris.

"We expected such would happen," Victor continued, "but we had hoped they would give Project SEEK more time to mature before making it so public. Are there any other questions?"

"Yes," replied Mikhail. "What's the big question?"

"Each of you have much to offer, many traits we could all emulate: the ability to deal with people, politeness, generosity . . . I could go on and on," said Victor. "But what they will mainly want to know is, has what you've learned about each other told you anything about the gulf between our cultures?"

"That's easy," answered Travis. "I think communication is the biggest gulf between us."

"He's right," Mikhail agreed." "Some of the English speaking natives, and I'll be careful not to mention any names, seem to delight in playing with word meanings."

"Others, while they can write well and clearly, are lost when they must struggle with a language," added Stefi.

"The gulf seems to be getting wider rather than shrinking," said Elizabeth. "I think we should be prepared to give examples."

"Any examples or comments?" asked Victor.

An embarrassed silence followed until Travis offered a solution. "Let's appoint Elizabeth as our spokesperson," he said.

Some applauded while others smiled their approval.

"The officials will expect each of you to contribute," said Victor. "So let's get the old gray matter working."

"It shouldn't be too difficult," added Julia.

Then, giving a little chuckle, she told them about the day she had gone for a walk with Stefi and Elizabeth and they had met an old fisherman at the river bend.

"When the old fisherman told us that Mister Grantley had lost his three sons," she said, "my immediate reaction was to reply, 'Well, let's go find them.' But it wouldn't have been appropriate timing on my part. Others may not share our sense of humor."

"Now you're getting it all together," said Victor. "Anyone else?"

More silence until Julia nudged Elizabeth to share some of her notes.

"I've jotted down a few experiences some of you have talked about while here," she began. "Maybe if I gave you a clue, you could recall the incident." Her eyes scanned one page of her notepad and rested on Andries' name. She then mentioned something that had been said by him during the field trip.

"Now I remember," said the South African member. "When we were at Agrirama, those boys we met on tour asked me how I found Johannesburg. I told them I used an atlas or road map. The pilot, however, had to rely on his skill to read the instrument panel. Those boys laughed, and now we're good friends."

"Give us another, Elizabeth," they chorused.

"There's one word we haven't been able to find a meaning to yet," said Elizabeth. "Maybe Stefi will tell us what it represents. Mikhail didn't find it in his bilingual dictionary that day in the bus. Remember the word?"

"F-L-U-N-S-A," they shouted.

"Just tell us, Stefi," pleaded Carlos. "We don't have all day to be guessing."

"Ironic, isn't it?" she began. " 'Flunsa' comes from Scandinavian roots. In Norwegian, it means 'to hurry.' "

She started to explain her phone call to the University librarian to verify her first interpretation when someone chided, "But the librarian didn't want to hurry!"

The spark caught, and others began to remember. Chris told about the salamanders thought by ancient alchemists to have the ability to withstand fire. Although not true, the idea continued in the language.

"Even today," said Chris, "a stove used by the construction trades to keep the chill off curing concrete or plaster is called a salamander."

"Then we agree," added Victor. "Language difficulty is the big issue. I think we have enough to fill the evening."

"What if someone should ask about the vandalism. That four-letter word that defaced Villa Sara?" asked Andries.

"Just tell it like it is," volunteered Lamar. "Y'all ignored it as a harmless prank. That took all the fun out of it for those punks who done it."

"Lamar, you'll never cease to amaze me," said Stefi. Then to Victor, "I do believe he has potential."

"Well, I'm ready," boasted Carlos. "Let's get the show on the road."

"Man, you're weird," said Lamar, punching Carlos in the arm.

The others laughed, and when no more questions were asked, Victor suggested they get something to eat and relax until the real performance started. Their wait was shorter than expected.

Villa Sara took on a carnival atmosphere as film crew tested and retested their equipment among a tangle of wires hours before the scheduled meeting time. The place was blanketed with security to ward off outsiders, but all efforts to confine activity to the outside was overruled. Officials moved nervously from one group to another giving directions in harsh and hushed voices.

Once the cameras were ready, reporters posed one group of children against a poster-filled wall. Quotations had been dispersed in art-gallery fashion along the hallway. This, they thought, reflected best the students' individuality.

The cameras zeroed in on one quote attributed to German writer Thomas Mann (1875–1955):

> Time cools, time clarifies;
> no mood can be maintained
> quite unaltered through the
> course of hours.

The confusion did not end there. As the cameras followed Chris, they saw what they could never have imagined. He blushed as he reached for the hook that opened the door with its carved crescent moon outlined against a recent coat of white paint. It had become a respectable tool shed with its red tiled roof.

Stefi edged her way up to the first microphone held by a startled reporter. "It's still a good place to rest and meditate," she said. "I'm not the least surprised that Chris chose to escape this confusion."

Carlos and Lamar doubled over with suppressed hysteria. Others stared unbelieving and embarrassed.

"Would someone mind telling us what's going on?" asked one official.

"Not at all," said Elizabeth, consulting her journal. "We got the Historical Society to recognize our efforts to save the outhouse. We met the code of the community by giving it a face-lift. Outside it's a tool shed. But you may not want to look inside."

"It's so yucky!" said Lamar before he realized a microphone had been shoved in his face.

"The hope, of course," continued Elizabeth, "is that this incident will not be dramatized in the media."

"Young lady, give us some credit, please," said one of the crewmen. "We know our job. You'll not find us negligent or misrepresenting the facts in any way."

"Yeah," confirmed Lamar. "Let the man do his job so we can get back to normal."

Carlos gave his friend a punch that almost threw him off balance.

"That's their normal behavior," said Elizabeth. "But if you want to capture something spectacular that everyone in any country can appreciate, try shooting that sunset as the rays hit the arrowhead beam of Villa Sara." She was touched and amazed when they followed her suggestion.

*   *   *

With the evening taping over, the University officials shifted positions in the comfort of the modular setting inside Villa Sara. As cameramen and reporters filed out to the respective vans or automobiles, Lamar turned and gave Carlos a hurried punch. Elizabeth, Stefi, and Julia began to giggle. Others beamed inward. Some expressed themselves verbally.

"It's good to see them go," said Andries. "Why do I get the feeling that our best features have been ignored? None of us generally behave like they had us pose."

"We didn't feel real," added Mikhail. "Do you suppose we'll be given a chance to edit any copy before it goes on the air?"

"Their creativity could sure use a boost," said Julia as she nudged Elizabeth.

"Granted, key scenes might have been avoided," explained Victor, "but you young people will be able to handle any misinformation. You know news is sometimes distorted to create interest from listeners who participate in the call-in portion of the program."

"You're right," said Elizabeth. "We all know Project SEEK is a huge success, so I think we should keep that thought uppermost in our minds."

"I told you she should have been our spokesperson," Travis reminded the group. "Now we've probably embarrassed a lot of people, and it wasn't our intention at all."

"I just hope the news releases don't worsen prospects for more students next year," said Julia.

"Some of you are over reacting," said Victor. "What we need is a good night's sleep, and everything will look brighter in the morning."

But there was little sleep for anyone that night. Those who still had final packing to do did it in sad, tired silence. It was a breaking-up time.

Chapter 17

or a moment Jayne faltered, lost in her own non sequitur. Then she reached over to help Elaine lift the humpback lid of their mother Sara Bocan Grantley's antique trunk. Bits and pieces of her material wealth dating back to her childhood now lay perfectly preserved in their cedarwood coffin.

"How long has it been since we dared look through her things?" asked Jayne.

"At least five years," answered Elaine. "Remember this beaded purse and all the fancy needlework? Pictures and letters. Even her report cards, charts, and drawings."

"And that cigar box with fool's gold," added Jayne. "We felt we had violated her image when we had Rick Steele have some items assessed for us. Would we have really sold them, do you think, if they had been valuable?"

"No way," said Elaine. "We'd go in Papa's things as youngsters, but we somehow knew not to invade our mother's privacy."

"It's ironic in a way," continued Jayne. "Instead of removing items to assess, we're putting in collectibles from this summer."

They removed the top three trays and pushed the hand-quilted bed covering to one side to make room for the new additions. In went Julia Niemcewicz's lace-trimmed *gorset* with its seedless stays.

"Julia's heroine would never have gotten through customs wearing this today," commented Elaine.

"We'd never have had this experience if security were as tight yester-years," said her sister. "I can feel our mother's presence even now. Can't you?"

"You're weird, Missus Reeder," Elaine said with affection.

217

"Thank you, Lamar," Jayne teased. "But coming from you, I consider it a compliment."

"Lamar does leave a deep impression on a person, doesn't he? This carved willow whistle he made should go right on top in the smaller shelf. Mamacita would be pleased, I'm sure."

Other sculptured gift items were wrapped carefully in tissues to be saved for later display in various rooms of Villa Sara. One gift, however, remained outside. Victor Griffith had searched antique shops religiously until he had found the cast-iron weather vane with a crude Don Quixote on his mount.

"Would Mamacita have approved of tonight's activity?" asked Jayne.

"She would up to a point," Elaine replied, "but there's no use dwelling on what happened. I think she might have excused herself as Chris did and seek the privacy of this mini-apartment."

"I totally agree with you. The boys thought of everything, didn't they? This guest room, walk-in closet, dressing room and bath with walk-through to our own sitting room. Reminds me of my first apartment."

"I'm sure my son Bill had elderly parents in mind when he added his own designs."

"I like to think of it as designed for efficiency with a retired couple in mind," added Jayne.

"I could live with that." Elaine made a face. Together they closed the trunk and replaced the Aztec blanket. "We're going to miss the young interns and foreign students," she said.

"I know. It's going to be lonely for Chris, too."

"He and Lamar will have a few hours together after the others leave. That should prove interesting."

"They'll be the first to hear the local news about last night's function. That should put a little spirit back into their lives."

"Remember when newspapers, and then radio, would simply report the local and state news?" reminded Elaine. "Back in the fifties, television began focusing on a few key issues. Now television crews go everywhere, and within seconds, have their reports on the air."

"What facts they don't find, they can certainly make up. All in the name of getting the news quickly to the listeners, right?" Jayne didn't wait for an answer. She plunged in with her next more important question. "Are we going to vote as a family whether to allow Warner

Brothers to film parts of Villa Sara when our best seller is made into a movie?"

"Dream on," said Elaine. "You know, some town officials are also afraid the fuss will scare away the estimated six million in revenue Warner Brothers would bring. We wouldn't want to disappoint the townspeople."

"You're right, but I've been told the Chinese symbol for crisis is the same as for opportunity. That is if Chang Han Sung has given us the facts. So bring on the crisis."

"I can hear Lamar saying. . . ."

". . . 'you're weird!'" they both said at the same time, laughing at their mutual thought.

"I wonder how Lamar will relate to his street chums after his ten-day experience with Project SEEK?" Jayne said.

"Maybe not enough was learned to turn his whole world upside down, but it'll make a few educational dents, I hope for the better. As for now, I've got to get some sleep if I'm going to drive some of the students to the airport tomorrow. Before you leave next week, we should schedule our family retreats."

Under her breathe, Jayne mumbled, "Young people are the future of the country."

"How's that?"

"Never mind. It was nothing."

"Then get some sleep."

* * *

The early morning arrival of a helicopter brought the sad, tired, travel-bound group out of their zombie state.

"Y'all seem surprised," a bubbly Rick Steele said as he waved the pilot his thanks.

This time the helicopter lifted off immediately. There was no need for the pilot to stay or take passengers for an overview. All those gathered below had experienced ten days or more of an inner view of Villa Sara. They had grown taller as a result, because Sara Bocan Grantley, the founder, was herself larger than life.

* * *

Chris sat in complete silence on the wrap-around bench contemplating the unplanted area of earth in the center. Neither he nor Lamar liked good-byes of the nature this day required, and being left behind made the pain even more unbearable.

Lamar whittled aimlessly at a piece of willow branch. When he had focused with it by degrees under the painful silence, he nicked ten notches in the stick to score the ten days he had been at Villa Sara. He blew the shavings out until he had a hollow sound. Then he worked his fingers over the notches as he blew.

In an attempt to soothe Chris, Lamar played a Dixie tune. Sad but effective. Chris reached out for the crude instrument and duplicated the melody. Suddenly Chris and Lamar were beaming. It was going to be all right. At least until Lamar's sponsor came to get him. And without Carlos's influence, he just might get to understand Lamar better.

*   *   *

Jayne Reeder, seeing the excitement of the preceding day fading to a dismal flicker, soon found herself infected with the same gloom. In an attempt to shake off the blues, she now stared numbly at a blank sheet of paper, mulling over the frustrations of her unfinished manuscript.

She punched a few keys as energetically as she could under the circumstances, but the sentences came out as gibberish. She hated good-byes, even though she felt she had reached a point in her life from which she never had to think about its pain. She compulsively picked up the morning newspaper and turned to the horoscope section. She could do with a bit of extra advice about now.

"I'm being put to a test," she said aloud to the noted astrologist. "Now is my chance to work uninterrupted, so why isn't it working in my favor?"

The columnist's words bounced out from the page:

> You will accomplish most today by working busily by yourself, away from the group. Avoid long journeys that can land you in a good deal of trouble. If you stick your nose out the door too early, you are likely to get pounced on by family members.

She chuckled aloud and had just moved to stick her nose out the door to defy fate when Chris sailed past with Lamar at his side.

"We're going to watch cartoons for awhile," he said without looking up.

"There's plenty of cookies left over from last night if you get hungry," Jayne offered. "I could pour you some milk."

"Maybe later," Chris said. "Don't bother none. We can get it. Grandma said we're not to distract you from your work."

"Aw, man," said Lamar. "Speak for yourself. I'd like some of them cookies and milk, Missus Reeder."

"You'll have to eat them here in the kitchen."

"Never mind then . . . I'll wait for Chris. He's got the cartoons on."

When Lamar moved into the living room, Jayne followed. She could do with a bit of extra rest anyway.

During one of the commercials, Chris began to complain. "I still don't know why we couldn't have gone along to the airport with the others."

"They explained that several times," Jayne reminded him. "Your mom wanted to introduce the girls to her other sister in Atlanta. They were going shopping and doing girl stuff. You wouldn't like that. You'll get to see your Aunt Daphne some other time anyway."

When Lamar started in with his questions about why three cars had to be used, Chris quickly changed channels.

"You know something, Auntie Jayne?" he said. "We won't need this remote control in a few years. We'll be able to change channels by voice command."

"Man, that's weird," said Lamar.

"Not weird, Lamar," she said. "It's very probable. Tell me more, Chris."

"You're stalling, aren't you?" he smiled. "You really don't want to type today, do you?"

"See, you've inspired me. I'm going back in the other room and show what I'm really made of."

*   *   *

Somewhere between the "Wuzzles" cartoon and "Disney's Adventures of the Gummi Bears," there was a news flash about a tragic fatality on the highway. It came at the exact moment the phone rang. Chris grabbed the receiver at the same time Jayne reached the extension in the kitchen. He babbled on and on about seeing Rick Steele with Carlos, Chang, and Nobuaki on TV until Elaine interrupted.

"Please, Chris," she said. "Hang up the phone and let me talk to your Auntie Jayne. I don't have much time."

Chris grudgingly hung up after another attempt to explain what he had seen went unheeded.

"Kids," sighed Jayne. "He's got Lamar believing he saw them, too, even though Lamar says they all look alike to him."

"It could very well be true," said Elaine. "There's a traffic jam just before the Macon by-pass. We were one of the lucky drivers near an exit. It was a long way off the interstate, and if I hadn't known the area, we'd never have gotten through."

"Where are you now?" asked Jayne.

"We took a pit stop near Forsyth. We've got plenty of time. Julia's flight isn't until five twenty-five this afternoon."

"Did you keep up with Rick Steele and John?"

"You know Rick. I expect he's in Atlanta by now. Carlos's flight was at nine twenty-five, and Chang and Nobuaki were scheduled for ten twenty. John has plenty of time. Travis, Andries, and Mikhail all have later afternoon flights."

"Can you hear the boys still arguing? Lamar is fidgeting because he hasn't seen himself on TV yet."

"Put Chris back on for a minute, will you?" I'll call back from Daphne's later this evening."

"Chris," Elaine said when her grandson came to the phone, "your Uncle John set the VCR, so tell Lamar he'll get to see whatever footage they decide to show later. Just relax and enjoy your cartoons . . . and try not to interrupt your Auntie Jayne too many times after Lamar leaves. I know I can depend on you to do that."

Chris made one last feeble attempt to tell about the traffic accident and about recognizing Carlos and the others, but his grandma's passengers were beeping the horn, anxious to be on their way.

"I'll call again from Atlanta, Chris," Elaine said. "Be sweet now."

As soon as Chris hung up the receiver, the phone rang again. This time it was an urgent Rick Steele.

"Bet y'all were surprised to see us on the news flash," he said. "But listen—I'm running late. We have a news helicopter with clearance to take our passengers to Atlanta Hartsfield International. That's so Carlos, Chang, and Nobuaki don't miss their flights. They're heroes now. It's been quite a day. Just wanted y'all not to worry." He was off the line before Jayne could voice any comments at all.

"Told you so!" Chris said firmly, then returned to flicking the remote control. He settled finally for "Real Ghost-Buster."

Jayne sat in suspense until eleven when "Headline News" gave a full report of the tragic traffic accident:

"Authorities on the scene say the semi-truck hauling molten aluminum spilled its load of twenty tons onto a car, killing two men inside. Both victims were burned beyond recognition. The car was nearly encased in hot metal before the gasoline inside its tank exploded. The dead have not been identified.

"According to Sheriff Damon Tifton, the truck driver was pulled from the cab by local businessman Rick Steele and his passengers, all exchange students from the Villa Sara Project SEEK. Carlos Moreno from Ecuador, Chang Sung from China, and Nobuaki Komura from Japan said it was only natural for them to assist, but they hoped they would still have time to make their flights out of Atlanta Hartsfield International Airport.

"The driver is listed in stable condition at Memorial Hospital. According to the police, no charges have been filed pending further investigation."

"*Told* you so," Chris said with emphasis.

"I'm sorry for doubting you, even a little," his great-aunt said. "Now will you let me redeem myself by fixing you and Lamar some lunch?"

"Yeah!" they both chorused. "You bet!"

*　　　　*　　　　*

While preparing lunch, Jayne mulled over the implications of the accident she had just viewed on television. Had the semi-truck been defective? Had the driver fallen asleep at the wheel? The two victims—what had been their destination? Who were they? Who were their families? The questions pounded against her brain until she finally shook them off.

"One thing I'm now sure of," she said to herself. "Any attempt the media had of magnifying our SEEK students' differences with the taping of the previous night will now have a balance with today's report and hopefully help perpetuate the favorable aspects between the countries they represent."

A cracking sound like dry twigs snapping came from the kitchen window.

"Chris, get the door for Littlejohn, will you?" she said. "I'm in the middle of Hellmann's Real Mayonnaise and Scot Lad Mustard."

"We're in the middle of a cartoon," yelled Chris. "Besides, Littlejohn knows his way in."

"We locked the doors from the inside as your Uncle John cautioned us to do while we're here alone, so don't argue. Please?"

"Oh, okay, but it had better be worth it."

Chris moved reluctantly toward the rear door while Lamar held on to the remote control and snickered.

"I didn't realize Lamar was still with you or I would have saved this surprise until later," Littlejohn apologized.

"Is it what I think it is?" said Chris.

Suddenly he was beaming. He reached for the Mason jar with a burst of energy. The sprig of a sweet lemon tree jiggled its roots in an underwater ballet.

"You did it, Littlejohn! You did it!" Chris shouted.

"Did what?" asked Jayne from the kitchen.

Lamar, also curious as to what was happening, came in from the living room.

"Come see," said Chris.

*　　　　　*　　　　　*

The sweet lemon tree took precedence over lunch, over cartoons, and over the manuscript, and somehow filled the void the trio had experienced during the morning hours. They all moved to the wrap-around bench and worked carefully to follow every detail of instructions from Littlejohn about proper planting. The boys raced for fresh soil from the creek to make a filling around the tender roots.

"It's like a jelly-filled sweet roll," laughed Lamar.

"You're weird," said Chris.

"Life will continue forward now." Littlejohn smiled at their efforts. "For awhile there, I thought it would never take root. Just shows you can't second-guess Mother Nature."

"How long will it be before I can climb the tree?" asked Chris.

"Let's give it time to grow under its own power now," added Littlejohn. "You'll see a big change by the time you get back next summer. But I'm not making any promises I might not be able to keep."

"You will protect the tree for me this time, won't you?" said Chris looking his friend straight in the eyes.

"That I can promise," he answered.

"Promises!" grunted Lamar. "You promised to tell me and Chris what you did with that grass field of yours. I know you didn't burn it or the whole county would be stoned."

"Yeah!" added Chris. "Will you tell us now?"

"I ain't leaving here until I know," insisted Lamar. "I won't let you off the hook like Carlos did."

"Well, fellows, I'll tell you this much and you can figure out the rest." Littlejohn paused for what seemed like an eternity to his eager listeners. "I buried it in a place nobody will ever suspect."

"If you buried it, man, it's going to grow again," snapped Lamar. "That's a stupid move."

"Not when it's buried under a ton of concrete. Now I've got work to do. That's all I'm going to tell you." Littlejohn turned away quickly so as not to see their puzzled expressions.

*   *   *

When Lamar left later that afternoon, Chris was not as alone as he thought he would be. He spent every moment between chores Jayne invented to keep him occupied shifting seating positions around the sweet lemon tree.

"It's time we got that plaque of your great grandmother Sara Bocan Grantley's and reset it under the tree," his aunt suggested.

Chris agreed at first, then thought seriously for a moment. "Not now," he said. "Let's wait until tomorrow when the family is here."

"That's a good idea," Jayne answered.

So they waited.

*   *   *

Elaine called shortly after the last flight at nine o'clock. Jayne and Chris reached for the phone at the same time.

"How's my grandson doing now that Lamar has gone back home?" she asked immediately.

"I'm fine, Grandma," Chris answered excitedly from an extension in another room.

Then, talking nonstop, he began to tell about Littlejohn bringing the sprig of the sweet lemon tree and the whole process of planting it and how he asked that they wait to install the specially engraved plaque until. . . .

"Sounds great, Chris," Elaine interrupted. "We'll have an appropriate ceremony tomorrow while the sun is just right. That way we can get some good pictures to send your ten new friends."

"Don't forget Victor and the others," he reminded.

"That we could never do. Now you'd better get some sleep. You've got a big day ahead of you."

"Okay, Grandma. See you," he said, offering no objections and displaying no curiosity about her day or the students' shopping spree in Atlanta or the final farewells.

Elaine continued the conversation with her sister Jayne. "I'm glad to know Chris is feeling chirpier," she said. "You heard he wrote to Castro about getting a cutting from the original sweet lemon tree in his great great-grandfather's backyard, didn't you? That's one letter that will never get to its destination, but the poor kid expects an answer."

"Oh, ye of little faith. Don't dismiss the thought too soon," cautioned Jayne. "Chris hasn't received the letter returned with an 'address unknown' sticker on it either."

"You're right, but let's not hold our breath."

"So how did your day go?" Jayne asked, but didn't wait for an answer before posing several more. "Were the flights all on time? See any famous people or not so famous? Were the last farewells painful? Did Rick and John get to the airport on time?"

When she paused for just a second, Elaine plunged in. "The girls shouldn't have any problem with jet lag. They'll probably sleep all the way to their first stop after all the shopping we did. Daphne was a big help in selecting items they could take with them as souvenirs. As for me, I'm ready to soak my feet and not move for days after shopping and walking all over the airport."

"All flights were on time then, I assume," said Jayne.

"Just about. We decided to spend the four hours right at the airport so we wouldn't have to juggle our time. There was plenty to see and do between Julia's flight to Frankfurt, her only stop between here and Warsaw, and Elizabeth's flight two hours later to London's Gatwig Airport. Stefi managed to get a seat with Mikhail a couple hours later on the flight to Frankfurt. Mikhail doesn't have much of a wait in Frankfurt, since he takes the nonstop to Moscow."

"That should prove interesting," Jayne injected. "The two of them together."

"I was wishing I could go with each one as their planes took off. Anyway, we all missed not having the other five members with us for our early dinner. We ate just before Julia's flight.

"Rick stayed through the whole thing, but John had to get back home. Rick told us all about the excitement during the rescue of the semi-truck driver. What details he left out, Mikhail was quick to supply from his viewing of the news on the TV at the station where he, Andries, Travis, and John had stopped for gas.

"Rick also said that Chang was thrilled to be on the same flight with Nobuaki and was looking forward to spending a weekend with his friend in Tokyo before leaving the following Monday for Beijing."

"You make it sound so adventurous," Jayne sighed. "I wish I could have been there at the airport, or better still, leaving on one of the flights. Just any of them would have suited me."

"Me, too," said Elaine. "You know, Travis was the only one to display little excitement or regret. He didn't blink, didn't smile. John said he thinks it's because Travis was the only student going west, or maybe because he was the first in the group to leave Atlanta."

"I know how he must have felt. Did anything else exciting happen? Any international crises?" Jayne asked.

"Nothing that airport security couldn't handle," Elaine said. "There was a purse snatching in the waiting section across from us, and a fistfight broke out at the same time. I wasn't even aware of it until what looked like the SWAT team rushed in and told us to stay put. I was concerned about Mikhail when I didn't see him with the others, but he was giving one of the officers a full description of the suspect. I was never so glad to see a plane take off as much as the one with Mikhail and Stefi aboard. I'm glad it was the last flight, too. Don't think my heart could have managed anything else that late."

"I'll be anxious for you to get back here," Jayne said. "Drive carefully now. Ya hear?"

"Don't fret none," Elaine told her. "Is Chris still up?"

"No. He went right down to his room after you talked to him," said Jayne. "I told him it was okay if he wanted to bring up his bedroll to the living room. Know what he told me? 'I'm a Grantley. I'm not afraid to be alone.'"

"Take good care of him for me, and I'll see you around elevenish. I'm glad his mother came along. Susan volunteered to do the driving after I get us out of this airport construction maze."

Chapter 18

The sweet lemon tree was planted in a sunny spot overlooking the creek. Elaine read the message that Sara Bocan Grantley had inserted in her Bible, the same quote Earl Grantley had had engraved on the gold plate and dated, "Summer 1920."

> For there is hope of a tree, if it be cut down, that it will sprout again, and that the tender branch thereof will not cease.
> (Job 14:7)

With reverence, Littlejohn mounted the plaque at the base of the lemon tree.

Soon after the short ceremony, it was Chris's turn to leave Villa Sara. He was so disgruntled, he clung to his grandmother Elaine. She held him at eye level and helped him to talk about the good things that had happened during his summer, things he could share with classmates when he got back to Wisconsin.

Reluctantly at first, then with enthusiasm slowly mounting, Chris began to remember.

"I could tell about Igu, my iguana, and how One-less became my dog. And how he helped me find Great Grandpa Grantley when he ran away from the church picnic. And how my Uncle Donald got stung by a bee. And how we entertained the elderly at Flunsa Rest Center. And how the loggers cut down my sweet lemon tree, but Littlejohn started another. And how. . . ." When he ran out of hows, Chris took a deep breath and started again. "And you know what else?" he said.

"What?" Elaine asked affectionately.

"When I come back to Villa Sara next summer, I'm going to give my sweet lemon tree a big hug."

Elaine struggled to hold back the tears. Then softly she whispered in her grandson's ear the one word that held a wealth of memories for both of them, "Skedaddle."

As he turned away, Chris wiped a tear from his own eye. One-less broke the leash that restrained him and buried his nose in Chris's weakening legs.

"That goes for you, too, pal," he told the frantic animal, giving him a warm tuck under the chin.

Chris then took a deep breath and entered the waiting family car, not daring to look back as it pulled away.

One-less cowered until the car was out of sight. Then he limped to the sweet lemon tree and relieved himself.